Back to Normal Series Book One:

PARADIGM RIFT

RANDY MCWILSON

Moving Images
Publications
Cape Girardeau, Missouri

Paradigm Rift

Published by Moving Images Publications
Cape Girardeau, Missouri
www.MovingImagesPublications.com

Lightning Photograph by Erica Murphy-Burrell

ISBN-13: 978-0615990606

Dedicated to

My family who encouraged me
My students who indulged me
My colleagues who supported me
Ron Pokracki who challenged me
Danny Janisse who motivated me

Special Thanks to

Janet L. Cannon, editor
Patti C. Whittington, editor
John LaRose
Alison Niermann
Bruce Boulden
David Dickey
Jonathan Fritzler
Jeremy J. Ford
Debbie Franklin

Friday, March 8, 1946

Journal entry number 1

There are two things you should know about time travel—
first, it's impossible, and second...it's terrifying.

I can hardly eat. I doubt I've slept more than two hours in a
row since I fell into this unimaginable horror. I've been throwing up
all over the place. I don't think I'm crazy, but insanity might be a
much better explanation. I would gladly accept a mental disease, at
least most of those can be treated. I'm afraid all the doctors in the
world can't cure my disorder. It's been three long, gut-ripping days
here in Normal.

Einstein said that the laws of physics created an impenetrable
wall that stopped any possibility of traveling backwards in time. What
about me, Albert? What about Phillip Nelson? Another brilliant theory
of a brilliant man ruined by reality. Who knows—maybe I did it
when the conditions went beyond the possible, or maybe I did it
when the Universe wasn't looking.

Unfortunately, I wake up every day tormented with the painful
realization that this nightmare is very real. I can't escape where I
am, or when I am, though I have rationalized both away countless
times.

Denial dies a lingering death when nursed by hope.

CHAPTER 1

Sunday, June 15, 2014 6:39 p.m.

"But, Daddy, how does the light in the sky make noise?"

Denver glanced up into the rear view mirror at the puzzled little ball of curiosity tucked away in the back seat of the SUV. Her attention was divided between a small tablet computer and the irregular flashes of lightning accenting the late afternoon urban landscape.

His mind raced for an age-appropriate and satisfying meteorological explanation. "Well, sweetie, the lightning kind of makes, uh, cracks in the sky, and the thunder is the sky cracking open."

The skeptical six-year-old leaned toward her rain-splattered window and stared, scrunching her little nose. Her blue eyes surveyed the thickening sky. "I don't see any cracks, Daddy, just clouds."

He looked back, somewhat disappointed, but not all that surprised that his makeshift weather tale was so easily challenged. Traffic, like his explanation, had just come to a total standstill, so he played every parent's ace card in these innocent bluffs. "Well, they're...*invisible* cracks. Big, invisible, cracks."

Jasmine's eyes darted around as she appeared to weigh her father's words. Whether it was actual satisfaction or just first-grade attention deficit, she leaned back, returning to her digital distraction.

Denver's seeming victory was disturbed by a series of quick rings. He grabbed his phone off the seat and checked the screen: JENNIFER COLLINS.

Denver looked away and tossed the phone down, but then reconsidered after eight rings. He shoved it to his ear. "Yeah?" He rubbed his forehead. "Listen, we're on our way, Jennifer. We got stuck in traffic...People act like it's never rained on the streets of New York before."

Denver raised his hand in silent protest, as if to stave off the verbal assault. "What? I get two weekends a month and you complain about me being fifteen minutes late? Whatever."

He threw the phone across the seat as the bumper-to-bumper traffic relaxed and the rain intensified.

"Was that Mommy?"

"Uh, yes, Jasmine. It was your mother."

She put her head against the window and enjoyed the cool glass on her cheek. She traced the paths of the large raindrops racing down with her finger.

"It's getting bad, Daddy."

"Yes it is, sweetheart. Yes it is. And it gets worse every day."

With considerable maneuvering, their SUV escaped the hectic New York boulevard, and minutes later the glass storefronts were replaced by brick apartment buildings. Denver pulled up to the curb, and hopped out, making his way around to Jasmine's door like a perfect gentleman.

He avoided eye contact with Jennifer, who was already outside waiting on the porch, as his little beauty emerged from the back seat. Her tiny umbrella popped up and her proud dad had to avoid being hit by it as she raced through the rain.

"Mommy!"

Jennifer latched onto her daughter and pulled her up into a rotating hug. "Mommy missed her big girl! I am so glad you're back home with me."

"Me too, Mommy!"

Denver walked up to the pair with Jasmine's small suitcase in tow. He looked around at anything but his wife, who released Jasmine and knelt by her. She fixed the child's ruffled collar. "Hey, you know what?"

Jasmine listened with great expectation.

"It's almost dinner, why don't you go wash up for Mommy, okay?"

Jasmine threw her arms around her mother's neck and gave her a smooch. "Okay!"

She started to go through the door, hampered by her kid-sized umbrella, but her father interrupted this severe breach of daddy-daughter-protocol. "Hey, wait a minute. How about a big see-you-later kiss for Daddy?"

She broke out in a grin and rushed back to him as he bent over to meet her. She wasted no time planting a sloppy kiss on his cheek and then disappeared through the doorway.

He watched her go, and he grew tired of watching her go, and always with the same fear. It seemed there was an irrational person co-existing within, always whispering that he would never see his daughter again.

Today was no different.

Denver shook it off. He had to shake it off, as he rose and started back towards his car, his rain-soaked shirt clinging to him.

Jennifer wasn't budging. "My lawyer said you still haven't turned in your paperwork."

He stopped cold.

He didn't want another fight.

What he did want though was a shower and a beer, but not necessarily in that order. Denver turned back. *She wants a fight? In the rain? Why not?*

He returned fire. "I love how you make it sound so cold and formal; like our lives are just...just *documents* that need to be neatly filed away."

She took a few steps towards him, just out to the dripping edge of the porch overhang. "I didn't start this whole mess, Denver, but I'm sure gonna finish it! For my own sanity, for Jasmine's. Just sign the papers!"

"I'm sorry if I can't erase the last eight years of our lives with just the magic wave of a pen, Jennifer!"

She spun away and shook her head in apparent disbelief, or rage, or probably both. The door cracked open, and a sculpted male with mixed-martial-artist written all over his attitude stepped out.

"Everything okay, babe?"

She put her hand on her forehead, not even looking at him. "Uh, yeah...it's, it's fine. I'll be inside in a minute." The men glared each other down, and Mr. Attitude moved back inside.

Denver pointed, "Lemme guess—latest boy-toy of the week?"

She stormed out into the rain and jumped into his face. "Look! I don't have to answer to you or to anybody else!" She marched back onto the porch, shielding herself from the rain. Jen glanced back one final time as the lightning began to unleash the storm's fury. "Now do the right thing for once, and *sign the damn paperwork*!"

She was gone.

He was alone.

He appeared paralyzed until a crack of thunder jolted him back to reality. But it was a fractured reality, a shattered existence he could never have imagined only eight short years ago. He glanced up at the apartment door, and then at the entire building. It didn't seem even remotely possible he had met Jen on an early summer night, in this very same building. In fact, the night they first met was almost identical to this night, minus the bitterness, of course.

If he hadn't been so miserable, he would have smiled as he reminisced about that first chance encounter. He had just begun to acclimate to civilian luxuries again after returning from his tour in Afghanistan when boy met girl. It was a simple case of, "Here, let me get the door for you," and he was never able to look at another woman again, though she did accuse him of it from time to time.

Jen loved the way he looked chiseled and manicured in his military uniform; in fact, she was adamant that he would wear it during their elegant but simple wedding ceremony. He wasn't keen on the idea, but he was keen on her. As far as he was concerned, she could have worn a tank top and jeans as she said, "I do."

But that was eight years ago.

Sunday, March 17, 1946
Journal entry number 4

I probably need to move to another hotel or motel soon. I've been at this one for 8 days, and I think that the staff is getting suspicious. I have been signing in as John Wilson, instead of Phil Nelson.

I am not sure how much longer my cash will hold out. I guess I was lucky that I had a $20 and a few $10 bills. I put some marks on them using a pen to disguise the dates. To research for a way to get out (if it is even possible) will require a considerable sum of money and equipment. For money, I have some ideas, if I can get out of Normal and head out West.

Facing a difficult task can be terrifying, even with the support of family and friends. But I am in this alone. I am trying to stay positive, I am focusing on Maryanne and Kurtis. I firmly believe I will see them again...the alternative is paralyzing.

Regardless, I need to come to peace with the absurd and horrific reality that I may never leave here. There is a difference between probable and possible. For example, lightning striking the same person twice is possible, but it sure isn't probable. The odds are nearly insurmountable. The solution? Pretty simple: Figure out where the lightning will strike.

And then be there.

CHAPTER 2

Sunday, June 15, 2014 8:07 p.m.

The empty darkness of Denver's studio apartment was interrupted by the erratic flurry of lightning flashes over downtown Manhattan. With a click, twist, and creak, Denver pushed past the front door and tossed his keys across a table in the tiny foyer. He peeled off his drenched shirt, replacing it with a comfortable if not entirely clean gray hoodie, then headed for the kitchen. A magnet-mounted photo of Jasmine greeted him as he snatched two beers out of the fridge.

He sipped as he migrated into the living room and sank into the couch, just as an uncomfortably close bolt of lightning made even this hardened soldier jump. The lights flickered as well, but stayed true as the thunder rolled.

Denver popped on the man-sized flat-screen across the room, creating sights and sounds to reinforce the illusion that he was not alone. The television rarely seemed to do that though...actually, it *never* did.

He reached across the coffee table and retrieved a framed photo of Jasmine riding atop his shoulders at the zoo. Pulling it in close, he studied the picture he had studied a hundred times before. His thumb traced across her ecstatic face as he took a long pull on his first bottle.

More lightning.

A weather alert blared across a red ticker along the bottom of his HD screen, but Denver Collins was far more concerned about the personal storm that raged deep inside of him. He set the picture back down as his eyes landed on a small stack of papers. They were documents he had made a deliberate effort to ignore for well over three weeks.

He stared over at the top page and then took further comfort in his bottle. A few lightning flashes, a few claps of booming thunder, and a few swigs of booze later, his courage and interest seemed to revive. He picked up the document and held it at eye level as he discarded the now empty bottle.

NOTICE OF DIVORCE PROCEEDINGS
Denver Wayne Collins   V.   Jennifer Lynn Collins

He flipped dispassionately through the sheets until he arrived at the signatory page. On the right side, in brilliant blue ink, was the signature of his wife (or estranged wife, or former spouse, or whatever fashionable term one uses these days to describe the last stage of formal, emotional disintegration). He looked to the left side, the line was as empty and flat as he was. He rubbed his thumb over the rough texture of the notarized seal below Jennifer's name.

So, that's all it takes. A signature, a witness, and it's over. How convenient. Marriage. A preacher in a black robe makes it; a judge in a black robe breaks it. Nice.

Denver tossed the offensive packet back onto the table, but most of it ended up on the floor. He pulled the second bottle up to his lips, hitting it hard, but the sight of his wedding ring inches from his nose froze him in mid-drink. He set the bottle down and rotated and removed the golden band.

Denver slid down on the couch and held the ring straight above his head. It was silhouetted against a tiny spotlight overhead, and he began spinning it like a craftsman. He flashed to the day he had proposed to Jen. Denver relived the exact moment she had looked out of the window of his friend's tiny Cessna at just over three hundred feet up. Peering down into the harvested fields right after sunset, she saw Denver's agonizing handiwork. He had spent fourteen hours, two hundred and twenty-seven dollars, and nearly five thousand Christmas lights writing the words "Will U Marry Me?" in letters twenty-five feet wide each, not to mention the eighty-five bucks to rent the gas generator, but at least his military buddy provided the plane ride for free as an early wedding gift.

After the "Yes" and the "I do's" there were happy days, even happy years, but they felt like someone else's life right now.

The intensifying electrical storm made the lights protest several more times, as Denver did his best to empty Budweiser number two. A strange blue glow filled the room.

Satellite dish is out, that's great.

He turned off the TV and studied the ring a bit more, before sliding it back onto his finger. He rolled to the side to finish off his beer, and in a matter of moments, Denver Collins was finished as well. Not even the incessant, window-shaking thunderclaps could disturb his fermented-barley-induced slumber now. He drifted off remembering the expression on Jen's face, but it was like a fading dream.

Nobody gets engaged like Jen and I did.

But that was over eight years ago.

Thursday, March 21, 1946
Journal entry number 7

Had to buy some more clothes. I will be out of money by week's end. I don't know of any other way to survive right now. I'm not proud of it, but I will probably have to steal (but I fully intend to make good on it once things improve). But cash isn't the only obstacle.

I have to not only look the part, but my actions, my words, my interactions, all must be authentic. I cannot let people find out who I truly am, and when I am truly from. For example—there's technology. I have been trying to cook my own food to save money and limit my exposure to the public. I went to the appliance store and asked the clerk to direct me to the microwave ovens. I had to quickly cover for my mistake (I am about a decade or so too early). They will be called Radar Ranges at any rate, not microwaves.

It's so weird to think there is basically only one computer in the world right now, ENIAC—and it's bigger than a small house! Back at the high school I teach at in Colorado, we had over ten Apple II computers in one building!

I have been immersing myself in newspapers and magazines. I haven't seen a TV here yet. I picked up a cheap radio. I can get a few local stations, and one out of Chicago. They carry a lot of sports. It's strange listening to games, at least the ones that I already know the outcome. A guy could make some serious cash with my knowledge, at least in the right places.

The ending and effects of World War II are still very fresh (I have found that most people refer to it as the "Second World War.") Everyone has lost someone, and some have lost everyone it seems. The only joys in this are the babies. So many babies, and expectant mothers (nobody uses the term "pregnant" around here). Many people say "In the family way."

It is so interesting to get to see the rise of the next world war, the Cold War (I need to be careful with that term, as well. If I remember right, Bernie—something, can't remember, coined it, not sure when). Immersion and education. These may be the keys to keep me from incarceration. I'm sure the Feds would love to get their hands on Phillip Nelson. I aim to make that difficult for them.

But first they have to find that a time traveler is among them.

CHAPTER 3

The images, colors, and sounds pulsed with intensity in Denver's tortured mind. Scenes and memories, or fragments of memories, blurred and blended. Nothing made sense, yet everything seemed important. *Children, the sounds of children. Are they playing?* The visual confusion and sensory overload escalated. The echoes of voices assaulted him with a haunting quality that made very little distinction between children playing and children screaming.

A flash. What was that? Is that blood? And the pain. Such pain. *Wait...who is he?* A frightened young boy passed before his mind's eye. *He can't be more than five years old!* Another face, an older face. *A new voice. What is he saying?* In low tones, words reverberated through the senseless nightmare.

Denver. Remember.

More pain. A knife flashes.

Rumbling and shaking.

More flashes.

Denver.

Remember.

A pale young boy stood before him. He couldn't have been more than five or six years old. The child screamed in terror, blood on his hands. A flash of hot, white light swelled brighter and brighter, blinding with the force of a hundred suns, followed by an explosive crash so loud it would not only wake the dead, it would surely rend them up out of their graves.

Denver snapped awake and thrust himself into a seated position, bathed in sweat as his heart pounded within a few beats of complete cardiac arrest. His head frantically spun about in the darkness, as a peal of thunder had just passed its crescendo and was retreating into the distance with all the subtlety of a squadron of low-flying aircraft. The entire building rattled and reeled beneath the onslaught, but soon everything around him returned to a dark, dead calm—with the notable exception of his nerves.

Lightning must've knocked the power out again. Looks like warm beer for breakfast. Terrific.

He sat frozen at first, transfixed by a new and unfamiliar sound—the curious sound of silence. Denver made an educated guess about the general location of his large picture window, and stared hard into the black nothingness in that direction.

Whoa. Whole city must be out. This is bad.

He sat and argued with himself about the merits of simply going back to sleep, but was interrupted by a question that refused to lie down.

Where are all the cars? Where are the lights from the cars?

Once again he studied the best-guess window area. *Still nothing. Lightning can knock out the city power, but not car headlights.*

His inquiry wasn't even close to being settled when a fresh mystery washed over him—the odor. It was different, heavy, almost oppressive—not entirely unlike an old, wet towel.

Denver ignored the foreign aroma and rubbed his hands on the couch, but something wasn't quite right about that either. He leaned over and groped all around. *Wait, this isn't my couch! It's my bed. When did I move to my frickin' bed?*

He got on his feet, his heart rate and breathing just about back to normal. *Oh, that's why I can't see the cars, I'm in my bedroom...duh.* He whisked his head around in all directions, and then he spotted it.

A light.

Not a city light, or a car's headlights, or a streetlight, but a weak, warm, incandescent glow. He could make out a straight line, actually two lines, maybe a doorway. He moved along the edge of the bed, disoriented, but now fully awake. Something hit him in the stomach and he stopped cold. He felt of it. *A chair? Feels like a wooden chair.*

Of course, there was nothing unusual about a chair, except for the fact he didn't have a chair in his bedroom.

He navigated around the foreign furnishing and progressed toward the light. It was spilling through a cracked door, and Denver pushed it wide open. The room that he saw both confused him and clarified his misgivings in the same instant. He had walked into a bathroom, but not his bathroom. In fact, not the bathroom of anyone he knew, or had ever known, for that matter.

This bathroom was...*different*. A porcelain toilet, rusty sink, and a plain tub with a hideous shower curtain furnished the tiny area. It may have been practical, but it was not pretty by any standard. He backed out with some effort and located a small light switch on the wall outside the bathroom. Nothing could have prepared him for what he saw next.

He wasn't in his bedroom. He wasn't even in his apartment. And he probably wasn't even in Manhattan. He stared into a long, single room—complete with a bed, a small table and chair, a telephone, a green door, and closed curtains along the far wall.

He was in a motel room.

Wednesday, April 3, 1946
Journal entry number 12

Something simple today triggered something fundamentally...
fundamental. I was walking across the grass in the town square and
had to cross over a section of soil, and then back to grass. Something
grabbed my attention—I think a car backfired—and I stopped and
turned. I looked down and saw my footprints clearly in the dirt, but
there were no tracks in the grass on either side.

And then it hit me. As a time traveler, as a man walking
somewhere he doesn't really belong, I need to be careful not to leave
any tracks, or at least, as few tracks as possible. My interactions in
and around Normal, my travels here in 1946, need to be like the
vanishing footprints we create in the grass. We push it down
temporarily, but moments later, the many blades of green snap back,
sweeping our tracks for us, all but forgetting our brief encounter.

If and when I am able to return home, I need to leave
Normal, Illinois, and the rest of this world, as if I were never here,
no footprints, no changes. My interactions with people, need to be like
walking in the grass. A quick, fleeting impression, then moments
later—nothing.

Maybe I need to write this mantra on my bathroom mirror, and
repeat it to myself several times a day:

Walk without Footprints.

This is my new axiom, my pledge. Walk without footprints.

Just over 20 years from now, another man, out of place, will walk on foreign soil. But unlike me, that man will intend to leave his mark, to make tracks for all to see: footprints that will be as clear and fresh at Judgment Day as they were (or will be) on that early Monday morning in late July of 1969.

Neil Armstrong misspoke on that important day, and no one ever forgot his famous line broadcast from the Moon's surface. But here in my journeys, also far from home, it would be better if no one ever remembered anything I said. Like an extra piece on a chessboard, I am not supposed to be here. Every move I make, every word I speak, anything I do could alter the game.

One small step I leave behind as a man, could create one giant disastrous leap for mankind.

CHAPTER 4

A motel room? What's going on here?

Denver was not just in any motel room, but a motel room that had been in desperate need of remodeling since at least the Vietnam War, maybe even the Korean. He was fascinated by the large, black phone by the bed and walked over to it. *A rotary phone?* He picked up the handset and listened to the tone. Just for fun, he spun the rotary dial, and it clicked back into place. He glanced around again.

No television? I gotta be dreaming.

He stepped toward the thick curtains and cautiously peeled the left side back a tad. He could make out a nearly-empty parking lot through the dirty glass, a few lights, but no activity. He grabbed the handle and the ugly green door opened under extreme protest. Denver moved out onto the uneven concrete sidewalk. There were about a dozen units along the wall, and a handful of cars were parked on his far right.

He strained to see the vehicles in the darkness. *Nice, looks like a '47 Ford on the end. Somebody dropped some bucks in that restoration job.*

There appeared to be some city lights straight ahead in the distance, though he couldn't tell how far due to the intermittent fog that hugged the ground. He grabbed his cellphone to check the time, and hopefully his location. The display was a disappointment except for the time, 9:34 p.m.

He pulled it closer. *Do I have a signal? How many bars?*

No and none.

That's great.

He put the phone away and felt his back pocket, relieved to discover he still had his wallet. He peered inside. *Good, at least fifty bucks.* He figured he would need at least that much just to get a cab ride home.

Denver took one final look around and made short work of getting across the parking lot, which dumped out onto a narrow, two-lane blacktop. He paused and looked up and down the road, lit about as well as could be expected in the mist and moonlight, and he began a brisk walk towards civilization.

The air was sharp and cool, not cold, but something bothered him as he trudged along. It was the weather. No clouds, no rain, no storm, no lightning, just a thin layer of fog. He was convinced it was a close lightning strike that slapped him from slumber mere moments ago.

But how? Where? If it was an explosion, where is the smoke? How did I end up in a motel? What's freakin' going on?

It was a mystery, but he reminded himself that a mystery is just an event that is yet to be explained. He began working through possible explanations, from an over-the-top office prank, to a far-fetched government conspiracy. He had a few friends who worked for the NSA, recruited right after Afghanistan. Those guys now operated in an entirely new region of reality, a region of unlimited information and limitless resources. They might be messing with him. Regardless of their individual merits, the potential explanations he toyed with at least served to pass the time.

He checked his phone again fifteen minutes later. *No bars, no location, no service.* As he shoved it back into his pocket—*a sound.* He perked up...in the distance, a low tone. He turned and spotted the muted glow of car headlights through the cool haze.

He thought about flagging them down, *but that would be almost crazy, right?* He decided against acting desperate and continued towards town, whatever town it was.

The car was much closer now, but he resisted the urge to look. The rumble of the engine revealed that it was slowing as it approached. Denver's shadow was thrown long and strong as a sudden pool of intense light surrounded him. He was being spotlighted and he just walked on, pretending not to notice, full knowing how ridiculous that proposition was.

A voice pierced the tension. "Need a ride son?"

He hesitated in his steps, still disoriented. "I, uh...I'm not sure."

Denver glanced back and was nearly blinded by the search light, now amplified by the mist. He couldn't help but shield his eyes as the gruff stranger continued. "A little early to be hittin' the sauce wouldn't you say?"

Denver was thrown for a bit. "What? Sauce? Oh, no...I...I'm not...I haven't been…" He tried to resume walking down the tiny shoulder.

The stranger rolled alongside in the car, matching his pace. "Lemme guess. You're not from around here, are ya?"

Denver shrugged as he plodded along. The conversation appeared innocent enough, but his military-sharp skepticism was on full alert. He managed a rough answer. "Well, if I only knew where *here* was."

The car pulled ahead of him a bit and Denver was shocked to see it was a police car, or at least it had been a police car, maybe fifty years ago. With huge whitewalls and large rounded fenders, it was an auto collector's dream. The man stopped the car and got out. His silhouetted form revealed a hat befitting law enforcement. Denver caught a glimpse of a pistol at the man's side and thought it best to attempt de-escalation. "I, uh, I'm not looking for any kind of trouble."

The uniformed figure stepped a bit closer. "Listen, son, why don't ya just get in my squad car, and let's figure out what's going on here."

Denver's fight-or-flight mechanism went into overdrive, and he chose the latter. He darted off the road, and flung himself across a shallow ditch, landing and tripping in a dirt-clod field. He recovered his stride and ran in the moonlight, navigating as best he could through the low rows of freshly harvested wheat.

The stranger lifted a gun. "Hey! Stop! Don't make me shoot you, son!"

Denver stumbled again, hitting face first into a patch of sharp wheat stubs, but recovered in a mess of dirt, sweat, and adrenaline, and took off again.

The man took aim. "Last warning!"

Denver's heart pounded out of his chest as he continued his mad and uneven pace. Then there was a flash, a crack of gunfire, and Denver was thrown forward with the impact. He smacked the bristled ground and rolled several times. The back of his left shoulder felt like it had been tagged by a scorpion's tail, burning and enflamed. He slid to a stop and reached around with his right hand. *What was this?*

His fingers discovered a large device buried into his flesh and yanked it out.

A tranquilizer dart?

He flung it away and moments later realized that these missiles were aptly-named. A strange calm descended over him, his muscles felt like lead, and his breathing slowed.

His vision started to defocus, and his eyelids weighed at least seventy-five pounds each. He saw something approaching and raised his head off the ground for a final time. In his crooked and blurred field of view, the man in uniform walked up and knelt beside him, holstering his weapon.

Denver tried to react and respond, but all of his military training collapsed under the weight of chemistry and biology. He stopped resisting and found it considerably easier to just fall asleep.

The uniformed assailant almost laughed.

"Sweet dreams, son. And welcome to 1956."

Tuesday, April 9, 1946
Journal entry number 18

I am not alone! This is unbelievable! Where to begin?

Wow, the last 24 hours have been terrifying, and amazing, and wonderful all at the same time...at least for me. His name is Ken Miller. He is from Texas, South Texas actually. And he is from 1979!

I just read those 3 sentences above again. I'm still almost pinching myself. Let me back up a bit, so much to share about what happened yesterday. You could hear it all over town, apparently. It rumbled the apartment pretty good. It was still echoing when I went outside. My next door neighbor stepped out and looked at me and said a strange word:
Thunder.
I looked around. A few clouds, but 99% blue sky. I started to go back inside, but then I remembered March 5. My Jump Day. Lightning, thunder, a severe storm back home, but no storm here in Normal. It brought back all those early questions—am I alone? Has this happened before? Can it happen again? Did it have anything to do with the storm that night?

I couldn't resist the possibility—and I walked downtown. There was so much at stake—so what if it turns out to be nothing? I got close to the diner, and there were some people talking and pointing. I asked about the thunder. A lady said a farmer she knows just on the north of town saw the flash. He had said it was close, real close.

I left them and started running. I realized that even if there was another Jumper, it didn't really help my case—but somehow—just the idea of it was thrilling, comforting. My misery would really love some company. It was probably thirty minutes after the blast. I hunted up and down the road beside the farm. And then I saw him.

Along a small creek to my left, there was a thick patch of trees, and there was a man lying on his stomach. He was in a nice gray suit, not terribly different than a 1946 suit, but you could tell it was out of place. I thought my heart was gonna come out of my chest!

I looked around for witnesses and ran to him. He was out cold, but breathing. He was breathing! I took some cold creek water and splashed his face. It took a while, but he came around.

There were a whole bunch of things that happened in the next 3 or 4 hours. Too much to tell in this little journal. He went through all the expected phases—disorientation, confusion, denial, more denial. A long walk downtown, a little television (I finally found one), and a few newspapers helped. It will sink in, but it won't be overnight. I hope I will be a good mentor. I am experienced, but far from an expert.

Ken is from Texas. He said it was June 20, 1979 back home. He is (or is it WAS, or is it WILL BE?) a salesman with Texas Instruments computing. Overseas sales, international stuff.

It will take some time to sort this out, to figure out where we go from here. Should we stay together here? What's the cover story? Brother from out of town? Second cousin moved in looking for work?

He is 31 years old, 7 years younger than me. Smart. Friendly. Married. No kids.

Ken's arrival proves at least three things:

1. These time jumps are almost definitely related to lightning somehow.

2. My own jump was not a unique event.

3. There might be more Jumpers in the future, and maybe there have been some before me/us.

There certainly are enough questions to keep you awake all night if you let them. We will head downtown tomorrow...I will be looking for clothes, he will be looking for answers.

So am I, Ken—so am I.

CHAPTER 5

Not quite 1,500 miles away and deep in the desert Southwest, an immaculate blue 1949 Oldsmobile made its way east on Route 66. The two gorgeous blondes who occupied the front couch seat (with windows down, scarves blowing in the wind) made the entire scene look like something right out of *Life Magazine.*

The passenger was engrossed in a tabloid, and she spoke without even looking up. "Are you positive this cousin of yours and I will...you know...hit it off?"

"Sharon, do you honestly think I would sacrifice my vacation to drive you all the way to Oklahoma, if I didn't think you two were perfect for each other?"

The passenger looked over; her skepticism barely assuaged. She thought about the answer, but soon got distracted by the dazzling silver ring with an impressive red stone adorning the right hand of the driver. "Where did you say you got that ring, Deb?"

Debbie smiled and showcased it. "It was a gift from my mother." She paused. "Sort of a going away gift, I suppose."

"Never seen one like it. It's really something."

"Thanks."

Sharon flipped the page on her magazine. "I've been on a few blind dates, but nothing like this. What if we don't—you know, *match*? This could be one awkward trip."

"Have I ever led you astray?"

"Well, no. Not *this week*, anyway." They both laughed.

Sharon discovered an adorable outfit on page seven and pulled the magazine close. The car started slowing and the right turn signal began flashing. She looked up at the empty vista, just miles of road, and a steep embankment off to the right. The car came to a smooth stop along the narrow shoulder. Debbie jumped out and the passenger leaned over. "What's the matter, Deb? Outta gas?"

"Nope, full of pee. I gotta go. Be right back."

The driver vanished around back and Sharon flipped her visor down. She rummaged through her purse and fished out some blush. Moments later she grabbed her lipstick and puckered for another alluring application.

The back door opened, as the vain occupant moved closer to the mirror for a better inspection. She heard the driver rumbling through the bags nestled in the back seat. "What're you doing back there?" Sharon inquired. "Looking for toilet paper?"

"Nah, just lookin' for a snack."

Sharon turned her head incrementally from side to side. "You know, my boss, Leon? He said he hates it when you and I walk into the store together. He says he has a hard time telling us apart."

Debbie stopped rummaging through the sacks. "Well, actually," she said, "that's the whole point."

Like a silent and lethal pair of snakes Debbie's hands slid from the backseat and latched either side of Sharon's head. With a ruthless and experienced twist, the young woman's neck was quickly and audibly snapped. The killer guided the beautiful and lifeless body back against the seat. She hopped back in the front and traded purses with the still-warm corpse.

With planned precision, she put the car in neutral and opened the door, jumping out and grabbing the steering wheel through the open window. The car began to accelerate downhill as she struggled to veer it to the right. With gravity and momentum now at the helm, the Oldsmobile plunged off the steep drop. In a disturbing cascade of metal, rock, and dust, the vehicle fell, hit, and tumbled its way down to the red-graveled valley below, eventually coming to rest upside down.

Debbie produced a small pistol and targeted the exposed gas tank. The car erupted in a small fireball and was soon engulfed in the blaze.

As if on cue, and almost out of nowhere, another dark sedan drew alongside her, coming to a calculated stop. She opened the passenger door and slid in.

"*Speshka, poydem comrade,*" Debbie said and shut her door.

The sedan accelerated away from the fire and the smoke, headed due east.

CHAPTER 6

"Mornin' sunshine."

The words echoed into the distance in Denver's mind like a dream, or was the voice real? He ascended back towards consciousness as if surfacing from a deep dive. He opened his heavy eyes, which snapped shut in the bright light. He attempted to sit up, but a blast of splitting pain through his skull ended that enterprise in short order. He laid back down, massaging his head.

The voice called out again. "I said, good mornin'."

Denver squinted and tilted his head to one side. He was greeted by thick, black jail bars, and just beyond that a large wooden desk with a grinning, late middle-aged policeman behind it. Denver tried to sit up once again. He grimaced. "Good isn't the first word that comes to mind. No offense."

"Probably got one heckuva noggin' splitter. Lemme guess—feels like a concrete truck is parked on your forehead?"

Denver managed to rise and sat on the edge of his cot, his face in his hands. *"Two* trucks."

The cop, or whatever he was, laughed under his breath as he rose out of his seat. "Hey, that one's on you, pal. I told you to stop runnin'."

Denver couldn't help but nod in an odd-sort of agreement. *What's this?* He looked down and was taken aback when he saw what he was now wearing. His new clothes were completely different than what he had been wearing last night, or at least, what he was wearing when he lost consciousness. He had no idea how long his drug-induced state had lasted. He examined his jail attire, not fashionable for sure, but he wouldn't have looked twice at anyone wearing it on any given sidewalk.

He reached around to his back pocket, then his front two. The stranger noticed.

"Lookin' for these, Mr. Collins?"

Denver glanced over as the cop opened a drawer and produced a familiar wallet and smartphone. He dangled them in the air and smiled. "Well, let's just say these ain't safe in this time zone."

He tucked the wallet away, but kept the phone out. "Trust me, ya got more bars over there, son, than you'll ever get with this. Well, at least not for another fifty years or so."

He stashed the phone in the drawer and strolled over to the cell, offering a steaming cup of coffee through the bars. "Here. This'll go a long way to clear things up. I hit you with enough happy juice to stop a small grizzly. But you'll be back to normal in no time. I promise."

The cop slid a chair over and leaned in as Denver took a cautious sip or two. "So, lemme ask you, son. When're you from?"

Denver didn't make eye contact. "New York, East side."

The cop paused. "I don't think you heard me. I didn't ask *where*, I asked *when* are you from?"

Denver froze and glared at him.

The officer grinned and leaned in again. "You heard me right, son. But wait, forgive me, Mr. Collins, I'll go first." The cop shoved his powerful hand through the bars. "I'm Police Chief James McCloud, but you can call me Jim. I'm from Atlanta, the year 1996. I jumped, local time, spring of 1950. Been here six years, actually a little over."

Denver returned the handshake, but only out of courtesy. He was doing his best to process the nonsense while recovering from a tranquilizer-accentuated migraine. He wagged his head. "Look, with all due respect to the badge, I really don't know who you are, or where I am, or what's going on here. So, if you'll just—"

"Hey, I know it's a lot to swallow, son. Heck, I remember my first day. Not much better'n yours!" The self-proclaimed police chief stood up. "I actually jumped naked and was found by a cute little gal, but that's another story for another time."

With considerable effort, Denver stood as well, and leaned against the bars. "I'm not sure whose idea of a funny joke this is, but you've got about five seconds to let me outta here, and even then I won't promise that legitimate law enforcement won't get a sudden and heated phone call."

The Chief reached back and snatched a folded newspaper. He slapped it against the bars by Denver's hand. "Check out the headlines, hotshot."

Denver retrieved it with some reluctance:

NORMAL JOURNAL FRIDAY, AUGUST 10, 1956.

He shoved it back, unimpressed. "You know what they say, don't believe everything you read."

The Chief appeared almost hurt, but shook his head as he stepped towards a console TV set. He muttered under his breath as he flipped it on, "I would get a stubborn Trailer right before a nice, quiet weekend." He smiled with confidence. "How about these TV shows, Ace?"

The black and white set crackled alive, right in the middle of a skit on *The Garry Moore Show*. Denver studied it for a few seconds. "Yeah, I think my soon-to-be-ex has that whole show on DVD. Now listen, I'm not kidding—you better let me outta here!" He rattled the door to the cell. It didn't give much. "I know people!"

The Chief marched over to the bars. "Know people? Not around here you don't. Listen! My name is Chief James McCloud. It is August the tenth, 1956. You are no longer in the heart of the Big Apple. You are in the middle of Normal,

Illinois. You are a Jumper, and I am too. And *we are not alone.*"

Denver stood there, half waiting for the punch line.

It never came.

He dropped back and plopped down onto his cot. Chief McCloud slid his chair closer. "Trust me—I know it's a lot to take in, but if you promise to play nice, promise you won't run, I wanna show you something."

Denver looked up into the Chief's wide-eyed, grinning face, as his own thoughts were in a desperate struggle to connect the dots.

This is way too elaborate for an office prank. Gotta be the government...yeah...it's got CIA or NSA written all over it. Maybe if I play along, I can get out quicker.

The cop pushed his right hand between the bars. "Whaddya say? Deal?"

Denver strained to take any of this seriously. "Uh, deal."

The Chief slapped his hands together, grabbed his key ring, and unlocked the cell. "Now that's my boy. C'mon!"

Denver took a few tentative steps out and sized up the Spartan room. A desk, gun cabinet, a few filing cabinets, chairs, large TV, concrete floor. He spotted a framed photo of President Eisenhower on the wall just to his left.

Nice touch. These government psychological testing programs are very meticulous. Can't wait to see the rest of this operation.

Chief McCloud trotted ahead of him towards the front door. As Denver got close, the Chief stepped aside and threw the door open for him, as if he were a visiting magistrate. "Right this way, Mr. Collins."

Denver exited the imitation police station into the bright sunlight of a late summer day, and was blinded for a few seconds. The Chief shut the door and flanked him.

"Welcome to Normal, Illinois!"

Monday, April 15, 1946
Journal entry number 21

Ken is approaching his one week anniversary. I think he is doing better than I was at Jump+7—no scratch that—I *KNOW* that he is doing better.

It is difficult to describe how immensely helpful Ken is, how much of a relief it is to actually be able to talk freely with another human being. It's like I have been trapped in a foreign country, and I barely know the language, and then suddenly, I meet another American, better yet: an American from near my home town.

We are about eight years apart (jump-date-wise), two states apart geographically, and politically only one president removed. He asked me yesterday if Carter won a second term. I didn't tell him, but I'm afraid my face did.

Having Ken around changes things profoundly. It's like having your own apartment, and then taking on a roommate. When you are alone, you really don't need formal rules, because, well...it's just you. And who cares? But then, there are TWO. An object alone can generate no conflict, but with two, friction is possible, rather...it is *probable*.

But it's not just about rules, or about formal agreements governing how we treat each other, or our respective responsibilities. Most of those things will arise naturally, organically anyway.

This relationship...it could change the world, and change it accidentally. We need policies, guiding principles. Especially if our group grows. Then everyone needs to agree to them, to be in accord with them. Like a micro-society within society, we would be a temporal subculture.

I like that word ACCORD. I guess I've already made one "rule": Walk Without Footprints. Should it be called: The First Rule of Phillip? Sounds a bit self-aggrandizing. How about this:

The First Accord: Walk Without Footprints.

Better. There is something comforting and stabilizing about rules, about boundaries. I'm not Moses, and I don't plan on making anywhere close to TEN of these, but I know there is value and virtue in them.

Oh, and Ken mentioned something the other day: Diseases. There are illnesses and diseases that this time period faces that Ken and I have not been exposed to, at least in a long time. I'm not sure the vaccines we've had will prepare our bodies. It's strange to think that an old disease could kill time Jumpers from the future. Almost like a version of the Old World diseases wiping out the natives of the New World 500 years ago. Not a pleasant thought.

But, if you think about it, Ken and I are diseases. We are foreign bodies injected into a 1946 host. We could poison and harm its natural future. Maybe a disease wiping out a disease would be nature's way of correcting its own impossible mistakes.

By the way, we are tentatively planning a trip to Vegas. Soon. We need money. I have some big plans.

CHAPTER 7

Normal? Normal, Illinois? Ain't nothing about this whole experience I would label as Normal.

Denver blinked hard and was compelled to squint as his eyes did their best to adjust. The sheer volume of intense daylight aggravated his headache somewhat afresh. As he acclimated, he found himself on a sidewalk in the middle of yesteryear.

This fake town's name must've been some bureaucrat's idea of a joke. "Abnormal" would be better.

The area appeared exactly like a community that time had long-since forgotten; indeed, much like any other Midwest town in the height of the 1950s. Vintage cars, people, clothing, and storefronts filled his vision. He was impressed.

Whoa, someone has really gone to a lot of trouble for this simulation. Maybe they will give me one of these cars as a consolation prize when it's over.

The Chief stepped around in front of him, grinning like an over-zealous tour guide. Denver would've almost laughed, if it hadn't been for the sidearm on the Chief's hip and the fact that he didn't have any idea where he really was or how long the powers that be were going to keep him for testing.

The Chief continued, proud and genial. "A beautiful Friday mornin' here in Normal. They're callin' for an even prettier weekend."

Denver concentrated on McCloud, wondering if that was even his real name. He studied his face, his demeanor, his costume.

He's a great actor, I'll give him that. A bit overplayed, but a good actor.

The Chief made his way toward a familiar squad car parked along the curb. "C'mon, I wanna take you for a tour. Technically your *second* ride in my car, but you probably don't remember the first one. You can sit in the front this time." The Chief started to get in the driver's seat, but raised his head over the roof. "For the record, you're heavier'n you look." He winked, and then motioned for Denver to hop in.

A vintage amusement park with rides, how nice, Denver thought. *At least I will be a lot closer to his pistol while I'm sitting in the car. That might prove useful later on.*

A well-dressed blonde sporting a summer hat passed Denver. Their eyes met and he nodded. "Hello."

The Chief tapped his horn. "Quit castin' an eyeball at that Dolly, lover boy, and get in here." Denver grabbed a final look around and slid into the passenger's seat.

The Chief dropped his voice. "Pretty sure she's circled anyway." Denver wrinkled his brow. McCloud explained. "You know circled…*married.*" The Chief held up his hand and traced around his ring finger several times. "Circled."

The squad car backed out of the slot and eased into the uptown lane. The breeze through the open window played with Denver's hair. "I do believe you are the very first stock broker I've ever had in this squad car," the Chief said.

Denver perked up. *I knew it. This is the government messing with me. Nice slip up, fake cop.* Denver smiled. "Now, how could you possibly know that?"

The Chief adopted a mischievous look. "I know people!" He glanced over at his passenger. "*Nah*—just kiddin'. I found information in your wallet. Detective work, it's my job. Or, one of my jobs."

Denver refused to be amused and took in the view, stunned at just how big this fabricated town was turning out to be. The Chief glanced over at the jaded stare in the eyes of his captive yet not captivated audience. McCloud changed the subject. "Jumpers."

"Excuse me?"

"Jumpers. That's what they call us, I mean, that's what we call ourselves. Me, you, us, we're Jumpers."

The Chief waved at a few of the locals as he slowed for a stop sign. Denver angled towards the Chief, willing to entertain this comical stranger for a little while longer. He glanced down at the pistol. It could've been in his hands in just over a second. That brought a strange sense of comfort.

"It started in the mid-to-late '40s," the cop began. "Now Doc and Ellen can explain it a whole lot better'n me, but it had something to do with nukes—"

"Nukes? Nuclear weapons?"

"That's what Phil and the others have told us. All that atomic testing did it. Manhattan Project they called it. Doc said those bombs created little holes, little rips in the space-time-continuum thing."

Denver called to mind another recent car ride and another conversation with a curious six-year-old less than twenty-four hours ago. He smiled as he glanced up at the sparse clouds. *"Invisible cracks in the sky."*

The Chief was on a roll and didn't seem to notice Denver's reaction. Denver, on the other hand, noticed just how smoothly McCloud delivered his little speech.

"Anywho...apparently these little time portals are pretty harmless," McCloud continued. "They don't bother anyone or anything. Well, at least not until they're supplied with huge, and I do mean huge, amounts of energy."

They made a wide left turn and the Chief's attention shifted abruptly to a couple of young men on the sidewalk. He slowed and leaned out the window. "Charlie Wilson! I better not catch you hotroddin' out on 66 tonight!"

The young men responded with nods and waves. The Chief chuckled and accelerated. "Kids! They all think they're the next Mario Andretti. Anywho...what was I sayin'?"

"Huge energy."

"Oh yeah...listen, lemme ask you a question. What's the last thing you remember before you came here, here to Normal?"

Denver gazed out his passenger window. "I was in my apartment. I had a few drinks, it was a rough night. I fell asleep and then I woke up in your little government-sponsored freak show here."

The Chief either ignored or dismissed the last little jab. "What else was going on? How 'bout the weather?"

"The weather?" Denver asked. "Well, it was about as nasty as my soon-to-be-ex: Rain, stormy."

McCloud motioned with his hands in an effort to get Denver to elaborate. "And lots of...?"

"Lots of...*what*?"

"Lightning, son! Lots of big, huge, lightning bolts."

He stared hard at the Chief, a man who now seemed a bit more credible.

McCloud continued, "Lightning. Guaranteed. Bet my life on it. It's the only common denominator for all of us Jumpers. Everyone has the same story. One second we're living our lives, then BAM! CRASH! Lightning bolt, and the next second, we're here. Right here, Normal, Illinois."

Denver decided to play along with this clever scenario, or maybe he was starting to buy into it; he couldn't actually tell. He threw the Chief a curve ball. "But why here, I mean, why *Normal*?"

The Chief didn't even blink. "That's the one angle our experts ain't quite nailed down yet. Some think it has to do with the geographic makeup of the area, something 'bout the land, and metal deposits—heck, who knows?" The Chief laughed and slapped Denver on the shoulder. "Hey, maybe there's a secret military program around here!"

Denver wasn't laughing. "There was lightning and thunder last night," he admitted.

"Not just a regular bolt of lightning, no sir. Doc calls it a Superbolt. Only one lightning strike in a million fits the bill. He says when a Superbolt hits one of those tears, those holes in the space-time-thing, it opens the portal wide enough to actually send an entire person back in time."

They turned onto a new street, and the Chief waved again at a driver passing by. "That's how I found you so quickly. That's how we *always* find 'em, at least, most of 'em." Denver shot him a bewildered look.

"The lightning and the thunder," the Chief said. "When a Jumper *jumps*, the portal carries a part of the lightning and a lot of the thunder back with it. We call it a FLaT. Being a cop and all, I hear about all of the strange stuff. When you jumped, heck, my phone rang off the wall last night—it was a snap to find you. Lightning and thunder on a clear night, dead giveaway, son."

Denver sat there, trying to take it all in. He could think of at least three good reasons why this was clearly ridiculous. The problem was, he could rationalize five better ones that made it believable.

As he became distracted in his thoughts, the Chief appeared to be distracted as well. A little commotion on the sidewalk in front of a soda fountain had snagged his attention. He slammed on the brakes, inadvertently throwing his passenger into the dash. The Chief jumped out, and then leaned back into his driver's window. "Stay here. I'll be right back. I can't wait for school to start back up next month!"

Three young boys were in a late summer scuffle, and the one on the ground was taking a severe thrashing. The Chief closed the distance, hollering at the boys. Denver looked over at the keys, still in the ignition. He glanced back up at Chief McCloud, who was occupied with diffusing the brawl.

It's now or never. I could be out of this psyche study in five minutes. Well, that is, unless there are armed guards posted along the perimeter. Denver slid across the seat. "So long, freak show."

He threw the car into drive and pressed the pedal to the floor.

Thursday, April 18, 1946
Journal entry number 23

Someone once said that knowledge is power.

But what about Future Knowledge? Maybe Future Knowledge isn't power. Perhaps it is DANGEROUS, like a nuclear bomb, powerful and dangerous. There are two issues at stake here, and neither is absolutely "knowable":

1. What happens if Ken or I accidentally reveal Future Knowledge to someone here in 1946? What effects will that have in the Time-Stream?

2. What happens if I accidentally impart Future Knowledge to Ken, and then (hypothetically) we find a way to get back home? He will return to 1979 with Future Knowledge, which then could impact the world from 1979 on, and then I will return to the late 1980s, into a world (potentially) changed by Ken.

This kind of thinking used to be a fun and fruitless exercise when I studied physics in college, usually leading to arguments in the frat house, especially after liquid-courage-enhancers in 12 ounce metal cans. But this is—real. These are real issues. To neglect them is to crack open something potentially far more destructive than the lid of Pandora's Box.

In war they say: "Loose Lips Sink Ships." But, honestly, a few frigates doomed to the depths is nothing compared to what we could possibly unleash with careless conversation.

We need our second axiom, another accord. Especially if our group grows beyond two. Something about keeping the future secret. We have to consider everything we say, or, rather, are about to say to each other, and to non-Jumpers (I've been calling them Locals). We need a type of screen, or a filter. I like that. A Filter.

Our Second Accord: Filter the Future.

After much planning, we will finally jump on the bus tomorrow, headed for Las Vegas. Easy cash awaits!

On a sad note, a cargo ship exploded at port in Texas City, Texas, a few days ago. Hundreds dead. Wiped out twenty city blocks. Close to where Ken grew up.

CHAPTER 8

My car! Son of a gun.

The Chief looked up in disbelief and darted out into the road as the squad car stole away, minus its rightful owner. He wiped his sweaty forehead. "You'll never get out of here, Mr. Collins. This thing is way bigger than you or me. You'll see."

Denver raced down the street, ignoring both the speed limit and ordinary caution. As adrenaline pushed him, he pushed the accelerator, his pulse pounding. He attempted to navigate the first corner and slid out of control, almost slamming into an on-coming car.

What's this? No power steering?

Denver corrected just in time to avoid hitting a second vehicle and then narrowly missed a few parked cars off to his right. The fleeing fugitive approached a four-way stop at full throttle and plowed on through.

The brakes and tires squealed as he made a hard right, struggling to compensate for the difficulty of sharp turns. The steering wheel seemed determined to fight him in a battle of wills. With the police station back in sight, he dropped his speed and rolled past, searching for something. Two doors further along he cut down a small alley on his left. He made another left at the end of the narrow lane and gunned the motor for the final stretch.

The echoing roar of the police sedan scared a stray dog scavenging through the garbage, and it bolted out in front of him. Startled, Denver cut the wheel hard to his right. He missed the malnourished animal, but caught a small tree on the edge of the alley instead, tearing a sizeable gash in the front end. He coasted to a stop behind the station and parked the squad car, yanking the keys out. He looked back at the lucky dog, who had already returned to his meal, then jogged over to the back door of the police station. He tried three or four keys before success, cursing himself for his trembling hands.

Focus, Collins. Focus.

The back door started to give way but then jammed on him. He slammed his shoulder into it and popped the door loose, nearly falling to the bare concrete floor in the process.

Denver scurried over to the Chief's desk and ransacked the drawers. Papers, folders, a few playing cards, and two packs of smokes became casualties of war in his mad scramble. He grabbed his confiscated wallet and phone and continued to pilfer the remaining drawers.

The lowest drawer yielded a bonus. *A pistol. Now that's more like it, McCloud.* He plopped the sidearm onto the desktop and rummaged for some ammo. He grabbed the gun, kicked out the magazine, loaded it, and shoved it back in with all the skill, speed, and precision of a trained soldier. He held it aloft for a brief moment.

Been a long time. Feels good. Finally something real around here.

The cold metal, clasped against his skin, took him back to a much different time. To what seemed to almost be another life. This whole fiasco was the second time in his young life that the government had taken him far from his comfort zone.

Of course, the first time it was voluntary, completely of his own choosing. The GI Bill was hard to ignore in the late 1990s for someone who needed college money, and whose parents and whose grades were incapable of offering much more than encouragement. He endured basic training, but he generally enjoyed the discipline and comradeship of Army life.

As the final month of his enlistment drew near, many members of his new military family put pressure on him to sign up for a second go around. It was strangely tempting, but he had his sights set on a degree in economics, paid for courtesy of Uncle Sam. He had always been fascinated with numbers, financials, and the global market. The Army had shown him what the world of implemented national policy looked like, but economics held the promise of revealing a much bigger picture.

Denver's family had planned a tremendous welcome back home party for early October of 2001. That is, until nineteen terrorists mercilessly obliterated two towers, four planes, part of the Pentagon, and over 3,000 innocent American lives.

More than airplanes were hijacked on that pivotal September day in America's national history—Denver's personal future suffered a violent takeover as well. Overcome with thoughts of justified revenge and brimming with patriotic fervor, many young men (including Denver and his younger brother, Dallas) either upped or re-upped. The attacks on the Twin Towers may have only temporarily crippled the U.S. economic system, but it indefinitely derailed Denver's dream of a future in financials.

In his mind, global economics could wait. It was time for global payback.

His marksmanship scores and spotless evals landed Denver a role in Task Force Dagger, a few weeks before Thanksgiving 2001. Cave-by-cave, town-by-town, tribe-by-tribe, his unit (one of many under the command of Colonel John Mulholland) routed the Taliban throughout Afghanistan. Once the last stronghold of bitter enemy resistance in Kandahar fell in early December, Denver's team relocated all across the unforgiving landscape until he left the army in the fall of 2005. It was a land of many contradictions, with nomadic herders subsisting in a culture that had changed minimally over thousands of years, yet communicating on satellite phones and email.

But four brutal years of sleep deprivation, innumerable late night raids, countless IEDs, and far too many flag-draped caskets were enough for the twenty-five-year-old boy from New York.

Like thousands who preceded and followed him, it was curiously difficult for Denver to make that sudden transition back to the soft civility of a civilian existence. The real world was an unfamiliar environment for those who had experienced the horrors of a land where life is cheap, and death is even cheaper.

And now, in the last twenty-four hours, it appeared that Uncle Sam had once again dumped Denver into a world he was totally unprepared for.

But this time, things were different.

He now had experience. He had combat skills. He had an overriding desire to get back to his daughter. Denver was more than a decent human being, but he feared for the safety of any man who would stand in the way of him achieving that goal.

Denver untucked his shirt and shoved the loaded pistol just inside his back waistband and jogged over to the jail cell. He pulled out the keys, removing the one for the squad car, and stuffed it back into his pocket. He locked the cell door, and then pitched the remaining keys into the cell. They slid along the smooth floor and Denver was halfway across the room before they came to a stop beneath the humble cot.

He locked the front door from the inside and sped over to the gun cabinet. Four rifles and a shotgun stood at the ready. He stepped back, kicked in the thin, glass door, and began grabbing the firearms. Denver slammed them, one at a time, onto the hard concrete floor. By the time he was finished, the arms collection was reduced to a twisted pile of steel and splintered wood. He snatched several boxes of ammo and chucked them into the jail cell as well.

He took one more look around and spotted the phone on the Chief's desk. He started to grab it, but then reconsidered. *They probably use radios or cellphones anyway.* He set it down and exited through the back door, making sure to lock it as well.

The foul stench of hot antifreeze assaulted him immediately. He glanced over at the car as radiator fluid drained upon the ground forming a tiny green river and volumes of steam rose above the hood. Saving a dog's life had cost him the regrettable loss of his easy ticket out of town.

He paused to consider his options. Flush brick buildings on the near side and towering shade trees straight ahead lined the narrow chasm, and Denver moved to his right along the tree line. About half a block down, a break in the trees revealed another short alley to his left and he took it, picking up his pace. He fished his phone out with some difficulty, hoping against hope for even a single bar.

But, hope disappointed. *Nothing.*

The shaded corridor dumped out onto another uptown street. A handful of vintage-era shoppers and an occasional dog-walker littered either side of the lane. Denver hesitated as a few more classic cars cruised by. He did a quick reconnaissance, looking for the location of surveillance cameras, on the light poles, and even along the tops of the buildings. The only thing he spotted of interest was a small restaurant across the road with a large, picture window. AMANDA'S DINER was painted across it in a gentle curve with two-tone lettering and a small OPEN sign dangled on the front door just to its left.

He crossed the street, attempting to be casual, and kept his head down. Denver had the irrational impression that everyone was staring at him, but no one seemed to be paying any attention to the out of breath newcomer.

A dull jingle from a broken bell announced his arrival to the diner, and none of the smattering of patrons even bothered to look up, except for one little girl in the nearest booth. She leaned out from behind the seat and smiled at him with a tiny wave, clutching a rag doll that was actually more rag than doll.

Denver caught her eye and managed to force a grin back. *About the same age as my Jasmine.* She held up her doll proudly, and then a momma's hand snapped her back into a more proper posture. Denver scanned the area, looking for exits and vantage points as he sized the place up. He glanced back out the window. *Business as usual out there. Odd.*

He grabbed a seat at the long bar as far from the front window as possible. He figured he could hop over the counter and make a break through the kitchen if he was forced to. Denver reached around to ensure that his gun wasn't showing.

That little piece of steel was his ultimate back up plan if things went south.

Monday, April 22, 1946
Journal entry number 25

I can't wait to visit the new Flamingo Casino. It just opened about 6 months ago. It looked great as we were coming in on the bus.

Hopefully Sin City will turn into Cash City for Ken and me. We need money to live on, and we will need large sums of money (eventually) for time-travel research. What better way to acquire large sums of money than gambling? We have weighed the pros and cons of this effect on the time-stream, and we feel like this will be a minimal impact on the future.

Our plan is to hit multiple casinos and bet on sports. Ken is a bit of a sports buff, and he knows the outcomes of a lot of games. I think we could spend a few weeks here and rake in a small fortune.

They say the house always wins.

Well—the house never met Ken and me.

CHAPTER 9

She had peered through that smudged window in the
swinging kitchen door at least a thousand times. Every time
the bell on the front door clanged, waitress Katie Long
peered out. She was always looking for something, never
sure what to expect, and never sure what she wanted it to be.

But today, she was intrigued, and grew far more certain
that she might have found what she had been missing. Katie
was so caught up in the moment that she didn't even notice
the close approach of fellow-waitress, Beverly Welker.

She examined Katie and then bent down, apparently
trying to locate the object of Katie's attraction. "What's so
interesting? Is Mayor Vorhees picking his nose again?"

Katie reluctantly stepped aside, allowing a better angle
for her coworker. Bev adjusted and spotted Denver over at
the bar. Her hands dropped to her hips. "Well, hello there,
handsome."

Katie shook her head with playful disgust and bumped
Bev away from the door. "You know the rules. First one to
the window wins."

Bev wasn't so easily dismissed. "That's never really been
a rule. More like a guideline, sugar. Let's uh, settle this one
the only fair way." She reached down into her mostly-
attached apron pocket and held up a quarter. "Heads he's
yours, tails he's mine."

Katie grimaced in mild protest, but her coworker flipped
the coin anyway, and it bounced and settled on the counter
nearby. They leaned in...*heads*. Bev stepped away from the
swinging door and stretched out her arm towards it.

"Go get 'em, you lucky tiger!"

Katie blushed a bit and stared at her fun-house reflection
in the flimsy metal door. She carefully teased and pulled a

few strands of blonde hair down and then straightened her outfit. She turned to Bev who surveyed her up and down like a proud mother inspecting her daughter before her first big social event.

Bev stepped back. "A goddess in a greasy apron, but hey—a goddess no less. Now get out there to this unsuspecting mortal!"

***

Denver noticed a well-worn tri-fold paper menu sandwiched between the ketchup and mustard bottles, and flipped it open. He was impressed by the incredible level of detail of this vintage, small town simulation. *Right down to the coffee stains on the menu, complete with 1950s prices…nice.* He turned it over, admiring the craftsmanship. He was running his finger down a ragged fold when a question startled his investigation.

"Don't get a paper cut. I think we're fresh out of bandages."

He nearly dropped the menu and looked up into the simply beautiful and wide-eyed face of Katie Long. He surveyed her figure and fashion, order pad in hand, complemented with a perfect cherry-lipped smile. It was a setting obviously borrowed from a Normal Rockwell painting. If the menu was an impressive prop in this little charade, the waitress sealed the illusion.

A little bit predictable, but I doubt they could've picked a better actress. I'll give 'em that.

She stood there while he judged her like a runway model. The tension became uncomfortable and she broke it. "Can I get you some coffee for uh, starters?"

He continued to study her, but he was thirsty, and he was hungry. "Oh, sure, coffee sounds good…black."

"Only color we got today," she said. "The blue brew
with pink polka dots doesn't come in from Chicago til next
week." She winked, tucked the order pad away, and turned
to grab a fresh pot.

"So, are you all serving the uh...the lunch menu yet,
Katie?" he asked. "I'm not really a breakfast kind of guy."

She donned a stern face, with just a hint of a smile and
leaned in. "Lunch? Oh, *dinner*. No, not for another half-hour,
at least officially," she said. "But I think I can sweet-talk Bob
back there to make just about whatever your little heart
desires. It's the middle column."

"Uh, sorry, the what?"

She pointed at the menu, and tapped it. "The middle
column. The middle of the menu, that's the dinner menu."

He blushed. "Oh, I'm so sorry, yes...just a bit out of it,
today."

Beverly passed by with a plate of food and a low growl.
Katie shot her a look and moved her own attention down to
Denver's wedding ring.

"While you're looking, should I set out another plate for
your wife?" she asked.

"Another plate?" He looked up. "For my....oh. Oh, no,
I'm not marri—I mean, we're sep—uh, it's *complicated*."

She retrieved her order pad again as the doorbell sang its
sad song and another patron strolled in. Denver's whole
body twitched at the sound, and he glanced over at the man
and back to Katie. She continued her picturesque stance and
smile, waiting for Denver's order.

"Well, uh, let's keep it quick and simple," he said. "Can I
get a burger, everything on it, and some fries?"

She began writing feverishly as she rehearsed it. "Put a
cow in the wheat field and run it through the garden, and a
side with eyes. Got it."

Denver contorted his face. "Sounds either delicious, or... *dangerous*. Guess it'll be a surprise."

She smiled and started to turn. "Oh, I'm full of surprises."

He watched her cute figure stroll towards the back.

Maybe this simulation isn't so bad after all.

Tuesday, April 23, 1946
Journal entry number 26

I may have jinxed us with my last journal entry. Who could have known?

Sports betting is not yet legal in Nevada!

Apparently that doesn't happen for at least several more years from now. I know my Dad talked about doing it in the mid-1950s. This is a disaster. Absolute disaster. We spent almost all of our remaining cash on this trip! I'm sure we could find some unsanctioned (illegal) outlets for this type of enterprise, but that is far too risky. I proposed that we should go back to my earlier plan involving the stock market. Ken thinks there is still hope with gambling. He said it involves horses.

CHAPTER 10

Denver enjoyed a few long sips on his cup, surprised and grateful that it wasn't *simulated* coffee. As he contemplated his options, he constructed a mental map of what he had seen of the area. The town of Normal, frankly wasn't normal. It was so picture perfect that it reminded him of those meticulously designed fake communities used in nuclear testing in New Mexico. Or was it Nevada? Or maybe both.

But the real difference, he noticed, was the people. Those model towns were meant to be destroyed. Their citizens and their pets were wood and plastic mannequins, but here, real flesh and blood. In those simulated communities, they were studying blast effects and radiation, but what about here?

What are you researching here, Uncle Sam?

He imagined they were studying a very different kind of bomb, a psychological blast. Perhaps testing the limits of human endurance and the breaking point of a person whose entire life has been replaced, down to the coffee stains on a paper menu.

It seemed so far-fetched, so fantastic, but it was the only possible explanation. *Right? The only one possible.*

But unlike the Army, he didn't sign up for this, for any of this. Maybe that was the point. After all, it wouldn't be much of a test if you knew it wasn't real. He had left active duty over eight years ago, but perhaps there was some clause, some fine print, a tiny caveat that gave Uncle Sam permission to conduct psyche tests, even without consent.

It didn't matter. *I'm not a guinea pig, and I've got enough trouble in my personal life. I don't need military trouble as well. I'm getting off this train.*

Katie navigated past with a tray filled with plates for a nearby booth. Denver snagged her attention. "Excuse me, Katie. Uh, what is the best way for a guy to get out of town, like, as soon as possible? "

She stopped on a dime, balancing her burden. "Hmm... what is it, Friday? Well, probably the ten-fifty to Chicago."

"Ten-fifty? What is that?"

Without a free hand, she tilted her chin at a clock on the wall. It was almost 10:30 in the morning.

"Ten-fifty. A bus for Chicago leaves in about twenty minutes, just up the block, corner of West Beaufort and Broadway," she offered. "I'll be right back."

She continued on with her delivery, and he grabbed his smart phone. Surprisingly, or maybe unsurprisingly, it read: 1:18 A.M., MONDAY. He studied it closer.

Still no bars, no signal. Not even GPS. How is that possible? You can't hide from satellites. Must be scrambling the signal.

Katie returned with an empty delivery tray dangling by her side. "Whatcha got there...a picture?"

"A picture? Oh, no, I was, uh, just checking the time on my iPhone."

"Huh? I'm sorry, did you say your *phone*?"

He glanced into her confused face, and shoved the device back into his pocket. "Well, yes...and uh, no...well, it's—it's—"

"*Complicated*, right? Well, look, sit tight and I'll be right back with your *uncomplicated* food."

He nodded with a forced smile. "Thanks."

CHAPTER 11

Police Chief James McCloud, out of breath, frustrated, and sweating completely through his uniform, rushed up to the front door of the police station. He tried everything he could think of to open it — except for kicking it in — but that did cross his mind.

It's locked, no keys, thank you — Denver Collins! He still yanked on the handle a final time anyway. He spun about and met the stare of two women transfixed by the unusual spectacle.

"Mornin', ladies," he covered. "Just a little routine security check. Nothin' to see here, folks."

They appeared satisfied, and he tipped his hat as they moved along. The Chief rounded the corner and jogged his heavy frame to the back alley, only to be greeted by a steaming mass that was once his fully-functional squad car. He leaned in the car window and searched for the keys.

Nothing.

He mopped his dripping brow and jerked vigorously on the handle of the back door to the station.

Locked, of course!

He scanned for observers in all directions, and stepped back. With gun drawn, he raised his right leg and kicked the door in, splintering the lock area with a loud crash. The commotion startled the stray mutt half a block down out of his summer slumber. The dog raised his head as McCloud was shocked by the mess inside.

What the…?

He caught sight of the mangled pieces of metal and wood that used to be his weapons collection. He looked up at the splintered remains of the door to his handmade gun cabinet. It was hanging on by a single, bent hinge. The entire scene reminded him more of tornado damage than vandalism. He stepped over the shattered chunks of glass and checked the bathroom, then the closet. *No one.*

McCloud went off high alert and secured his weapon into his underarm holster.

Wait…what's this? He moved towards the cell and leaned over, spotting his keys on the floor under the cot, and the contents of his ammo boxes littering the area. He picked up a loose shotgun shell and then tugged on the cell door.

Locked, of course.

The Chief couldn't help but smile. *This guy is good, real good.* He hurled the shell against the cinder block wall. It broke apart and tiny pieces of lead bounced and rolled all across the floor.

"Nicely played, Mr. Collins, nicely played."

CHAPTER 12

The swinging metal doors burst open and Katie emerged from the kitchen with Denver's steaming dinner plate. He may have had trouble believing his eyes here in Normal, but he couldn't deny the reality of the home-cooked meal that his nose conveyed.

She eased the large dish down in front of him with grace. "One cute little cow in the wheat field..."

He smiled and lifted the bun, revealing the vegetables hidden below. "And then run it through the garden," he said. "I get it now."

She pointed at the fries. "And a side with eyes."

He couldn't decode this clever culinary clue. She appeared almost hurt. She pointed again. "*Potatoes.* Eyes."

He shrugged in ignorance. She waved her hand. "Forget it. Anything else I can get for ya?"

"Uh, yes—and no, I mean, no I don't need anything." She began to walk away, he reached up. "Oh, wait, actually yes. Can I have my bill now? I have to literally eat and run. Maybe even run and eat. Sorry."

Katie pulled out her pad, scribbled some barely decipherable math and slipped it face down by his plate. "You can just pay me when you're ready."

He thanked her and devoured his food, eyeing the clock several times. He plucked the bill and turned it over. *Sixty-two cents.* He shook his head as he continued to wolf it down.

Katie and Bev converged in the kitchen and watched him eat, with all the base interest of a couple of adolescents at a peep show. Bev broke the silence first. "You know what they say—healthy eaters make healthy lovers!"

"Would you stop it! No, he's in a hurry, said something about getting out of town."

"You know, a man like that has a girl in every port," Bev said. "Probably headed to the next one now."

Katie faced her cynical companion. "You don't know that. Anyway, he has a wedding ring, but he kinda got strange about it."

Beverly backed up and began collecting a few items. "Definitely a big danger sign, Miss Katie Long. He is a walking, talking heartache. I can smell it from here." She paused for a second. "A *handsome* heartache, but it all hurts the same in the end, no matter how they look."

Katie continued to study him, and leaned in closer to the window. "I dunno. I somehow feel sorry for him. He seems kinda out of place, almost...*lost*." She paused and pushed through the door.

———————————

Denver was finishing his last burger bite as Katie appeared with a pot of coffee. "Fresh cup for the road?"

He protested with his hand as he reached for his wallet. With some difficulty he managed to swallow. "Oh, no, no thanks. I really have to go."

Denver thumbed through his cash and tried to pull out a five dollar bill. It snagged on something and almost tore the corner off. He held it up and frowned. "Well, it all spends the same way." He slid the bill across the counter as he stood and wiped his mouth. "This should cover it, and keep the change."

She was wide-eyed and nearly speechless as he made his way out. "But, you, you can't be serious!" she protested. "This is too much mon—"

He waved with a "don't mention it" look and was gone before the dysfunctional doorbell finished clanking.

Katie remained staring, almost frozen. Bev drew up beside her, and grabbed her co-worker's shoulders.

"If you love someone, you gotta let 'em go—and if they don't return, well, then you need to hunt them down and strap 'em to a crop duster."

CHAPTER 13

Chief McCloud plopped his frustrated and tired frame down at his desk and began dialing his desk phone. *At least he didn't cut my phone cord!* He scooted back and partially opened a drawer, then jerked it out all the way. *Of course! He came back for his wallet and phone.* He shifted the phone to his left hand and examined all the drawers. Disgusted at what he didn't find, he slammed them all shut and leaned back.

"Hey Leah, I need Shep." He rechecked a few of the drawers. "It's me. Listen. We have a situation. He's gone." He tapped on the desk. "Denver Collins is *gone,* and he is armed." He scrubbed his chin. "Yes. And there's something else—he found his wallet and his phone."

He rolled his eyes and rubbed the sweat off his wrinkled brow. "I know...I know that, too. I am well aware of what this could mean...I will find him, we will find him...I've called O'Connell in." He looked up at the ceiling. "I know this is a bad time!"

McCloud leaned in and fished a liquor flask out of the bottom drawer. He nodded a few times and took a quick hit on the bottle. "No, he only knows what I've told him." He put the cap back on the bottle. "No, he doesn't know 'bout that. Don't worry! We will clean this up. I promise you, I promise you: I won't let *them* get to him first."

He returned the flask to its hiding place. "I will eliminate this threat. Period." McCloud slammed the phone down into the cradle.

He pulled out his gun, and checked the chamber. It was full.

CHAPTER 14

As he made his way back to secure a seat, Denver thought that the 10:50 to Chicago idled more like a freight train than a bus. With each step, he debated the rationality of this escape plan. Surely the bus was as much a part of the grand charade as the rest of this psychological experiment.

Where will it take me? Back to jail?

To Chicago? Hardly believable.

A fake Chicago? Even more absurd.

Halfway back an open seat to his left came into view, and he slid into it carrying nothing but a list of questions. A few stragglers poured in as the bus prepared to leave, and with a deafening release of air brakes, the lumbering vehicle eased onto the road.

Denver scanned the passing streets. There was no sign of Officer McCloud, let alone any evidence of a manhunt. He never really considered himself as important, but the idea that a disoriented psychological test subject was loose on the streets of this pretend Midwestern town surely demanded more of a response than this. *This is so odd.*

The uptown district was gradually replaced with various neighborhoods. The yards and houses were absolutely convincing, down to the children at play, erratic sprinklers, and pets of all shapes and sizes. Denver couldn't even begin to imagine what a setup like this was costing the taxpayers. It had to be in the multiplied millions.

And for what purpose?

He strained to see beyond the residences and eventually caught sight of the outskirts. It looked like farmland: flat, dirty, and rows upon rows of corn with no end in sight. He half expected to see miles upon miles of desert. Denver had convinced himself that this was probably a new addition to

Area 51 somewhere in Nevada. The temperature was about right, but the humidity didn't match at all. The air wasn't oppressive, but it was much heavier than it should be.

But where are the fences? The guard shacks? The checkpoints?

There were no fences, or guard shacks, or checkpoints, just vast stretches of rural landscape. The pleasant smells of the countryside drifting in through his cracked window offended him strangely. Visuals could be faked, sounds could be imitated, but the nose was virtually impossible to deceive.

A child giggled and Denver's attention abruptly snapped inward. He straightened up to survey those around him, hoping that perhaps one of them would hold a clue as to his current predicament.

Behind him sat a distinguished-looking, older gentleman in a nice suit, scanning a Chicago newspaper. A soldier— probably home on furlough—was just ahead, with a large rucksack leaning up against him. To his left and up a row, he caught sight of a young couple engrossed in each other. *Get a room.* He turned and stared across the aisle at a young mother holding a baby girl wrapped like a doll in a quintessential pink blanket.

Wow, actual babies. They really are serious about this illusion. Wait, maybe it's just a fake baby, a doll. The tiny infant blinked a few times and fussed. *Wrong again, Collins.*

The sweet sight across the aisle triggered a sweeter memory a lot closer to home. He retrieved his wallet and pried it open, and with loving reverence pulled out a photo of his daughter. It was his favorite picture of her: goofy party hat, tooth missing, and a bit of icing on her tiny nose. He turned it over, greeted by a message in smeared blue ink: JASMINE, 5th BIRTHDAY 2013.

Denver flipped it back over and traced his finger across her face. *First, your momma tries to keep me from you, and now the government is doing the same. But don't worry, I'll be home soon, sweetie. I can handle Jennifer, and I can handle them.*

He blinked hard to stave off a tear or two. Now that things had calmed down, the repressed emotions of the past twenty-four hours refused to be ignored any longer. He stared at the photo for a few more moments, and carefully hid it away in his front shirt pocket.

Palming his wallet, his head rolled to one side and he glanced out at the green and gold patchwork quilt of farmland. *Where is this? Where am I?*

It seemed that the sheer burden of unanswered questions forced him to slump down in his seat and close his eyes. The relaxing trio of a rocking bus, the almost comfortable seat, and the exhaustion of continued uncertainty, all knocked him out almost as fast as McCloud's tranquilizer dart.

He had no idea where or when he would wake up this time.

Sunday, May 5, 1946
Journal entry number 34

Yesterday was my first time at a horserace, and it was the Kentucky Derby, no less! Ken's knowledge of sports history has really paid off. He remembered that 1946 was/is a famous year in horseracing—he remembered that Assault won the coveted Triple Crown—Kentucky Derby, Preakness Stakes, and the Belmont Stakes. (I've learned a lot!)

Assault was an underdog (or is it underhorse?) with only 8-1 odds going into the Derby yesterday. This was great for us. We walked away with nearly a thousand dollars! It's not as much as we could have won in Vegas, but it's a start. We can bet again at Preakness, and Belmont, and maybe invest money in the stock market.

Anyway, the best thing about all of this is that we don't have to steal anymore.

We can finally make an honest living by cheating.

CHAPTER 15

"This latest test data can only go so far, gentlemen, but I want to know: *what exactly are the risks?*"

Doc Stonecroft stared across the table at the impatient redhead who was at least three decades his junior. His mind raced for a satisfactory reply for her. Being at a loss for words was rare for the eloquent former college mathematics professor.

He glanced over at the balding, spectacled man seated next to him, and then back at her. "This is clearly uncharted territory, Miss Finegan. The list of potential...*unintended* consequences is formidable."

The windowless room was lit by several incandescent bulbs dangling from the ceiling, supplemented by the pale blue glow of several electronic control panels nearby. Besides the three occupants, a large round table, and a few upright cabinets, the featureless chamber resembled more of a large prison cell than a meeting room.

Ellen Finegan, with her shoulder-length red hair pulled back, and sporting a long white lab coat, adjusted her glasses. She glanced up from a handful of papers. "I'm not asking for an exhaustive list, Dr. Stonecroft. I'd be satisfied with top tier threats."

He traded quick glances with the other gentleman and turned back to her. "Worst case scenario?"

She nodded. Doc took off his glasses and massaged the bridge of his nose. He cleared his throat and gave her a smile that would have warmed the heart of a serial killer. Before he could speak, the other gentleman gesticulated wildly and almost shouted.

"*Il pourrait devenir un* wormhole *incontrôlable!*"

Doc Stonecroft was polite but firm. "While possible, Dr. Papineau, that outcome is highly improbable, sir."

Ellen interrupted their exchange. "What outcome?"

He stood and moved towards her. "My esteemed colleague is over-estimating, in my opinion, the possibility of a CUTA. A cascading, unidirectional, temporal anomaly: a *wormhole*."

"And why is that a problem, Doc? Sounds like the solution we've been hoping for, even praying for."

"This is not a stable rift, Miss Finegan—it is an expanding, cascading rift. It is a temporal anomaly that could grow exponentially—uncontrollably."

"Meaning?"

"*Meaning*, that once ignited, it could expand outward, both in space and in time, and even in velocity. Dr. Papineau shares my concern."

Papineau pounded on the table. "*Aussi vite que la vitesse de la lumière!*" Most of it appeared to be lost on them. "*Lumière*," he repeated. "*Light.*"

"Yes, Emile," Doc said. "Theoretically, the rate of expansion could accelerate up to near the speed of light. Nothing can reverse it. All of creation would...would necessarily *implode*."

Dr. Papineau spread his hands far apart and then clapped them together. "Singularity *intervertir*."

Ellen looked to Doc Stonecroft for the interpretation. He kept it short but not very sweet.

"Backwards Big Bang."

CHAPTER 16

"Mr. Collins? Mr. Collins. *Denver Collins.*"

The female voice continued to echo in the distance, but it seemed to be getting closer. "Wake up. Wake up, Mr. Collins."

Denver's eyes popped open, and he leaned forward, disoriented, and blinking hard in the sudden, bright light.

"Mr. Collins? Over here."

He directed his gaze to the right, and as his eyes adjusted he discovered that he was in a hospital, in a waiting room to be exact.

The voice belonged to an older African-American nurse framed in a doorway, she took a step closer to him. "Congratulations, Mr. Collins. You have a beautiful baby daughter. She is healthy and your wife is doing fine. It was kind of touch and go for a while, but you can come back to see them now."

Without warning, streams of hot tears began to cascade down as he rose to follow. He rounded a few corners and the large, glass expanse of the nursery window came into view. The nurse tenderly maneuvered the newborn's cart into a nearby room.

She opened the door into the hallway and motioned for Denver to come inside. As he walked across the threshold time literally seemed to slow. He glanced down at the baby.

That's my daughter.

He wiped his wet face again and again. The nurse transferred the precious package into his trembling, inexperienced arms. He had held everything from wild women to dangerous weapons, but this was new, fragile—outside his experience.

The nurse almost laughed as she guided his arms into the cradle position. Once he felt comfortable, and with careful precision, he sweetly brought the newborn close and kissed her forehead.

The nurse patted his shoulder. "She's a very pretty baby, and trust me, I'm an expert. I've seen quite a few."

He struggled to speak, but what came out was more crack than voice. "Jasmine." The nurse leaned in. He swallowed and made a stronger second attempt. "Jasmine, her name is Jasmine." He attempted to wipe another tear with his right shoulder...

...Without explanation, Denver found himself standing against a bed in ICU Recovery. His wife was hooked up to a spaghetti maze of tubes and wires, looking more like she had recently survived a car accident rather than a hard delivery.

Jasmine was nestled up alongside her, with just her little face peeking out from the wrap of blankets. Jennifer stroked the sleeping infant with no more pressure than a gentle breeze. Denver bent over and graced his wife's cheek with a light kiss, and then turned his head to see the newest member of the Collin's clan.

Almost on cue, baby Jasmine began fretting, her eyes tried to open, and then settled back to sleep. Denver smiled and stared into Jennifer's tired but thankful face. He mouthed the words "I love you" and clasped her hand, being careful to avoid the IV. Suddenly, the light in the room grew brighter and brighter until Denver was blinded...

...As his sight returned, he saw the kitchen and dining area in their first apartment. Jennifer was storing the remnants of a late meal in the fridge, as a young Jasmine played in the floor nearby. Denver had almost forgotten how cute her Shirley Temple blonde curls had been. The back door opened, and he saw himself walk into the room.

Jennifer glanced up and turned to the toddler. "Oh look, Jasmine. It's the guy who sleeps here occasionally."

"Babe, I told you it would be a couple rough weeks," he said. "We've got new software, and a new—"

She cut him off. "A couple of rough *weeks*? How about a few rough *months*!" She pointed at their daughter. "I have to show Jasmine your photo just about every night—sure don't want her to forget what her father looks like!"

He started to say something, but reconsidered, and bent down to the cutie on the floor. He put his arms around Jasmine, and as he raised her everything began to blur out...

...There was darkness and then more blur...

...And then he was holding a smart phone. By the hot emotion he felt, and the look on Jennifer's face, he ascertained that they were in the middle of another argument.

Arguments came quite frequently and with more intensity in those days.

He shook the phone in her face and said, "So what am I *supposed* to think!"

She wasted no time. "It's none of your *damn* business!" Jen made a quick move to snatch the phone and he grabbed her arm.

"I think that a strange man texting my wife on a daily basis falls under the *'my damn business'* category, Jennifer!"

She yanked hard against his grasp and moved away, grabbing a small shot glass. She downed it like a pro. "At least he *tries* to talk to me every day. More'n I can say for my own husband!"

Denver took a step towards her. "What *else* does he do for you every day?"

"Just shut up! *Shut up!*"

With all the force of a major league pitcher—but the accuracy of an enraged and intoxicated spouse—she hurled the cup at him. The shot glass crashed into the wall behind him and exploded into hundreds of sharp shards.

Denver snapped awake as he felt the bus brakes engage. The loss in momentum almost threw him into the back of the seat just ahead. The nightmare had been so vivid, so tangible, that he jumped up, out of breath, veins pulsing. As he grabbed the seat to steady himself, he scanned the rows of unfamiliar faces for his drunk wife and precious daughter.

Very few of the passengers seemed to even notice his desperate state, as most of them were craning to look out the windows at something. The bus continued to decelerate and Denver heard the wail of a police siren approaching.

With the hiss of air brakes and a strong lurch, the bus came to a dusty stop on the side of the road. Children began to fuss, and loud chatter rippled row-by-row. Denver dropped back down and pressed his face against the window, but the plume of dust obscured most of his view.

But the dirt couldn't obscure the unmistakable voice of Chief McCloud. "We know you're in there, Denver Collins."

Denver jerked back from the window. It was an uncomfortable and new experience for him. Back in the Middle East he had marched probably hundreds of Taliban sympathizers off of buses or out of the beds of pickups, even dislocating several out of cramped and dusty automobile trunks.

He was now on the receiving end, and he wasn't receiving it well.

Some of the passengers exchanged furtive glances, some clutched their children, others mouthed silent prayers. But the taunting call would not be silent.

"This will go a lot easier if you surrender peacefully, Mr. Collins. The good and decent people on the bus with you don't want any trouble. We don't want any trouble."

A slim young man, sporting dark sunglasses and a hat, emerged from the unmarked police car behind the bus. He made his way towards the driver's side, with his sidearm drawn and ready. His awkward mannerisms and gun insecurity betrayed a lack of police experience. And though he tried to hide it, he didn't fool anyone.

A little boy peered out the window at him and pointed, but the child's mother ended her son's excitement, yanking him down into her lap.

McCloud donned his own pair of sunglasses and plain hat, and moved to Denver's side of the bus. "So the way I see it, there's only one way for this to end," the Chief said, obviously enjoying the drama. "I'm gonna count from five, and before I get to *one*—I want to see your smiling face, with hands held high, stepping off this here bus."

McCloud's inexperienced assistant rounded the front of the vehicle and took up a position, gun aimed, near the closed door. The driver hesitated between opening it, or leaving it be. He didn't want to make any sudden moves.

The Chief was unrelenting in his ultimatum. "*Five...Four.*"

The passengers became deathly still, eyes darting around. Even the children were quiet, or were at least forced to be.

"*Three...Two.*"

There was some activity, some sort of movement on the bus. The door opened. McCloud paused, struggling to see through the filthy glass. "*One.*"

In reluctant protest, Denver emerged with his hands just above his shoulders, staring straight ahead. He stepped down to dirt level and froze. They approached him with all the stealth of a big game hunt, guns aloft, taking measured steps.

"On behalf of the great state of Illinois," the Chief boomed, "I would like to thank you for making the right choice, Mr. Collins. Please step away from the bus."

The young officer waved his gun to the left a few times, signaling the direction for Denver to move. The Chief looked up at the driver and waved. "Let's get this rig outta here, pronto! Nothin' to see here, folks! Show's over."

The driver appeared thrilled and quickly shut the door. Moments later, with a loud release of air, and a knocking engine, the Greyhound pulled out onto the blacktop, leaving the awkward trio in a mushroom dust cloud.

"Officer O'Connell," McCloud said with an unusual air of respect and formality, "would you please search the suspect for weapons?"

At least half a dozen scenarios of how this could go down passed through Denver's mind, and more than a few of them involved the death of two supposed policemen. With his military training, he imagined waiting for the wannabee to get close, and then grabbing his arm and shooting McCloud with O'Connell's gun, then turning it back on the young fool.

It would be over in all of two and a half seconds.

The only thing stopping him was the near certainty that this was all part of an elaborate government experiment. These men were just playing their part, following orders, even difficult orders. He himself had been there more often than not. It sickened him to think about how many children he left fatherless overseas or all of the widows he had created just following orders. His already sickened gut felt even sicker.

A lot of guys had come back from Afghanistan having lost their hearing, or sight, or even a pair of limbs. But

Denver had lost something both intangible and crippling; he had forever lost the right to ever judge another human being.

As O'Connell got close, Denver kept his fight-or-flight instinct locked in a tight cage. He knew the two cops had no clue how close they had come to meeting their maker. Even added together, they were still woefully out of his league.

Officer O'Connell began patting him down nervously, and within moments located the small pistol. With trembling hands, he lifted Denver's shirt and retrieved the firearm as though he had found a coiled rattlesnake. He held it high and the gun swung from his fingers like a trophy kill.

The Chief stepped closer and screamed, "On your knees, Collins—*now!*"

Denver lifted his head and shot him a glance. McCloud wasn't playing games and spoke each word again separately and clearly. "On...your...*knees!*"

Denver sank down, almost wishing he would've taken a different option moments ago.

McCloud continued his predictable and harsh barrage, "Hands behind your head!" Denver complied, but he wasn't in any big hurry to do so. His body language announced to them that his acquiescence was strictly voluntary. The Chief scooted through the gravel and placed the business end of a rifle near Denver's temple.

"I don't know about you, Billy, but I'd say this criminal here has had a pretty busy day." He cocked his head and spat in the dust. "Woke up this mornin' in jail, committed grand theft auto by dinner, and has a loaded gun to his head before supper."

Denver had had enough of this ridiculous charade and retorted. "I just want to get home to my daughter!"

The Chief moved in an arc and engaged him face to face. "You wanna go home?" He pulled the bolt back on his Remington. "I can definitely help you with that." The Chief continued to stare at Denver as he called out over his shoulder. "Is that bus outta sight yet, Billy?"

Officer O'Connell lifted his sunglasses, and strained his eyes. "All clear, no witnesses, Chief."

McCloud shifted his weight. "Good."

Friday, June 14, 1946
Journal entry number 41

It's still hard to imagine that our sudden financial fortunes have revolved around a four-legged steed carrying a tiny jockey. Assault won the Triple Crown (just as Ken "predicted"), and using the nice pool of money we won at Kentucky, we made a much, much bigger pool of cash. We are now the proud owners of a late 30s sedan.
(It would be priceless back home!)

We have also purchased some promising corporate stocks, which required a trip to Chicago, a few hours north of here. The 1946 skyline of the Windy City will take some time to get used to—and the lack of jets. All the commercial airliners are prop planes at this time.

We decided that sharing an apartment, combined with our erratic schedules of coming and going, could lead to many uncomfortable questions from our neighbors. We found a house on the outskirts of town for sale, fairly isolated...no prying eyes, and no prying questions. It has a large garage, which could possibly be used for research in the future. Just dreaming.

We close on the house sale on Monday. I still can't get over the price—$7600! It sits on 3 acres, on the north side of town, not far from where Ken and I both jumped.

A fat bank account, a reliable vehicle, and a secluded base of operations...at least, at some level, some things are starting to get back to normal.

CHAPTER 17

Denver shut his eyes.

He wasn't a coward, and he sure wasn't going to beg. He had been in enough "we're-not-getting-out-of-this-one-alive" firefights that he had become numb to thoughts of his own sure demise, even a real demise in a fake world.

He was always amazed at how the other senses seemed to become heightened once vision was denied. The cops' exact positions were as clear as day. Their subtle movements were betrayed by the sounds of cloth upon cloth and shifting footwork upon gravel. He could even discern their attitudes and emotions by changing patterns of breathing and tiny vocal inflections.

He weighed his options. He was fast, but with two guns roughly two yards apart trained on him, the chances of avoiding a mortal injury in a scuffle averaged somewhere within two standard deviations of dismal.

Regardless of his options, there wouldn't be time to enact any of them. Without warning, Denver felt two sets of hands raise him up to a proper standing position. He was almost positive he had heard a subtle chuckle in the process. His eyes opened to two grinning faces with sunglasses removed.

"Sorry 'bout this dog 'n pony show," the Chief blurted out. "But we have to keep up appearances around these parts. How 'bout some introductions—Mr. Denver Collins, this is my right hand man, Officer Billy O'Connell."

Billy plainly forced a grin and stepped forward with hand outstretched, but Denver locked onto the distance with a cold stare. He remained motionless. O'Connell glanced over at the Chief, then back at Denver. He withdrew his hand. It was more than obvious that a dangerous level of rage was not too far below Denver's surface.

McCloud cleared his throat. "Look, Mr. Collins, we're the good guys."

Denver exploded, "Why can't you people just leave me alone? I am minutes from Chicago, and hopefully a few hours from a flight back home. So, whatever government psychological experiment or whatever it is you are conducting, I didn't sign up for it, and I want my life back! This *game* ends now!"

The Chief hesitated for few moments after Denver's diatribe. "Government experiment? A *game*? Is *that* all you got? Heck, I thought I was on a Hollywood movie set when I first jumped! Billy, get me the dang binoculars!"

McCloud stepped up to Denver and grabbed his shoulders, turning him to face north, more or less. He pointed a stubby finger at Denver and then at the city in the distance. "Let me ask you, Mr. *I've-Got-It-All-Figured-Out*—when's the last time you were in Chicago?"

Denver had no intention of answering, but he couldn't think of a good enough reason to stay silent. "Fourth of July, last year," he muttered.

"Well, good, cause I'm sure you couldn't look up at all them fireworks in the sky without seeing a few hard-to-ignore little buildings. Uh, let me help your architectural recollection—namely the Sears Tower or the Hancock building?"

Billy returned and offered the field glasses to McCloud.

"So, Mr. Answer Man," the Chief continued as he transferred the binoculars over to Denver, "take a good look through these field glasses at the skyline of the windy city."

Denver was stoic.

"Go on," the Chief encouraged.

He didn't want to, but he raised them anyway, and the distant metropolis came into view. McCloud began to wax condescending. "Well, wait a minute. Where's all those big buildings? Something's wrong here, ain't it?"

Denver lowered the binoculars. He was growing uncomfortable with the fact that the fake police chief was making some real sense. He raised them again and panned the hazy horizon a few more times. It wasn't a painting, or a mirage.

How could anyone make a simulated city on this scale?

Building on his probable success, the Chief played his next card. "Hey Billy, what day is it?"

"Friday, Chief. All day."

McCloud put a hand on Denver's shoulder. "Wait, isn't the second busiest airport in America here in Chicago—O'Hare International? Now, correct me if I'm wrong, Mr. Denver Collins, but these ol' eyes of mine don't see any jet contrails anywhere. It's Friday, Friday afternoon to be exact. This sky should look like a crossword puzzle by now. But, they ain't there."

Denver dropped the binoculars once again, and surveyed the empty sky.

This is wrong, this is all wrong!

McCloud leaned in. "This may be a nightmare, Mr. Collins, but it sure ain't no friggin' dream!"

The Chief grabbed his rifle and held it up, shaking it. "This, this is a real gun." He fired it into the air and stared a hole through Denver. "That was a real bullet." He ejected the casing and tossed the weapon over to Billy—who almost dropped it—then knelt to cup a handful of roadside dirt. He rose and let it drain slowly out of his hand just inches from Denver's face. "This is real dirt. It's all real. This is *real*…as real as it gets, son."

Denver paused for a moment and bent over and amassed his own fistful of reality. As he stared at the falling dirt, it seemed his former excuses began diminishing as well. All at once, coffee stains on ragged paper menus and tiny babies in pink blankets didn't seem to belong to a well-crafted illusion anymore.

In his mind's eye, he recalled rows of houses, children and pets at play, and vast stretches of Midwest farmland. He remembered a flash of lightning and a rushed layman's explanation in the front seat of an amusement park ride that looked awfully close to a squad car.

The impossible had been eliminated by the strange fortune of becoming probable. That which remained was a truth too terrible to comprehend, at least, all at once. He rose dejectedly and sulked about.

McCloud adjusted his tone and spoke with a depth of compassion obviously nurtured by experience. "The year is 1956. I am from 1996, and O'Connell here jumped to Normal from 1965. Like us, you're a Jumper, Mr. Collins. You've come to us from the year 2014." He cleared his throat and spat again. "The quicker you accept it, the quicker we can get on with our lives, and the quicker we can get to fixin' this mess."

Denver began shaking his head and picked up his pace. His walk morphed into a run, as he climbed up a steep dirt bank which dumped out onto a field. He couldn't restrain himself, and started yelling—nothing discernible—just wordless cries expressing his bitterness and loss.

The Chief muttered to Billy as he pointed in Denver's basic direction, "Here we go again. Have you ever noticed that Trailers are way harder than Priors?" He slapped the younger officer on the back. "Come on."

"Go ahead, let it out. All of us have done the same thing," McCloud called out as he topped the bank, out of breath. "And neither of us will think any less of you, trust me. I promise."

Denver crumpled to his knees in the dirt, clutching his daughter's photo in his right hand. His screaming may have subsided, but the emotion was still alive and raw within his chest.

Billy hung back, but the Chief eventually walked down to the broken man, a man out of time. He put a sympathetic hand on Denver's heaving shoulder. Denver shook it off with the force of an offended high school steady.

"C'mon," the Chief urged. "We're the good guys. I promise. You are *not* alone."

Minutes passed and the Chief remained at Denver's side. Standing silently with his head bowed, it was as if McCloud observed some sacred ritual, a painful rite, not unlike a graveside service. Denver was passing through his own valley of the shadow of death. There was evil…and he couldn't help but fear it.

Several cars passed by, and a motorcycle with a hole in the muffler rattled down the rural stretch. Denver rose to his feet and wiped his hot face, leaving a dirty streak across his temple.

McCloud walked around and stood in front of him, though eye contact was apparently still out of the question. "Listen to me. Listen. *Hey!*"

It took several seconds, but Denver's attention refocused and he locked eyes with a man who, in his opinion, shouldn't be smiling. A man who should be as resentful and angry and bitter as he himself was at that very moment.

If McCloud believes the boatload of crap he has been saying, then how can he exude such hope and such irritating confidence? These questions plagued Denver, but he was incrementally warming up to the possibility that the Chief might be worth listening to. *Might be.*

McCloud punctuated every word. "We are going to get home, all of us. *All* of us!"

Normal's newest time traveler looked away as the Chief started heading back to the car. "C'mon Mr. Collins," he said. "I wanna show you something." The Chief hesitated as he pulled a rock out of his boot and dusted off his pants.

"And this time, it won't be a jail cell."

Tuesday, July 2, 1946
Journal entry number 52

Incredible. Truly, amazingly, wonderfully—incredible. A THIRD JUMPER HAS ARRIVED!

It may be 2 days until the 4th of July (they call it "Independence Day")—but there are already fireworks of celebration in our house in Normal. Actually, it sounded a bit like the 4th of July early this morning as Lawrence Etherington arrived, and arrived in a big way.

3:30 a.m., sound asleep, and boom! Ken said he only vaguely remembered waking up and then passing out again. Me—I woke up, and within milliseconds, my heart was pounding with the excitement of THE HUNT!

I knew it was cloudy last night, but no storm. I looked outside: no stars. I waited for a good 2 or 3 minutes, scanning the horizon for flashes of lightning. Pitch black, except for the town lights to the south. I ran back inside and shook Ken. I told him what happened. He eventually came around and we got dressed. One problem was that we had no sense of direction. I knew it was close, but that could be 3 square miles of search-and-rescue, if there even was anyone to find.

The second problem was/is the "small town factor." If it was New York City, no one would think it strange to see people out and about in the middle of the night, but here in Normal, in 1946—you could end up in jail or being shot. Neither of those sounded good.

But, on the other hand, looking at night would make it easier—less people around to confuse you. We decided that the benefits far outweighed the risks. If there was a Jumper, we needed to get to him/her first. A dazed and confused time traveler walking around asking questions would definitely violate the First Accord, threaten the Second Accord, and severely complicate matters.

We put on the darkest clothes we had, hoping not to look like outright bandits, and drove around with our headlights off when we could. I was never a hunter, but I can understand the rush, the thrill of the chase. There were so many thoughts that raced through my head—what if the time Jumper was from later than me? Maybe the year 2000, or even 2025. Maybe from the past—why not? 1930, or 1830...how about 1530???

We made several passes around town. First around the outskirts, starting on the north edge by our house. Ken jumped near there, and I had jumped several hundred yards from there. We hit uptown, and then almost all of the residential areas. We had probably been out for almost an hour and a half. The early glow of the rising sun was just winking at us from the East. I was driving, and it was Ken who had the eagle's eye this day.

We were in our third pass uptown and he saw something dart between the buildings. He told me to stop, and he jumped out, about a block from the police station. I slowly followed in the car, and he ran into an alley next to the grocery. I circled around to the next street and made a left and hit the alley from the backside and turned on my lights.

And there he was. Lawrence was hiding behind a stack of pallets. Ken probably would've missed him, but my headlights made the dark into day. He was scared (I remember what it felt like!) and that made him very defensive. He almost took a swing at Ken! I won't go into all the details right now, but it was a very tense 30 minutes or so until he calmed down enough to really reason with him.

That was about 18 hours ago. It is around 11 p.m. right now. Larry (he insists we call him that) and Ken are in the living room looking at some newspapers and magazines. He hasn't eaten much. He is from Indianapolis, more or less, and he jumped from the year 1978. It seems each Jumper is from earlier and earlier....I don't know yet (obviously) if this is a trend or just a peculiarity.

Speaking of trends, it looks like we are averaging a Jumper about every 45 days or so. Could this be a trend? And all men. No females. Should be 50/50ish split, right? Odd.

I'm going to head to the best place to find deep answers to deep questions—my soft bed.

CHAPTER 18

Ellen watched Dr. Papineau work, as he hunched over and studied a few small, round gauges. Without so much as even looking up, he waved his hand in deliberate motions like an orchestra conductor. Doc Stonecroft responded like a trained musician, with one eye focused on Papineau and the other on the potentiometer he was adjusting. Papineau's right hand began a slow sinking motion, and Stonecroft matched the change with perfection.

The pair of scientists may have been born on different continents, spoke different languages, and raised in different times, but they were of one mind most days.

The French physicist straightened up, though it didn't make him much taller, and lowered a pair of heavy duty, dark goggles. *"Juste un peu plus, arrêter!* Stop."

As if on cue, Doc Stonecroft rotated towards Ellen Finegan, who stood at the ready near a large metal door fitted with a thick plate window. His hopeful eyes met her hazel ones, and he nodded. Her right hand gripped a bar that resembled a gear shift. She slid her own set of goggles down, though she always despised how they made her look, and Stonecroft followed suit.

She could hear his oft-repeated admonition in her mind: "Safety before beauty!" Ellen took a half-step forward and peered through the thick glass. She engaged the control bar.

A distinct hum formed and intensified. At the outset it was more felt than actually heard as it permeated the floors, the walls, and the glass. Like a caged beast, the deep rumble increased powerfully and fearfully.

Then it began—erratic flashes of pale green light poured through the tinted window. Startled by the luminous development, Ellen recoiled. She glanced over at Stonecroft who calmed her with a reassuring nod. He raised his right thumb, beckoning her to go higher, and she deferred to his wisdom, but not without trepidation.

As the bar progressed, the reverberating hum became almost deafening, followed by an even more intense and unstable light show. She imagined it would have been beautiful had it not been so unpredictable and terrifying. The bar passed the 50% marker, 55%, then 60%. Everything was progressing in accord with their projections.

Even Papineau was smiling, and that was rare.

But the elation among the trio was premature, for exactly four seconds later the palpable hum exploded with an ear-splitting compression wave, a blinding green flash…then darkness.

Ellen said what they all probably felt. "Uh oh."

Katie Long dried the last few dishes before the onslaught of the late afternoon rush at the uptown diner. The lights flickered, then dipped to a rich amber, and then the entire kitchen went almost black except for the bluish glow from burners on the gas stove.

Beverly broke through the swinging doors, flooding the small space with sunlight from the front windows. Katie popped her with the damp dish towel for scaring her. Bev laughed it off and threw her hands up.

"Wow, *another* power outage on a Friday? I am so surprised."

Sunday, September 8, 1946
Journal entry number 87

We've been talking a lot about our need to get help from the scientific community. We need a physicist or engineer that thinks outside the box, maybe even outside of time.

Ken mentioned Albert Einstein. I shot down the idea: he's too famous, too connected with the government. Can you imagine what would happen if he met us? He always said that time travel is only theoretically possible forward into the future, not backwards.

But I know three men who would disagree. Not only would we make him look like a fool, but there are no guarantees he wouldn't turn us over to the Feds. Think about it: he gave, arguably, the greatest discovery of all time to a president. What would keep him from delivering us to another president?

In a sense, Einstein created atomic warfare to stop the Nazis. What would keep him from giving us up to end atomic warfare with the Commies?

So, in my opinion, Einstein is out.
Larry brought up Tesla.
He's perfect, except...he's dead.

CHAPTER 19

The unmarked police car kicked up a growing cloud of dust as it careened off the paved county road into a gravel parking area just on the outskirts of town. Denver, once again sharing the front seat with the Chief, peered out at the unimpressive beige building more or less in the center of the lot. The front of the establishment had a few large windows and a single door at the entrance. Several cars were scattered about and a delivery truck had backed up to a small side dock.

The Chief pointed at a waist-high sign out by the road flanked by shrubs. *"See?* Nelson Manufacturing. This is where the magic happens." Denver noted the excitement in McCloud's face, but he found it hard to drum up any of his own.

Billy tapped on Denver's shoulder from the back seat. "Trust the Chief—you'll see." Denver nodded, but only as a courtesy after this bland first impression.

Of course, he knew that exteriors rarely matched interiors. He had seen enough command and control centers in Afghanistan that looked like abandoned dives, but housed millions of dollars of techno wizardry about six feet past a cloth door and several guards armed to the teeth. Spooks from the CIA had delighted his unit with tales of rusted, broken-down fishing trawlers off the coast of North Korea housing sophisticated listening stations that rivaled the cockpit of the Space Shuttle.

Denver suspended judgment for the moment.

McCloud came to an abrupt stop directly in front of the entrance and hopped out. Before Denver and Billy had even shut their doors, he continued his explanation. "It's a genius set up, really. Pretty well all the Jumpers work here, right here, well, except for Billy and me. We'd planned a big meet and greet for you today at the factory during dinner, but, uh, your little stunt with my squad car and the bus…well, it kinda changed that. But, you'll meet everyone soon enough."

"Sorry to screw up your party," Denver replied. "I was— having issues."

The Chief laughed, "You ain't the first, and you sure ain't gonna be the last. Don't worry about it."

Denver studied the building. "What do you make here?"

Billy piped up. "Oh, windows."

Denver was further deflated. He had hoped for something a little more exciting. "Windows?"

"Windows. At least upstairs," the Chief said as he opened the front door. It took a few seconds for Denver's eyes to adjust to the light or the lack thereof as he entered the spacious but Spartan foyer area.

Still not impressed.

The Chief guided Denver across the dim room to a desk occupied by a middle-aged Asian female and a teenage girl. They were studying a large book.

"Afternoon Ms. Swan, Tori," the Chief said as he looked up and around at the ceiling. "Lemme guess, Shep's trying to save a few bucks by turning the lights off again?"

Leah Swan turned a page, pointing at something for Tori to read. "Hey Chief, uh, no—we lost power earlier, probably two hours ago. We're on battery backup. Again."

"Price of progress, I reckon," the Chief observed.

Leah muttered something to Tori and then rose to meet them out in front of the desk. The teen was unflinching and gave no indication that she even noticed their arrival. Denver thought it was kind of odd.

Chief McCloud initiated introductions. "Denver Collins, Ms. Leah Swan. Ms. Swan, Trailer Denver Wayne Collins.

Leah here is our receptionist and, uh, she will be your teacher—"

Leah interrupted. "*And* accountant. *And* HR Manager. *And* whatever else Shep needs done. A real pleasure to meet you, Mr. Collins." They shook hands and she motioned towards the desk. "And this, this is Tori."

There still was no reaction from the teen. "Tori," Leah called out, "can you stand up and say hello to Mr. Collins, please?"

Tori rose mechanically and stared at Denver. "What's your birthday?"

Denver was caught off-guard and looked hopelessly at the others. Leah nodded towards Tori. "It's not a difficult question, Mr. Collins. Would you care to answer her?"

Denver took the rebuke in stride and cleared his throat. "Uh, January twenty-first, 1979."

Tori continued to stare, and bobbed her head a bit. Denver wondered if maybe there was an inside joke going on at his expense. The pause was more than awkward, but no one else seemed to care but him.

Tori broke the silence. "Sunday, you were born on a Sunday."

He thought for a moment. "Well, yes, that's right. It was on a Sunday." He broke out in a smile, his first in a good while. "That's…that's amazing."

"Tori is an amazing person," the Chief offered.

"Calculating dates is only one of her many exceptional skills," Leah boasted. "You should view some of her artwork. Simply inspirational."

Denver was still trying to analyze the young lady's parlor trick, but McCloud kept things moving. "Well, now that introductions are good and over, Ms. *Whatever-Else-Needs-Done*, would you mind locking the front door? We're about to have a VIP tour, and I sure don't want any interruptions."

Leah brushed past them, and the Chief motioned for Denver to follow him in the opposite direction. As they arrived at an unmarked door in the back, he unlocked two different sets of heavy deadbolts.

What do they have in there? Denver wondered. *A T-Rex?*

McCloud shoved the large metal door open, and escorted the impromptu tour group out onto the production floor of Nelson Manufacturing.

The foyer had been dark, and Denver discovered that the somewhat noisy assembly area wasn't faring much better. The gymnasium-sized expanse was sporadically lit by a handful of lights scattered above. Denver scanned the vacant walls.

Interesting—a window factory that doesn't have windows. Nice.

Several employees were occupied in various capacities throughout. Only a few of them seemed to notice the newcomers. The Chief whistled toward one small group. "Shep! Yo—*Shep!*"

One of the workers tapped a large male on the back. Denver guessed that the man was likely in his early fifties. Shep looked up and waved at the Chief, and after giving some final instructions, jogged over to meet up with them. Denver could tell by the way that Shep carried himself that this had to be the boss, the top dog (that is, if they had bosses here at the magic factory). Even his flat top haircut somehow gave the impression of authority.

The Chief leaned over and confirmed Denver's suspicion. "That's Shep. Plant manager."

The out-of-breath boss arrived and McCloud spoke first. "Mr. Sheppard, I present to you Normal's newest arrival."

Shep extended a strong hand with an even stronger handshake. "Robert Sheppard, Mr. Collins. Pleased to meet you. Absolutely pleased."

"It's Denver."

Robert smiled broadly. "Then, it's Shep, Denver. Now we're even!"

Everyone minus Denver seemed to find that marginally humorous. "So, McCloud," Shep asked, "what does he know about the operation?"

"Only the bare minimum," McCloud replied. "I saved the juicy details for you."

Shep corralled a very tense Denver by the shoulders and moved him down through the middle of the factory. "Hey, loosen up," Shep said. "You are among friends here."

Denver clenched his jaw. *Easier said than done, buddy. You didn't have a gun to your head a few hours ago.*

He studied Shep's clothes: a pair of dirty khaki pants, and a short sleeve, white dress shirt that was way too tight.

It looks like too much man shoved into too little shirt.

Shep's name badge caught his eye in particular: Robert Sheppard, Plant Manager: 0191966.

Shep halted the tour. "Sorry I don't have your badge yet. Maybe Monday or Tuesday. Everyone gets a badge." He pointed at the ID number. "The last four digits reminds everybody here of the year you jumped from."

"But I thought this place was supposed to be a safe haven? If everyone here is a Jumper, then who cares what year?"

Shep postured like a college professor who was just asked a typical first-week freshman question. "Well, Trailer Collins, your question reveals the problem."

Denver sensed a well-rehearsed exposition coming. Shep elaborated, "All of us are from *sometime* in the future. As our research advances, hopefully, all of us are going to go back to our same future one day. And we want it to be the *same* future, *capiche*?"

"I'm sure it all makes sense to you, but, uh, I'm a little new at all of this."

Sheppard grinned and nodded. "Trust me, we were all there at one time. It'll get easier. You can bet your bottom dollar on that one. But I don't want to steal too much of her thunder. Leah will go into more detail with you when you start your TOC"

"Sorry, TOC?"

"Temporal Orientation Classes. Yeah, sorry. We got more damn acronyms around here than the Army. The TOC—it's like time-school. She will get you up to speed on everything from money to politics, even top-forty music. Everything."

Denver shrugged. Acronyms didn't bother him, the Army didn't bother him, but school—well, that was something different.

They started moving again. "It ain't as bad as it sounds," Shep declared.

"I'll take your word for it, Mr. Sheppard."

"Please, it's Shep. Anyway, we have rules, Mr. Collins." He caught himself. "Sorry, *Denver*. Protocols have been set in place to protect each of our futures. No one is allowed to share information involving future knowledge with a Prior. Even the slightest bit of improper information can have, as Doc says, *disastrous temporal consequences*."

As Denver tried to digest the complexities of it all, they were interrupted by a stocky African American male with greasy hands and rolled up sleeves. He handed Shep a large, oil-covered bearing in a handkerchief.

"Load wasn't being distributed properly," the worker said. "It was only a matter of time. We probably need to order at least two more." Shep studied it for a moment, then wrapped the bearing, returning it.

"Denver Collins, this is Terrance Gaines. Terrance is our plant mechanic and head of maintenance."

Terrance rolled his eyes. "It's usually a department of *one*."

Denver shot out his hand, but Terrance held up his wiggling dirty fingers and smiled. "I'll have to take a rain check, Mr. Collins. Welcome to Normal...at least, your *new* normal. Nice to have a new Trailer."

"Uh, thanks, Mr. Gaines. And, it's Denver." He looked at Terrance's badge. *1983.*

"Hate to leave good company, gentlemen, but it's late on a Friday, and stuff has piled up. Especially with the power problems." Terrance gave a rough military salute and departed.

Denver started to move again, but Shep held up his arm to stop him. The plant manager leaned in close and spoke in low tones. "You will soon learn, just exactly the kind you can trust, and the kind that you shouldn't."

Denver looked into his serious eyes, and then glanced back at Terrance in the distance.

Shep stepped over and blocked his view. "You know what I mean?"

Denver thought about it.

No. No, he didn't know what Shep meant, and this time, it was getting uncomfortable as he considered what Shep *might have* meant. Denver was rescued from the intimidating exchange by the arrival of the Chief and his sidekick. It was the first time today that Denver was actually glad to see McCloud.

"The original Jumpers set this whole shootin' match into motion, back in the late forties," the Chief said. "They realized that it was too dangerous to try to merge Jumpers into the community."

Shep wasn't going to let the Chief wrestle the tour from his control so easily. "I was getting there, Chief. Anyway, the more interactions between Jumpers and Locals, so to speak, and you increase the likelihood of something said or done that exposes us, or that endangers all of our futures."

McCloud moved directly in front of Denver. "Imagine what people would do, if they knew, they really *knew*, you were from the future. The fear, the mistrust, the, the—"

Shep broke in. "*The Exploitation*. No thank you."

Officer Billy started to fall back. "Hey Chief, I'm gonna go to town and lock up the station and take care of the back door, and clean all the mess up. See you at breakfast! Be seeing you around, Mr. Collins!"

Denver nodded, and Shep didn't miss a beat. "Our founder, Mr. Phillip Nelson, built the plant in forty-nine. Its function was to give all the Jumpers a job, a daily cover story if you will, while we actually work on something much more important to all of us."

"Your founder? What do you mean?" Denver inquired.

"Uh, Phil was our leader," Shep said. "He was the very first Jumper, at least, we think he was. It's really hard to be sure about such things."

Denver's interest was piqued. "Where is Mr. Nelson?"

Shep looked long and hard over at the Chief. Denver noticed the solemnity of the silent exchange. The Chief took the lead once again. "He, uh, had an unfortunate *accident*." Shep shot him another look, but McCloud never missed a beat. "But, uh, in 1950, when I jumped, the leadership decided that a few of us Jumpers should try to get highfalutin jobs in the community. My police background was perfect, and with a little *budgetary* persuasion, the mayor appointed me just over four years ago."

"So," Denver began, "all of the Jumpers, except for you and Billy, work here?"

The Chief deferred to Shep on this one. "The simple answer is, *yes*." Shep paused. "All of the Jumpers living in Normal, that is. Well, and then there's Grandma Martha. But she's retired."

Denver stopped. "Wait—there are *others*?"

Shep gave the Chief a "we-ain't-going-there" look. McCloud smiled big as the outdoors and cleared his throat, placing his hand on Denver's back. "So many questions, as to be expected. But trust me, Mr. Collins, there'll be plenty of time to answer 'em all. We ain't gotta write the whole Bible in a day."

What are you hiding, McCloud? Denver thought.

With a strange popping sound and a few flashes, electricity returned to the factory, albeit with some reluctance. The lights hummed and began to grow brighter, and a few machines chirped and whirred. A small audible celebration erupted throughout the staff, just as a hint of burning oil drifted by in the heavy air.

Shep smiled with a helpless shrug. "Yep, power's back on, just in time to shut down for the weekend. Well, sir— *that's business.*"

Denver looked at the equipment to his left as they approached a door on the far wall. "To be completely honest, I've never worked in manufacturing before. I've broken a few windows, but never made one."

Shep chuckled. "We have a saying around here— windows are a *pain*." He searched Denver's eyes. "Get it? Pain. Pane."

It was clever, but that's about all it was.

Shep pointed at a palletized bundle of finished product. "So, yes, we do make windows here, but that's not the whole picture, Mr. Collins," he said. "It's true that we make lots of windows *upstairs*, but *downstairs*, well, we are just making *one* window."

Denver cocked his head. *"Downstairs?"*

Shep produced a key and opened a door to a much smaller side room. They stepped in and Denver saw a couch, coffee table, and a few magazines. He imagined it was either a break room, or a meeting room for clients and vendors.

The Chief was beaming with pride. "It's time to show you...*The Basement*."

"No offense, but I've seen quite a few basements, Chief."

The Chief just grinned as Shep unlocked what appeared to be a wide door to a shallow closet. Inside the useless space he inserted another key into a small hole. Denver wasn't prepared to see the entire back wall of the closet open outward. Shep spun about with an almost arrogant smile. "Oh, you've never seen a basement quite like this one before, Mr. Collins. *Trust me*."

He was right.

CHAPTER 20

Deep down inside her, something yearned for simpler times. *The days before electricity would probably be a good start,* she thought. Katie Long hurried behind the counter toward the register in a mad dash to make up for the lost time caused by the annoying power outage.

Simpler days.

Grandma Long used to talk about them quite often. Katie chuckled inside as she remembered Gram-Long, as she called her, ranting and raving about all the new-fangled machines and such. She could still hear her, clear as day: "They will be the ruination of us all, I tell ya." Well, today, granddaughter Katie was beginning to agree with her.

Katie glanced up from her final duties over at a dark-haired woman several seats down the bar. "Now that the power's back on, I'll get you a fresh cup of coffee, Miss Larson. I'm headed out in a minute, but Bev'll take care of you when I'm gone."

The middle-aged patron acknowledged her without even looking up from the copy of *The Pantagraph* newspaper she was glued to. Katie finished getting the coffee started, and turned to the register and fished her tips out of her apron. Amanda, the owner, had always told the girls to count their tip money in the back. She said it wasn't proper to do that in front of the customers.

Katie surveyed the room. First off, Amanda was down in Bloomington for the day, and secondly, the only customer close enough to see her was obviously more interested in local gossip than Katie's personal business.

She looked down at her daily haul—a motley assortment of small change: a pile of pennies, several nickels, a few dimes, and two quarters. She paused and checked the room again: no one was looking. She reached into her front pouch once more, and retrieved a single five dollar bill. At least, it *resembled* a five dollar bill. She held it up cautiously, examining the strange design and colors. It was a five dollar bill, but then again, it wasn't.

Miss Larson looked around the corner of her page as she turned it. "What'cha got there, Katie?"

The waitress was so lost in the moment that the question startled her like a kid caught with her hand in the cookie jar. She hesitated and then hid the bill down beside the register. "What? Oh, nothing."

Miss Larson set her paper down. "Katie, you forget that as a seasoned newspaper reporter and as this town's editor, I can spot a story a mile away." She paused, then continued. "Plus, no offense, but you are a terrible liar!" She winked at her.

Katie dismissed her own concern and raised the bill, or whatever it was, back up into clear view. "Oh, I don't know, Betty, but it, uh, it's probably nothing."

The inquisitive reporter stood up and moved closer. "Katie, *today's* secrets are *tomorrow's* headlines."

For just a fleeting moment, Katie felt like she was being scolded by Gram-Long. She could "cut you to the quick" with a word, sometimes just a stare. "It's, it's just this— something's wrong. I've never seen money like this before."

"You got some funny money? Or is it some Confederate cash? I've seen some of those floating around of late."

Katie handed the bill to her. "Maybe. I dunno."

Betty flipped it over a few times. "Colorful. Creative—I'll give 'em that. Who gave it to you?" she asked without looking up.

Katie turned to check on the coffee. "Never saw him before. Outta-towner. I think he hopped on the bus to Chicago just before dinner. A shame, he was a looker."

"A handsome counterfeiter...hmm." At last she glanced up at the puzzled waitress. "Seems like the good ones are always criminals."

Katie forced a laugh. "Just my luck. I'm always attracted to the wrong kinda man. Tall, dark, and *Wanted*." She checked the coffee. It was steaming, and she grabbed the pot.

The newspaper editor continued to study the fascinating piece of paper. The date near the bottom seemed to catch her eye—2013. She stared at Katie for a moment, then went back for her purse. Katie poured her a fresh, hot cup as Betty cracked open her billfold. She slid some cash across the counter discreetly and dropped her voice down considerably. "Tell you what, let's trade money."

Katie looked down and saw seven one dollar bills on the counter. Betty patted the hand of the waitress. "With a few extra to, uh, just keep this between us for now."

Maybe it couldn't buy love, but it appeared that Betty was counting on the fact that money could still buy silence.

Saturday, September 14, 1946
Journal entry number 91

Our profound need may have just been met in a tabloid (When was that term coined?)

Ken was reading *Popular Science* magazine yesterday and stumbled upon an announcement for the 9th Washington Conference of Theoretical Physics. The annual gathering in DC is a Who's Who of eminent scientists and researchers. It said that several dozen physicists from around the world will converge the end of this October and early November in a post-World War II think tank. This sounds like a godsend.

Of course, the perils and pitfalls are many. None of us can even begin to imagine how awkward and potentially dangerous that first contact will be.

What do we say?

How can we prove our backstory?

Why should they be willing to help us?

What if they turn us in? (This is a huge risk.)

Is money enough to motivate them?

Is the current state of theoretical physics able to help us?

In addition to all of these questions, how can we, in good faith, seek help from a scientist without violating the First Accord? And once we have them, how can we avoid trampling all over the Second Accord?

Hypothetically, if we did acquire the help of a physicist, and if he was able to help us all return home, imagine the size of THAT footprint? We would return to the proper time stream, yet we would leave behind a physicist with an immense cache of futuristic information, even if we did minimize interaction.

There is a counterpoint. The benefits of returning a group of time-displaced persons, as soon as possible, is in the best interest of the First and Second Accord. The shorter our intersection is with this time period, the less possibility of adversely impacting it. Perhaps the cons of accidentally influencing a single theoretical physicist is far less dangerous than three or more time travelers loose on the streets of mid-America. And that leads to another uncomfortable thought: I don't see myself as breaking it (who knows?), but what happens as this whole time-drama wears on? What happens if one or more of us kind of "snaps" and breaks the Second Accord?

Potentially, as hope fades, and our minds acclimate to a no-return ideology, then the temptation to capitalize on our knowledge could prove overwhelming. I pray that day never comes.

Funny thing about temptation, it doesn't seem tempting...until it's you.

We are planning to discuss the Washington Conference strategy tomorrow morning. We will need to make a decision soon, and we will probably need at least one more trip to the races to secure a sufficiently attractive financial portfolio, at least Ken thinks so. We could offer thousands of dollars of 1946 money, which, adjusted to 1980s dollars, would be over a hundred thousand, maybe more.

In all of our confusion and uncertainty, it's good to know that, even in 1946, money probably still talks. It's not much of a virtuous reference point, but it does feel a bit like home.

CHAPTER 21

"The contractors who built the basic structure of The Basement were told it was going to be a bomb shelter," Shep called out over his shoulder as he, Denver, and McCloud descended a long concrete staircase. His voice reverberated as if in a drain pipe. "Bomb shelters are in fashion right now. Cold war. Perfect cover story."

Denver's tension started to rise again as they descended. Combining the idea of going down into a concrete tomb while sandwiched between an enthusiastic cop and an athletic alpha-male certainly didn't elicit any warm-fuzzies.

In fact, the whole scenario of being a part of a trio of men, carefully navigating concrete steps in the dark, made him flash back to any one of several missions in Afghanistan. Only this time, he had no weapon, no advantage, and no concept of an exit strategy if things went south.

Just play this one by ear, Collins...one step at a time.

"Almost there," Shep announced as they reached another door. He inserted a key and pushed it open.

Chief McCloud leaned forward and whispered, "I know you're not Alice, but, uh, welcome to Wonderland."

The door opened, revealing a medium-sized room with a tall ceiling, large table, a smattering of electronic consoles, cabinets, a few doors, and three researchers.

Not quite Wonderland, Denver thought. *Still not impressed.*

Three researchers glanced up from a schematic discussion, and one-by-one walked across the room to meet them. The Chief pushed to the front. "Dr. Papineau, Ms. Finegan, and Doc...may I introduce Trailer Denver Wayne Collins: stock broker turned armed, dangerous fugitive." The Chief smiled at Denver with an oversized grin and slapped him on the back.

Ellen Finegan reached them first and examined Denver head to toe, then circled him like chum in a shark tank. He actually felt like a piece of meat, but she was attractive enough that most men wouldn't have minded. He examined a little of her as well, just more discreetly.

"So this is how they grow 'em in the twenty-first century?" she observed with a sultry smile. The Chief looked over at Shep's concerned face as Ellen continued. "You know, we were a bit worried that you would be one that got away." She came to a smooth stop just inside his comfort zone, and locked eyes with him. "I, for one, am glad you *didn't.*"

Shep cleared his throat and interrupted Ellen's admiration. "Denver, this is Ellen Finegan, one of our friendly researchers here in The Basement." Denver nodded to her, then Shep pointed. "Also, Dr. Emile Papineau..."

The short, French researcher bowed a bit, and Denver nodded in return, but wondered if perhaps he should have bowed as well.

"And finally, Dr. Glen Stonecroft."

Doc pushed forward and grabbed Denver's hand with all the enthusiasm of a rock & roll groupie. "Indeed, it is a rare pleasure to make the acquaintance of a fellow New Yorker, who has been temporally displaced within a reasonable distance from my own time zone!" Denver didn't actually shake as much as he just merely held on. The energetic stranger provided all the necessary motion.

For whatever reason or reasons, Denver immediately liked this one. Doc's genuine demeanor, his obvious command of language, and his appearance as the quintessential scientific sage, all played their respective roles in Denver's positive reaction.

Denver noted Doc's name badge. *He Jumped in…2005. Getting closer. He will know about 9/11, the wars in Iraq and*

Afghanistan. He'll know Presidents Clinton, and Bush, but not Obama. Hmmm...he may or may not know about Hurricane Katrina. I think that was 2005, or was it 2006?

"This lab represents the true heart of our operation," Shep boasted. "But at this point in the tour, I will defer to Doc's overwhelming expertise and presentation skills." With that bit of flattery he motioned at Stonecroft who blushed and waved his elderly hand in modest protest.

Stonecroft laid hold of Denver's arm and led him towards a door to his right. Doc lowered his glasses and looked up at Denver. "Did they retrieve a radiation sample from you yet, Mr. Collins?"

"Excuse me, a what?"

Stonecroft halted and called out to the group. "Did anyone bother to initiate his TRS sample?"

It took a moment for all of them to stop chatting and look up. The Chief apologized. "We're sorry, my friend, what was that?"

Dr. Stonecroft took a deep breath then enunciated every word. "I said, has anyone bothered to gather the requisite TRS from Mr. Collins? Perhaps last night in the detention facility, or sometime early this morning?"

One-by-one they either looked away or began pointing playfully at each other in a blame game. Doc waved his hand at them in faux disgust. "*Incompetents,* the whole lot of them. Come with me, my dear Mr. Collins."

He led Denver toward a tall storage unit with double doors standing against the wall to their left. He unlocked it and opened the right-hand side. Denver wasn't expecting the rush of cold air that invisibly poured out of the refrigerated unit. The door was filled with multiple rows of test tubes, many of them capped and labeled. Doc donned a pair of thin gloves and retrieved an empty tube, and shut the door. He opened a smaller drawer nearby and grabbed a pair of tweezers, spraying them with a clear liquid. He waved them in the air for a few seconds and stepped up to Denver who, understandably, had grown a bit nervous.

Denver broke the tension. "Lemme guess...*urine* sample?"

Doc was puzzled. "Urine? Oh, no, no, my good man, wrong end." He moved around behind his nervous victim and started running his fingers through Denver's hair. "You may experience a slight nervous response," he said dryly.

Denver began to ask for clarification when a sharp pain in his scalp provided all the clarification he needed. Doc circled back around holding a sizable clump of Denver's hair in the tweezers.

"Don't tell me you can't afford a cheap pair of scissors in this research lab?" Denver complained as he rubbed the back of his head and his eyes watered.

Doc let out a controlled laugh as he inserted the hair into the test tube. Ellen came alongside and started capping and labeling it. She leaned towards Denver. "It's not really the hair we need. It's your *roots*."

"The roots?"

"Once mammalian hair protrudes from the scalp," Doc explained, "it is necrotic tissue. We need living, viable cells."

Denver didn't like the sound of that at all. "Viable cells?" Nazi-era medical procedures flashed through his mind. "Wait, are you trying to clone humans down here?"

Ellen smiled, and leaned in even closer. "Not clone, *capture*. We need to capture your radiation chronology stamp." She looked into his hopelessly lost eyes. "It's a temporal marker embedded in your cellular structure."

Denver spun around and faced the group. "Um, I'm supposing someone actually speaks *English* down here?"

Doc nodded at Ellen while he placed the sample in the cooler.

"Okay, English," she said. "Well, you were pulled here by a particular temporal rift, a time portal—"

"Yeah, the Chief told me about the cracks in the space-time-thing, and the lightning."

She grinned. "Excellent. Well, the cracks that each of us were pulled through have highly specific signatures, like a fingerprint. As you passed through, your living cells were imprinted with this unique marker."

Doc ripped off his gloves and took control once again. "We can extract the specific radiation signature from your follicles. Dead hair cells cannot retain the pattern, but these follicles, now separated from your body, will expire, consequently leaving them with an immutable temporal marker."

Denver struggled to interpret and organize this information into layman's terms. He attempted to recite it back. "So, hair roots are alive, living cells, and when I jumped, they received a stamp, a pattern of radiation or something."

Stonecroft pointed in his elation. "Yes. Yes. Spot on."

Denver's confidence increased. "And then, those hair cells will die, but they will have a permanent pattern locked in them."

"Correct again, Mr. Collins."

"So, uh, why do you need hair cells and stamps and all that?"

Ellen interjected, "Dr. Stonecroft, may I?" He nodded. She locked arms with Denver like a young crush, and led him straight ahead to a large door with three locks. Stonecroft and Papineau walked over and each of them pulled out a key and unlocked a tumbler. Ellen waited for them to step aside and she inserted the final key.

Oh, wow, three locks. This is gonna be a triple disappointment.

As she opened the door, Denver looked above it and noticed a small plaque:

IN MEMORY OF PHILLIP NELSON 1946 - 1953.

The Chief cleared his throat. "All this tech talk makes my head hurt. I'm headed topside and check up on a few ballgames on the radio. Holler if you need me." A few of them waved and he vanished up the stairs, heavy footfalls echoing the whole way.

Ellen turned back to Denver. "If and when we are successful creating a sustainable, temporal rift—"

Denver interrupted, "Which is a...?"

"A wormhole, a time portal, Mr. Collins," she offered. "Once we achieve a successful rift, we can use your TRS, your signature, like an address, to send you back, or actually *forward*, to the same moment in time you jumped."

Denver was wide-eyed. "You're, you're serious?"

Ellen smiled and shrugged. "Well, at least...in theory." She winked.

"But, my good man," Stonecroft added, "don't let uncertainty cloud your appreciation. The mathematics behind it are quite sound, I assure you."

Denver shook his head. "So you're telling me, you're trying to create a *time machine?*"

She donned a mischievous grin. "Not trying, Mr. Collins. *Perfecting*. Wanna peek?"

He raised his eyebrows. *This I gotta see.*

She shoved on the heavy door and motioned for him to proceed inside. After a deep breath, he stepped through, hoping to finally see Wonderland.

He would have settled for something, for *anything* that would give him hope that he would one day see Jasmine again.

Wednesday, November 13, 1946
Journal entry number 117

I can't imagine what he is going through. I mean, all three of us Jumpers have come backward in time—that is traumatic enough—but we gain nothing in terms of knowledge. We went into the past.

But now we have taken this man, this older physicist into our confidence. It has taken a real effort to win him over. If this journal is ever found, we have a responsibility to protect his identity. He is risking everything to help us, and ultimately, he must remain behind once we are able to jump back home. His unique secret must remain uniquely secret.

We will call him X. The letter X is similar to the first letter of the Greek word Chronos, or TIME. X is fitting. He is unmarried, with few family ties.

It has been a difficult process recruiting him, on many levels. First, there is the language barrier. He is French, and let's just say that his fluency in English lies somewhere between crippling and tragic. (His credentials, though, are off the charts.) The money, predictably, secured his attention, but it took considerable persuasion to convince him who we were, and WHEN we were from (and rightly so).

Larry took what I call the "Biblical" route—using prophecy to confirm veracity. We selected certain events that are not really predictable in the ordinary sense, and then told him the outcome ahead of time.

Ken's internal sports encyclopedia really helped once again. Last Saturday, on November 9th, it was the famous football "Game of the Century" between Army and Notre Dame at Yankee Stadium. The game, in a rare event, ended in a tie: zero, zero. Ken wrote it all down, on Friday, the night before. X was very impressed, but still, we sensed, needed more.

My geological index sealed the deal. I told him last Thursday that there would be a devastating earthquake, over a 7.0 in Chile, killing well over a thousand people on Sunday. Sporting events might be able to be predicted, since you know there will be a game, and the relative strengths and weaknesses of the two teams, but precisely predicting a geological event, in 1946, that is well-nigh irrefutable.

News travels a bit slow, but by late yesterday, reports of the destruction in South America started coming in. X was convinced. And if he ever needs more, we will be more than ready. Winners of political races, discoveries, tragedies...all at our disposal. Our problem is not in proving that we are from the future, our problem is enabling X to help us get back there before anyone discovers us or betrays us. We can't be naive; he will have to be monitored continuously. Many corporations in the world would offer millions, and some governments even billions of dollars for access to our knowledge.

It is a paradox. We have to trust him with our futures, yet we can't trust him—period.

We are leaving tomorrow to head back to Normal, now as a group of four. The plan is for X to live at my house, at least for now. He can't really interact with the people of the town, so I will take care of him, and he can start "setting up shop" in my garage.

Larry has already been attempting to give X our limited knowledge of time-jump-phenomena, mainly the lightning part. It's hard to understand what he says, but we think it is something about studying the issue of why NOW? Why 1946? Why not earlier or later? Eventually we will have to answer the other big question: WHY NORMAL?

Of course, there could be Jumpers elsewhere. Who knows? Well, time to stop writing and time to start packing for the train ride home. Goodbye, Washington, D.C. (And no, I did NOT get a chance to see or meet President "Give 'em-Hell Harry" Truman. That would have been amazing.) He might be in Florida at the Little White House anyway. I know he liked (likes) to spend winters there.

CHAPTER 22

He had seen her act like this before, so he shouldn't have been surprised.

But it was quite obvious that Shep still didn't like it.

In the big scheme of things, it didn't really matter. Denver was just the latest toy in Ellen's toy box. The newness would fade.

Shep joined Stonecroft and Papineau as they gathered near the doorway to gauge the newcomer's reaction.

Denver crossed the threshold into a surreal environment, not quite Wonderland, but definitely a room to make one wonder.

He stepped out onto a suspended metal mesh transom about four feet wide and roughly fifteen feet long. He peered up and around. The room was almost spherical, about twenty feet in diameter, and white. Very white. *Interesting…a reflective coating of some sort.* He felt like he was inside a huge, hollow ping pong ball.

Ellen hung back, arms folded, and called out, "What do you think of our little baby?" She motioned toward the far end of the metal walkway.

The contraption was elegantly simple, triangular in shape, and roughly seven feet high. The sides were composed of three shiny metal tubes, each a little wider than a baseball bat, with thin fins spaced along their lengths, not unlike a large radiator. Thick, insulated wires branched out of each of the three vertices and disappeared into the curved walls. Denver eased up near it, but not too close.

"It won't hurt you," Ellen yelled, making him flinch. She stated the obvious. "It's not on right now."

Denver waved. "Uh, thanks." With childlike curiosity he traced a finger along the fins. He wasn't sure why he did it, but he stabbed his arm timidly through the open air in the center of it. *Nothing.*

In his concentration, he didn't sense Ellen walking up right behind him and she whispered into his ear. "What did it feel like?"

This time he was pretty sure both of his feet left the floor.

"Lemme guess," he said. "You double majored in college. First, in Physics, and then in the Psychology of Human Surprise?"

She feigned a cute, coy look. "You read my resume!"

"You shouldn't have wasted your money on your second degree. Trust me. You're a natural."

"Well, you might be *right* about the second one, but you're definitely *wrong* about the first one. Nurse. I have my RN."

He rolled his eyes. "Great. With your natural talent you will probably give me a heart attack, and with your education you can...revive me."

"Hey, a girl's got to have a hobby. Especially a girl trapped over ten years in the past."

He glanced down at her badge. *1968.* She moved past him and caressed the fins herself. "I liked Custer."

Now that was an odd statement. Denver stared. "Come again? The Little Big Horn guy?"

"Custer. Somehow no one thought that the name Continuously Sustainable Temporal Rift had any endearing or memorable qualities. It kinda spells Custer. CSTR, so we just call it our Jump Portal."

Denver thought for a moment and smiled. "It was probably for the best. I mean, who wants to step into a machine whose name is synonymous with meeting your doom?"

Ellen rolled her eyes at his morbid humor.

He stepped back and raised his arms in admiration. "It's like something from a fantasy, or, or science fiction."

"In this subterranean ward," boomed an approaching Doc Stonecroft, "magic and science are essentially synonymous. With each successive iteration we employ, our result approaches a more stable rift. You will see, Mr. Collins, that the term *fantasy* is merely the temporary placeholder for immature technology."

Ellen nodded in agreement. "Once we dial this thing in, once we work out all the problems, and we have a stable wormhole, we should be able to just jump right in."

Denver glanced at her, then at the contraption. He muttered to himself.

"Just call me Alice."

CHAPTER 23

It wasn't all that uncommon on a Friday, but it was much earlier than usual for Betty Larson to shut down the office of the *Normal Journal*. As she dropped the last set of blinds, two shirtless little boys chased a wayward puppy, dragging its leash, past the front windows. She paused for a brief moment and grinned at the fool's errand as it unfolded. Normal was a small town, but *Meandering Mutt Dodges Detention* was not too high on her list for an upcoming headline.

Not that she hadn't written and used some catchy but worthless alliterations over the past three years, but there are limits, even for a reporter. One can only stomach for so long all the various combinations of Perplexed Police, or Big Business Breakup, or, her personal favorite, Female Fescue Farmer Finds Famous Photos. But every newspaper editor knows that the first rule of reporting on a slow day is: "news is what you make it."

Drumming up credible stories hadn't been her only challenge since she took the editor's position three summers ago. Just being credible at all had been a daily, uphill, and often, *losing* battle. All else being equal, she started her role with two strikes against her from day one. First, she was fairly new to the area and outsiders in Normal are on an unspoken scale somewhere between Greedy Lawyers and Horse Thieves, and secondly, well, she was a *she*. The Second World War had begun to erase some of the stigma surrounding professional women, but in the Midwest, gender bias was often elevated to an art form.

She caught her own reflection in the glass just before the blinds went down. Her black hair was pulled back, making it look shorter than it actually was. She turned gracefully side to side, considering her appearance. She didn't look masculine, and she had no desire to be treated just like a man, but in 1956, maybe a little less like a woman.

The blinds finally dropped and she slapped her hand across a wall switch, extinguishing the foyer and front counter lights. As Betty moved towards the back, she stopped and examined a few invoices and tickets at the counter.

I probably should work on these.

But after a few seconds of trying to drum up desire, she just filed it all away loosely in a small box below the register. She wasn't a procrastinator, for sure, but neither her head nor her heart were within fifty miles of accounting paperwork this day.

She moved down the short hallway and turned left into her office sanctuary, heading straight toward a large oil painting of a desert sunset on the far wall. It was a leftover relic from the previous editor, and as far as she could determine, from two or three editors before that. The only thing Betty had changed was the frame a year ago. She stopped mere inches in front of it and grabbed the artwork like a steering wheel. With a modicum of effort she lifted it up and over and gently set it down against the wall at her feet.

She wasn't thrilled with the canvas painting, but it made an adequate cover for her small office safe embedded in the wall. Betty spun through the first three numbers in quick succession, but had to pause on the final one.

Oh, yes, 31. Click.

She turned the handle, and the thick metal door slowly swung outward. She retrieved a cigar box-sized wooden chest, and transported it to her cluttered, yet functional desk. A small key from her top desk drawer released the tiny padlock adorning the front.

She set the lock down and cracked the lid with all the anticipation of Christmas morning. She peered down at a random collection of mysterious objects that no person from that era could ever be expected to fully understand. It was, perhaps, the most unique assortment of items in the world, bar none. Betty had spent hours playing out scenarios and deducing potential explanations for them individually, and for the collection as a whole.

All the common question words, including Who, What, Where, and Why, were probed, over and over. But a new investigative word was gaining momentum in her mind— *When*.

Her latest acquisition may have held the key to that very issue. She popped her purse open and withdrew Denver's hastily tipped and torn five dollar bill. She scanned it for the date once again...2013.

2013. Nearly sixty years into the future.

Is that what all this is about: the future?

The olive-drab phone on her desk started ringing and it jolted Betty back from her reporter's thirst for that next big story. She looked over at the phone with no intent of answering.

She lowered the money, or whatever it was, down into the box and locked the lid back in place. In that moment, all of the private struggles and public hardships she had endured over the past three years were, at least for now, worth it after all.

That five dollar bill didn't just represent buying power: it could very well represent *power* itself.

CHAPTER 24

Denver squinted and bit his bottom lip. "This is all so incredible. But, how are you funded? This stuff must cost a fortune. I doubt you could sell enough windows to pay for all of this. Do you guys cook meth down here?"

Shep glanced over at Doc. "Uh, *cooking*?"

"Narcotics, Mr. Sheppard," Doc clarified as he looked up from his work. "*Drugs*."

Shep got it. "Oh...oh, no, no. We use a method a lot more fun," Shep explained, "a lot less dangerous, and only *slightly* more legal." He leaned in, and Denver matched his move. "We *gamble*."

Denver was almost disappointed. He had expected a more mysterious or exciting source for cash flow. *Gambling? Roulette wheels, blackjack, and slot machines?* Denver vented his misgivings, "But, how? Everyone knows that in the long run, the house always wins. It's called gambling for a reason. It's based on uncertainty."

Shep raised his eyebrows and raised a wagging finger. "Correction, the house always wins; unless, of course, the house is being *cheated*."

"Well, tell me, Danny Ocean, what's your method— stacked cards, rigged dice, loaded roulette balls?"

Shep grinned and lowered his voice. "Nope. Sports scores."

The rest of the crew seemed to be waiting for the inevitable moment that the light bulb would come on in Denver's mind. It took a few moments, but it did.

"Because you know the future, you know—"

"We know the final scores of big ball games," Shep replied. "Winners, losers, sometimes even total points. You name it. In the old days, it was horse races. But now, we send a couple of guys out to Las Vegas whenever our funds get low. We win big, but not too big, we keep it under the radar, and we switch up who we send each time." He slapped Denver on the shoulder. "Who knows, maybe you can go with us next time. Lights, girls, lots of action. Did I mention girls?"

Ellen Finegan grabbed a clipboard. "I'm sorry to break into your delightful discussion of dancing girls, dancing lights, and boatloads of easy cash, but we have fixed our power problem and are about ready to begin the next phase of our test. You can stay for the show, if you'd like."

Shep jumped up, and Denver was left in the dust as a sudden flurry of activity and tension developed in the chamber. Dr. Papineau muttered with indecipherable diatribes, and Doc Stonecroft and Ellen intermittently conferred with each other and adjusted equipment.

Denver caught Ellen between duties and followed her around. "So what's going on?"

She slowed down moderately to bring him up to speed. "We're testing our synchronized capacitor relays. It would've been finished earlier, but we had a little power outage issue." She messed with a large dial and looked at her clipboard.

"Anyway, within the next several minutes our reactor will complete its current charging cycle. Here, you're gonna need these." She snatched a pair of dark goggles and dropped them in his hands.

"What happens after that, charging, capacitor, sync thing?" he asked.

She stopped moving and turned to face him. "Lightning, Mr. Collins. Beautiful, powerful, *predictable*—lightning."

He didn't even know how to respond, but before he could, Dr. Papineau began making wild motions.

"Viens ici, maintenant!"

Ellen and Doc rushed over to him, concentrating on the meter he was pointing at. Denver only knew three words in French, but the terror in the eyes of the scientist required no interpretation.

Even Doc's confident and positive appearance collapsed as Ellen hurried over to another device and made several adjustments. Denver was sure he saw the remaining color drain out of Ellen's already fair skin.

Papineau shook his head violently. Just above Ellen, a red light flashed, and a warning alarm's piercing wail added to the confusion.

Shep scrambled over to Ellen. "What's wrong?"

Her eyes darted around a console. "There's been a failure in the primary reactor cooling system. Doc! Doc! Engage the backup!"

Stonecroft flipped a small lid and depressed a button. He glanced up at the warning light. It continued flashing, and the alarm increased in intensity.

Denver had to yell to be heard. "Just how bad is it?"

"Well, Mr. Collins," Doc offered, "to put this potential catastrophe into perspective, consider a nuclear meltdown that, if gone critical, would puncture a gaping hole into the very crust of the earth, poisoning the water table, and perhaps unleashing enough magma to inundate the area with several meters of lava and ash!"

Denver backed toward the exit, trying to stay out of the way of the emergency response. He came close to colliding with Chief McCloud who was bounding down the stairs and burst into the room. "The alarm, what's wrong?"

"We are in the late stages of a Level Three Emergency," Doc called out over his shoulder.

"Should I evacuate the town?" McCloud demanded.

"It would be an exercise in futility, Chief McCloud. If this goes critical, everyone within a few miles radius is, well…" Doc hesitated and adjusted his spectacles.

"To put it bluntly, my friend, everyone is dead already!"

Tuesday, December 24, 1946
Journal entry number 129

I am about to spend my fourth major holiday in Normal. It is Christmas Eve. The undeniable fact that three outsiders like us have stepped through time, almost miraculously, brings the essential tenets of Christmas into the arena of discussion. The idea that the ultimate outsider, God, has stepped into time, miraculously, well, Ken is highly uncomfortable with that prospect.

Larry largely avoids any theological or philosophical implications of our plight, but Ken and I, especially of late, seem to approach these topics regularly, and with passionate and mostly polite differences.

The tradition of gift giving, of a selfless act to benefit others, has made me evaluate our situation here. Our accumulating financial successes and our potential time-travel successes which may grow as well—are unintentionally creating an environment of temptation.

Wealth and the ability to manipulate time could combine to create unimaginable power. We need safeguards against this dark path of personal exploitation, the lure of using our knowledge, our wealth, our technology for strictly personal or harmful purposes. It is time for a new accord.

The First Accord: Walk Without Footprints
The Second Accord: Filter the Future

How about: The Third Accord: Prevent Personal Profit

CHAPTER 25

For the second time in less than five hours Denver faced the strong likelihood of his own death. It occurred to him that perhaps these good old days weren't properly named.

The Chief looked down at his watch. "How much time do we have?"

Doc probably didn't give him the answer he had hoped for. "At the current rate of acceleration, I would anticipate somewhat less than seven minutes."

"*Engager les tiges du réacteur, manuellement!* Manual!" Papineau demanded above the noise.

Ellen looked over at Doc. "What?"

"I believe that my French colleague is insisting that the control rods will have to be manually engaged."

"Where is the manual override?" McCloud asked as Ellen rushed over to the window in the reactor room door and pointed.

"There!" she yelled.

Denver, Shep, and the Chief caught up to her. "But the temperature in that room is over a hundred and thirty degrees," she cried out, "and the caps are becoming unstable. Just the right conditions could lead to an electrical discharge that would level the factory and potentially scatter highly enriched uranium for miles, depending on the weather and wind."

They huddled close and peered through the thick, plate glass and spotted a red lever, about twenty feet away on the far side of the steaming hot room.

Denver dropped back from the group and pulled out his photo of Jasmine. As his heart raced, he couldn't begin to imagine the prospect of not seeing her again. He had endured the daily horror of several years of a bad marriage, and he had put up with the ridiculous demands of an estranged spouse, just to gain a few precious hours with her.

He longed to reminisce about all the milestones of watching her grow up, but now, in a fit of ironic cruelty, for this time traveler there simply wasn't *time*. He traced a finger across her face, and whispered to her in his heart, as if across time itself.

If any of us survive this, people will probably think that I was brave for what I'm about to do, but actually, I'm just terrified that I'll never see you again. This is for you, sweetie.

He stashed the photo away, and made a move for the reactor room door.

Ellen lunged in front of him. "*Denver!* What're you doing? You could die in there!"

"Like Doc said, if someone doesn't pull that lever, we're all dead anyway." He pushed toward the door a second time.

"Wait," Ellen pleaded, "you'll at least need to wear a protective suit. That room is hot, and not just the temperature."

She ran to a freestanding closet and grabbed a bright yellow reactor suit. Everyone pitched in to help him don the gear.

"It won't be very comfortable," she admitted, "but it should give you a few minutes shielding from both the heat and the radiation."

Doc raised his voice above the commotion. "We have less than three minutes! And Mr. Collins: whatever you do, do not initiate a voltage discharge!"

Denver paused before sliding his awkward helmet down. "*English?*"

"A *spark*, Mr. Collins," Ellen clarified, "don't cause a spark. Hurry!" Ellen shoved the mask down and sealed it. He gave her a fast thumbs up as Shep and McCloud opened the heavy reactor room door, just enough for him to squeeze through. Everyone lowered their goggles as he entered and the thick door was immediately secured behind him.

The heated vapors in the chamber instantly steamed up his helmet, making an already difficult task a hopeless cause. He attempted to wipe it away with his gloves with miserable and varying results. He glanced to the right and saw rows and rows of large cylinders with heavy-duty wires crossing and crisscrossing them.

Must be the capacitors. Okay, avoid sparks. Get to red lever.

His feet slipped and slid in the cumbersome boots. *Marbles on glass have better traction than these boots! Focus, Collins. No sparks, red lever. Probably less than two minutes. Concentrate.*

He hadn't felt it before now, but the rising heat had become suffocating. Almost intolerable. He hoped that the tingling on his skin was from nervousness, the temperature, or stress—anything but nuclear radiation.

Don't be distracted, soldier. Red lever. That is your mission. Red lever. Objective dead ahead.

Just outside the heavy door, Doc studied his watch. "Sixty seconds!"

Denver could only hear his own heartbeat, his labored breathing, and his own mantra: *No sparks, red lever.*

He wiped his facemask once again. The manual override was less than three feet away. *Mission nearly accomplished. Focus.*

He raised his heavy right arm and reached out for the bar. But, in the confusion of urgency and his near blindness, he did not see the sudden change in the floor's elevation. His right boot struck the ledge, jarring him off balance, and he crashed face-first into the wall. Denver fell, scraping all the way down, missing the lever by inches.

Ellen cried out, the rest just shook their heads.

He was not injured, but the thick coating of hot moisture coupled with the unforgiving suit transformed the simple process of standing up into a heroic feat. He made several valiant attempts, but failure dogged him.

Doc heralded their desperate state. "Thirty seconds!"

Denver fell against the wall once more. His prize was in sight.

Red lever. Focus.

He screamed out and lunged upwards with his right hand. His glove graced the lever, but failed to latch on, and he crumpled down upon his right knee. A blast of nauseating pain shot through his thigh, almost blacking him out. He recomposed himself, gritting his teeth so hard he was sure his molars would shatter. He couldn't see the lever through the agony, steam, and condensation, but he knew exactly where it was.

Red lever. Focus.

He managed to get one leg under him, and he found just a hint of traction for his right boot on the lip of the step. Denver's internal clock was basically accurate: *Last chance, Collins.*

He raised his right arm and thrust himself skyward with everything he had left within his tortured body. His hand caught hold of the lever just as his boot broke free and careened out from underneath him. He hung from the bar and swiveled from side to side until he was able to get some semblance of footing.

A small round of nervous applause broke out beyond the door, but it faded when Doc cried out, "Ten seconds!"

Denver managed to get both hands onto the bar as he stood up all the way. He took a deep breath and shoved down on the rod with a massive push. Denver thought he heard it creak, but the lever refused to budge. Years of moisture, oxidation, and the lack of use had all but fused the mechanism.

"Five seconds!" Stonecroft lamented.

Inside the reactor room, Denver pounded on the lever. *Nothing. What do I do?*

In a final act of desperation, and with a right knee on fire, Denver jumped as high as the suit would allow. He locked his arms straight out as a ramming rod and came crashing down upon the handle. He wasn't sure if it was his bones breaking or the bar giving way, but he heard a distinct pop, and the red lever reluctantly tripped downward with a sickening grind. Carried by his own considerable momentum, Denver slammed into the hot floor, chest first and bounced. He gasped for breath that wouldn't come.

"Two seconds!" Doc cried out.

Ellen peered through the window as the control rods descended. She knocked the Chief backward as she spun about and rushed to the panel to her right, shedding goggles along the way. She made a rapid survey of all of the gauges as Doc Stonecroft drew alongside. "Well, Ms. Finegan? Will it be Chernobyl all over again? Are we among the living dead?"

She frowned. "Uh, Chernobyl…what?"

Doc adjusted his glasses. "An unintentional slip, sorry my dear. But back to the question at hand…"

Ellen hunched over and watched a meter with great interest. She smiled and grabbed an unprepared Doc Stonecroft. "It…it worked! Radiation levels appear to be returning to normal! They are returning to normal! He did it! He did it!"

Doc collapsed into a nearby chair and removed his sweaty glasses with trembling fingers as hugs and handshakes filled the room. He mopped his brow with a handkerchief and spoke to himself, "Well done, Trailer

Collins. Well done, indeed. Perhaps Providence has sent you to us for such a time as this, my friend."

Dr. Papineau reset several switches and the piercing alarm was silenced, along with the incessant warning light. Ellen hurried back to the tiny window. Through the sauna-like conditions it was possible to discern that Denver was sitting on the floor with his back against the wall.

What no one could see was that he was still struggling to catch a full breath. Glancing up through a condensation-covered helmet and the lessening mist, he could barely make out the exit door. His throbbing knee and bruised chest were the least of his concerns at the moment. Denver knew that each second he lingered was adding to what could already be a lethal radiation exposure.

With considerable effort, he clutched the manual release lever and hoisted himself to his feet. It felt as if a red-hot knife was being plunged into his right knee cap. He almost went down again. He gasped.

Mission accomplished, soldier. Not with grace, or with style, but accomplished, nonetheless. Thank God.

His arms and legs felt like buckets full of lead. He remembered from his military training that severe fatigue often follows high doses of radiation. He rationalized that his condition was due to emotional and physical exhaustion.

Denver took a few unsteady steps as Shep watched through the thick glass. "Can we open the reactor door yet? Is it safe?"

Doc rose and examined some instruments. "I would not recommend opening it until I absolutely had to, Mr. Sheppard. Radiation levels are still elevated, but not lethal. But every moment helps," Doc said. "Of course, there's no way of predicting what our dear friend's body has just been exposed to."

Ellen shot him a hopeless glance. The Chief spoke up. "How long til, um, til we will know if…he will make it?"

Ellen rubbed her forehead. "It's, it's hard to guess, Chief. Acute Radiation Syndrome can sometimes take weeks or months to manifest itself. Even years."

"Or it can be fatal in less than twenty-four hours," Doc added grimly. They all turned to him. "But that's in very rare cases, only the most extreme of accidents. And our dear friend was shielded…to some extent."

Shep faced the reactor room again. "So, you're telling me that he could be a walking dead man? That guy right there! The one that just saved all of our sorry asses?"

Doc framed it in the best light. "He could be as healthy as you or me, Mr. Sheppard, God willing. Only time will tell."

In the reactor room Denver had expended a tremendous amount of energy just to reach the midpoint back to the door, fighting injury, fatigue, and slippery conditions the entire way. He paused for a moment and was encouraged when he saw Ellen nodding through the window. He smiled back, but with the hazmat helmet concealing his response, he could've stuck his tongue out, and she never would have known the difference.

He caught his second wind and began moving again. The pain forced him to favor his left side, creating an irregular waddle. Three steps later, his left boot slipped outward in a small puddle and collided with a capacitor wire running along the floor. He looked down in terror just in time to see the cable break loose from a terminal.

No sparks, Collins was the last thing that went through his mind. There was a spark, triggering a blinding flash of sizzling, white hot light, followed by an explosive shockwave that sent the hero hurtling back across the room. His body slammed directly into the concrete wall like a projectile and he bounced off and plummeted to the floor in a crumpled and scorched heap of melted plastic and burnt skin. The force of the blast cracked the glass in the door and sent many of the capacitors cascading across the wet floor like so many bowling pins.

Ellen pounded on the door in horror. "Denver!" She screamed at Shep and McCloud, "Get this door open, *now*!"

The two men yanked hard on the release, but something was wrong. Shep examined around the edges. "The explosion must've warped the door somewhere." He turned around and scanned the area. "Get me that rope over there!"

Papineau retrieved it, and Shep secured it to the handle. "Everyone grab ahold of it, we will pull on three." They all obeyed. "One, two….*three!*"

The massive door was jammed, but it was no match for the combined force of five people powered by pure adrenaline. The hinges protested, and creaked, and then gave way as the door opened with an unearthly sound. Doc would later describe it as being akin to the screech of a foot-long nail being pulled through a piece of dense wood by a claw hammer.

Ellen dropped the rope and darted into the suffocating heat of the chamber, warily navigating around possibly-live wires and displaced capacitors.

"Careful, my dear Ellen!" Doc called out.

She hopscotched over the remaining cables and arrived at Denver's motionless body, lying face first on the ground in a twisted pile. The Chief caught up with her, and together they tenderly rolled Denver over onto his back and straightened his angled limbs. Ellen removed his cracked helmet with extreme care, revealing a severely blistered and pale face. A lifeless face.

The Chief knelt, and placed two fingers on the side of Denver's neck, checking for something, for anything. Ellen leaned in, listening and feeling for even a hint of breathing.

She didn't.

Ellen looked up through her tears and the Chief locked eyes with her. "I'm sorry Ellen. He didn't make it."

"Denver Collins is dead."

Saturday, January 25, 1947
Journal entry number 138

Today is my wife's birthday. It's so bizarre to think that she is turning 41 today, but in reality, Maryanne hasn't even been born yet.

I miss her terribly. And Kurtis, too. If I think of the time of the year here as matching back home, then he is in his second semester as a junior in high school. It's the weekend, and it's January—he's probably hitting the slopes at Breckenridge right now.

You have to think about time this way or you will go insane. It is a strange paradox—on the one hand you want to imagine your family is okay, that they can move on with good and happy lives, but then, there is that part of you that cries out, that demands for the whole world to stop turning and wait.

Is time still "moving forward" back home?

There is a now HERE, but is there a now THERE?

Have I been missing for 10 months back home in Colorado Springs, or is that world trapped in the moment that I jettisoned?

Either seems plausible, and both seem impossible. But our experience seriously calls into question the whole notion of impossible.

I need about 6 hours alone with Albert Einstein to sort things out. He has a Theory of Special Relativity, but I need a Law of Personal Relativity. Mathematical theories may satisfy the mind, but they woefully miss the mark when it comes to satisfying the heart.

Happy birthday, Maryanne, my love. Tell Kurtis to hit a couple of black diamonds for me. I'll be home soon. Actually I'm hoping to be back before you even miss me.

CHAPTER 26

All of us have one.

They may be different places, with different people, doing different things, but we all have at least one.

We all have a perfect day.

And today was Denver Collins' perfect day.

Denver spun about, trying his best to process the unbelievable view. The weather, incredible, the feeling, enjoyable, the location, just...wonderful. He touched his arms and legs and looked at his clothing—*no hazmat suit*. He felt his face—*no helmet*. Even his right knee was pain-free.

A warm and sensual breeze greeted him and he closed his eyes. He breathed to capacity, and dissected the individual aromas wafting his way: freshly mown grass, a touch of pine, perhaps just a hint of honeysuckle.

The sweet sound of children at play in the distance caused him to open his eyes and survey the scene again. Beautiful rows of trees in nearly every direction, and rolling expanses of emerald green grass filled his view.

The perfect day.

A familiar rumble from above made him look up, as a large passenger jet bolted across the sky, the sun glinting across its metal hull, a white contrail marking its path. Three more could be seen in the distance.

Jets? Jets.

He looked to his left and noticed that the tall trees were surpassed by even taller buildings miles away.

I'm in New York again, Central Park. But how? But when?

He fished the phone out of his pocket and turned it on.

SUNDAY JUNE 15, 2014

12:30 P.M.

He even had four bars of signal but no Wi-Fi. Questions flooded his elated mind. *I'm home? I'm back? But how?*

He double-checked his phone, 2014.

Amazing.

He bent over and ran his fingers through the soft grass. *This is real.* He pulled up a small handful and let the blades drain through his fingers as they floated down.

He rose back up and rubbed his forehead.

Was it all a dream? But it seemed so real. The lightning, the dark motel, the policeman, the tranquilizer, the jail, the town, the bus, the factory, the research lab, the crisis. Was it just a dream, just a nightmare?

But, what about those people? The Chief, and the cute waitress, and Shep, and Doc, and Ellen. And all the others.

But what happened?

Think Collins, think. What is the last thing you remember?

He flashed back to the impending crisis in the reactor room. The heat, the steam, the red lever, the pain, the urgency of it all. He recalled the failed attempts to move the bar, but then, success! Mission accomplished.

There's more Collins. C'mon. Remember!

He closed his eyes and pieced it back together. The painful victory lap back to the door. Ellen smiling. *Wait. Something happened. What happened?* He concentrated harder.

My foot. The boot. I slipped…it slipped. I hit a wire. Ellen said NO SPARKS! Oh, no! A spark! A flash of light.

Then…here.

Here.

Wait, what was it that Ellen said they were doing? She said predictable lightning. They were trying to create LIGHTNING. The Chief said it could send a person through those cracks in the sky. What is a spark?

A spark is…lightning. And now, I'm home.

I'm home!

Powerful joy overtook him. He stood frozen in the moment, lost in wonder, until a welcomed voice added to his euphoria.

"Daddy! Push me, Daddy!"

That sweet plea could have only come from one sweet source. *JASMINE!*

He spun about and beheld his precious daughter on a swing, not quite twenty feet away. His ability to speak was almost beyond him. "Jasmine?" He stared at her—white summer dress, her tiny shoes, her beautiful face.

"Push me, *Daddy*! Up high this time!"

Well, of course I will! Of course I will push you, sweetheart!

He wasted no time running towards her when another familiar voice stopped him dead in his tracks.

"I'll have lunch ready in just a minute, you two!"

As if in slow motion, he turned about to see his estranged wife, his gorgeous wife, smiling at him, busy with bread and deli meats on a colorful blanket nearby. He stared at her in shock, and she glanced up at him. "Everything all right, baby?" she asked.

Baby? Everything all right? Everything hasn't been all right for years!

She finished composing a masterpiece of a sandwich, and looked up. "Really...is something wrong?"

Something was wrong, but, then again, it couldn't have been more right. He was transfixed.

Jennifer cocked her head and lowered her voice. "You're staring at me like I'm laying here naked or something." She blushed a bit.

"No, nothing's wrong," he said. "It...uh...couldn't be better. Really."

Jennifer waved him off and pointed over at Jasmine. "Well, it isn't going to be *better* if you don't give that six-year-old some daddy-sized pushes on the swing." She reached down for a mustard bottle.

Denver blinked and nodded. He started walking towards Jasmine as she struggled to pump her legs in a vain attempt to gain altitude. He stepped front of her, with tears in his eyes and studied her lovable little face.

She greeted him with a wrinkled frown. "But Daddy, you can't push me from *this side!*"

He grabbed the chains, slowing her motion, and dropped down. He pushed back the hair out of her face. "I love you so much."

Jasmine was happy but clearly frustrated. "Well, I love you, too, Daddy, but swing me! Swing me high!"

There was no sense in delaying the simple request of someone so cute and yet so demanding. He rose and maneuvered his way around behind her. He wiped his eyes and then grabbed the sides of her seat and gave her gentle pushes. But, like her father, she was a thrill-seeker. "Faster, Daddy! *Higher!*"

Laughter poured out as he dutifully obeyed his pint-sized boss. In under thirty seconds, Jasmine was flying high as requested and he took a few steps back to enjoy the sight on this perfect day.

Nothing could make this day any better, he thought.

He, of course, was wrong.

Almost on cue, soft hands with passionate red nails slid across his muscular shoulders. Goosebumps rippled across his arms as he glanced down at his wife's delicate and manicured hands.

Jen encouraged him to turn around, as she gazed into his still-misty eyes. "Thank you for taking the day off to spend some time with us." He beamed as they both turned to enjoy the swinging spectacle for a few moments.

"It means so much to her," she said. A soft hand grabbed his chin and turned his face towards her own. "It means a lot...to *me*." Her face lit up with a smile he hadn't seen in years.

Nothing could make this day any better.

He, of course, was wrong once again.

She rose to her tiptoes with a slow kiss that turned passionate at just the right moment. He was almost awkward at first. Denver couldn't remember the last time they kissed like that.

The perfect moment on that perfect day was rudely interrupted by a perfectly needy six-year-old. "*Gross Dad! Gross!* Push me again!"

He didn't want to stop. But, as he thought about it, he was in a perfect win-win situation. He could keep kissing, or keep swinging. He couldn't lose on this one if he had wanted to. Two different women controlled him, and he couldn't have been happier.

Jennifer smiled and rolled her eyes, as she released Denver. She pointed at his chest playfully. "That's the only other woman I ever want to share you with! Got it?" She winked and strolled back toward the blanket, as he took a few steps, giving Jasmine another couple of daddy-sized pushes.

He reached up and tickled her sides as she passed by, and uncontrollable giggles soon followed. He gave her another extra-long push and ran under her, taking the fun to a whole new level.

But it was right then that another distinct voice from his past created the first crack in this otherwise most perfect day.

"I beg your eternal pardon, sir, but would you happen to have the time?"

Doc?

Denver turned toward what sounded like his imaginary, dream friend from an imaginary nuclear-powered research lab, in an imaginary 1956.

A smartly dressed elderly gentleman with a miniscule terrier on a leash stared up into Denver's incredulous face.

"Doc? *Doc?*"

The impossible visitor appeared puzzled. "Did you say clock? Yes, my good man, clock, I was asking for the time."

Denver shook his head. "No...no, not clock. *Doc*. Doc Stonecroft. Doctor Stonecroft? Don't you remember me?"

The distinguished gentleman strained his eyes, and adjusted his glasses. "Can't say that we've met. But then again, at my age, the mental processes are not what they once were. But, uh, back to the temporal question?"

Denver was frozen. The man leaned in. "Temporal. The *time*. Do you have the time?"

The time. Temporal. Doc? What is happening? Denver snapped out of his inner deliberations. He took out his phone. "Oh, yeah...the time, sure, it's, it's 12:41."

The polite senior bowed his head in gratitude. But something on the other side of the gentleman caught Denver's attention. A young boy walking by had been abducted by an older man, who had clutched the child's arm. The boy began screaming as he was dragged to a car nearby.

Denver panicked. *What is going on?*

"Thank you, my good man," said the Doc Stonecroft look-alike, temporarily distracting Denver.

"Oh, yeah—uh, don't mention it." Denver glanced back up and they were gone—no child, no abductor, no car. He spun around wildly. *What?* The crack in his otherwise perfect day, had just widened to a considerable degree.

"Where—where did they go?" he demanded.

"I'm not entirely sure whom you are referring to, sir, but I can assure you that we all need to go for shelter at once."

Denver looked down at him. "Shelter?"

"Oh yes. My canine companion loves the park, but Napoleon cannot abide a severe storm."

"Excuse me, did you say a storm?" Denver scanned the sky: *nothing but blue.*

The man smiled and chuckled, "And I thought that I was the one with degenerative hearing loss. Yes, sir, a *storm.* An *electrical* storm." The elderly man motioned toward Jasmine on the swing set. "You'd best remove your child from that infernal metal entertainment contraption. It's a veritable lightning rod. Good day, sir."

Denver nodded in return, and watched Jasmine, who was having the time of her life, as the old man and his mutt hastened away. Without warning, the colors and shadows around Denver muted somewhat, and the temperature dropped at least ten degrees. He studied the sky once again.

What the—?

Brilliant blue faded into a dull, gray overcast, and violent clouds of varying shades jockeyed for positions above. His meteorological observation ceased when a wayward Frisbee slammed into his shoulder.

An apologetic voice called out through the increasing breeze, "Sorry! We are so sorry!"

He bent down to retrieve the toy when waitress Katie Long ran up to him, adorable and breathless. He rose and handed it back to her, and she smiled with her trademarked red lips. "Thanks! Must've been the wind." She turned around and tossed it back towards her friend.

Denver followed her every move, and called out, "Katie?"

Another familiar female voice behind him made him jump. "I'm not Katie, handsome, but you can pick me up like a Frisbee any day of the week."

He turned on his heels as Ellen Finegan seductively stalked toward him, her vibrant red hair dancing as if it were alive in the steady breeze. Before he knew what was happening, she threw her arms around his neck and pulled him in for a long and deep kiss. He resisted and pushed back, breaking free for a moment, but she refused to be refused. She hauled him back in as the strong winds wrapped her wild hair about his face.

Denver shoved her away, but she seemed to find that as an irresistible challenge. A lover's game. "Oh, I love a fighter!" She pawed at him again, but he managed to get all but one arm out of the danger zone.

A few rumbles of thunder in the distance revealed the storm's impending fury and the wind kicked it up another notch.

What was that?

Denver discerned another strange sound above the roar—it was giggling, but not from Jasmine.

Jennifer?

He gazed to his left and was horrified that his wife was rolling around on the blanket in a passionate exchange with Chief McCloud. He was groping her aggressively and kissed her bare neck.

There was no doubt she loved it.

"Jennifer? *Jennifer!*" Denver yelled.

Neither of them seemed to notice him and Ellen pulled on his arm with all her lustful might. "C'mon! Let's show them how it's really done!"

The harsh wind made forward progress all but impossible as he tried to reach his willingly violated spouse. He called out again. *"Jennifer! What is going on?"*

The storm intensified in dramatic surges as lightning flashed and popped around them. Large drops of cold, intermittent rain drops pummeled his face. He escaped

Ellen's improper advances as a horrific scream from the playground pierced the turbulent air.

"Daddy! Help me, Daddy!"

The violent wind tossed Jasmine about in the stinging rain. She struggled to hold on as she flung about, twisting, screaming, and crying out. A bolt of lightning slammed into a large tree nearby, and a huge branch exploded downward as the crashing thunder drowned out all competing sounds.

Denver fought hard to reach his daughter, shielding his face from the driving rain that struck like thousands of liquid bullets within the maelstrom. His leg struck something on the ground.

What's this?

He nearly tripped over a boy who was rolling around in the wet grass, writhing in horrible pain. The boy screamed, clasping his right side. Denver attempted to lean over to assist him, but another close bolt of lightning flashed, and the distressed child was gone. Denver spun about in every direction, hunting for the boy.

He's gone!

He caught sight, yet again, of his currently-unfaithful wife in her blatant blanket debauchery. It literally sickened him, but Jasmine's desperate cry refocused his resolve.

"Daddy! Help me!"

He strained to reach her, but the hurricane-force gale made standing a lost cause, let alone forward motion. Another blinding flash of lightning arced all across the sky and instantly Ellen was standing before him. She grabbed him and shouted into his ear, "You'll never get back to your daughter. *Never!*" She roared with laughter.

With a swift motion he heaved her aside, sending her tumbling across the ground. He could hear her laughter echoing above the noise and confusion. He grasped once again for Jasmine as the terrified little girl attempted to reach out to him, but the wind jostled her in a dozen different directions.

"Jasmine! I'm coming! Hold on, I will save you! I promise!"

But he couldn't, and he didn't, and he shouldn't have.

Time slowed all at once. It was as if Denver could trace each individual raindrop as it hurled through the air and splashed into the ground. He looked up in disbelief as a tremendous bolt of lightning branched out from a menacing thundercloud just overhead. Time slowed further, nearly to a standstill as Denver watched the lightning's erratic, fiery path down, down to the Earth below. The white-hot bolt hammered the swing set, vaporizing the metal and rending the entire playground in a violent explosion of light, heat, and despair.

Denver wailed, but no sound escaped his terrified lips, *"Jasmine! No!"*

They were the last words of Denver Collins' perfect day.

Friday, March 14, 1947
Journal entry number 153

Just past my one-year anniversary as a Jumper, and time just
sent us an anniversary gift: Grant Forrester. And a few days ago,
President Truman bequeathed a gift to the whole world: the new
Truman Doctrine.

Our exclusive club has now grown to FOUR. Yet another male.
Grant is officially the youngest, coming in at 24 years young. He
jumped from 1972, and with his thick sideburns and nearly shoulder-
length hair, I probably could've guessed his era within 3 or 4 years.
He kind of reminds me of a young Lee Majors. He is a medical
student and apparently from a family of money and power. Enough of
both to keep him out of Vietnam.

Grant was a tough one to track down, and we almost didn't. We
have spent many hours discussing the mechanics of time displacement,
especially with the more scientific perspective of X when the language
barrier allows us. We have concluded that FLaT, our little acronym
for Freak Lightning and Thunder doesn't necessarily have to always
bring a new time Jumper.

Yesterday, approximately 10:45 am., FLaT came to town. Ken,
Larry, and I fanned out. We agreed to meet a few hours later at

12:45 in front of the Normal Theater uptown. (I was just there a few days ago and watched *Angel and the Badman* with John Wayne and Gail Russell. Fifteen cents for a movie, and popcorn for less than a dime!)

Those two hours came and went with no luck. We jumped in the car and hit a wide perimeter, almost into Bloomington to the south and Kerrick Road to the north. We drove back into town about 2:00 p.m. and went over to the college campus area, parking on Locust Street. We walked all over the campus and luckily, Larry spotted him. Grant was inside Milner Library.

Obviously, our greatest concern is the amount of contact and amount of observation, i.e. which Locals has a Jumper talked to, and has anyone seen a Jumper in their non-period clothing?

Grant said that he had stopped a small group of college girls and asked them where he was, and what was going on. He said they laughed at him, and kept walking. He reported that he had quite a few stares, but no other worrisome conversations.

He was hungry for both food and answers, and we took him to the house. We filled his stomach quickly, but his appetite for information is still pretty strong. It is fascinating how time displacement affects people differently. I couldn't stand the sight of food, and he can't get enough of it. He appears to be fairly self-confident and pretty sharp. A good addition to the family.

I'm worried about the first haircut for this "pretty boy"—time to introduce him to Vitalis Hair Tonic.

Now that we are at 4 men, from diverse backgrounds of knowledge and skill, it is starting to feel a bit contrived. Is our predicament the result of natural accidents, or unnatural selection? Did we jump here, or were we brought here? Are we being studied like a bizarre zoo exhibit? But who, why?

On another note, X seems to be making some real progress. I've noticed a lot less obvious fits of profanity and quite a few more "bon's" and an occasional thumbs up.

CHAPTER 27

The distant look in his eyes suggested that he would rather have been just about anywhere rather than at work. Dr. Ferrel Montgomery slid into his oversized chair and rolled up to his over-cluttered metal desk. The springs in the seat protested, but he wasn't embarrassed in the slightest. He combed thick fingers through salt and pepper hair (more salt though than pepper) and closed a folder, sizing up the immaculately dressed, eager blonde sitting opposite him.

She seemed almost *too* eager.

They always seemed eager at this stage.

"I've had a final meeting with the hiring committee," he said. "We have decided to move forward with your employment if you are still interested in the offer, Ms. Beussink."

He noticed that she was trying to mask her excitement. It didn't work.

"Oh, yes, absolutely, Dr. Montgomery. Thank you."

He leaned back. The chair felt almost at the breaking point. "Now, as we do with all nursing positions, there is a probationary period, usually twelve weeks."

"I understand."

He selectively withheld the fact that most new hires didn't make it one month, let alone three.

He glanced up and removed his glasses, like a gambler contemplating how to play his difficult hand. He wiped the smudged lenses, and then locked eyes with her. "This isn't a job for everyone, Ms. Beussink. It can be...more than a little *challenging*."

The news didn't seem to concern her, so Dr. Montgomery tipped his cards further. "We've found that most nurses with your type of traditional hospital experience have a little difficulty in...*adapting* to our specialized type of clientele."

"Oh, I completely understand," she said.

But he knew she didn't.

Silently he gave her three weeks.

He peered down at some paperwork, and collected a small folder's worth. "There are certain rules and policies here at Chicago State Hospital that may be a little unfamiliar to you."

She nodded. "That's to be expected."

He half-stood to hand her the packet. "Such as our prohibition regarding jewelry." She reached out to accept the information. "That pretty silver ring you are wearing—"

She beamed as she showcased it.

He wasn't impressed. "That ring could be turned into a deadly weapon by one of our more...*unstable* clients."

If she heard him, it didn't show. She caressed the red gemstone. "It was a gift from my mother."

He raised his eyebrows as he sat back. "Well, Nurse Beussink, I'm sure your sweet mother wouldn't want her precious daughter injured...or, heaven forbid, *killed* by her own gift."

Her tone grew more serious as she bit her lip. "I, uh, completely agree. Yes. It won't be a problem. I just want to thank you for this job. And trust me, I can adapt to just about any situation. I'm so excited to work here."

Montgomery nodded as a polite gesture and revised his estimate of her employment longevity down a whole week. He signed some required paperwork.

She lowered her voice somewhat. "And, uh, don't worry about my mother. She died a long time ago."

He looked up briefly. "I'm sorry to hear that."

"Oh, it's okay. I know that she would be proud of me, getting this job." An inappropriate grin spread across her painted face.

"This is something that I've trained for my whole life."

CHAPTER 28

Monday, August 13th, 1956 4:52 p.m.

Ross had always hated Mondays as far back as he cared to remember. He despised them long before he transitioned to the CIA from the OSS nearly ten years ago. Some people hated them because each Monday represented undeniable evidence that the weekend was over. To add insult to injury, Monday was also, statistically, the furthest point possible from the *next* weekend.

But that was not why Howard Ross detested Mondays.

Being a project chief in the most sensitive CIA program ever developed, rendered the concept of a weekend meaningless for all intents and purposes.

Intelligence and espionage did not differentiate or cater to any particular twenty-four hour period, regardless of where it fell on a calendar. In fact, Saturdays and Sundays only varied from the other five days in terms of the sheer volume of meetings. The so-called "weekend" had statistically 18% less of those unpleasant bureaucratic encounters.

But all of this was not why CIA Project SATURN Chief Howard Ross hated Mondays, per se. The first day of the work week represented something far more humiliating and frustrating for the double-decade intelligence veteran. Monday represented his weekly progress update phone call with Allen Dulles, Director of Central Intelligence. Every Monday at 4:30 p.m. Dulles called—in sickness or in health, rain or shine, progress or no progress. And for the last few years, it had been *no progress.*

Recently, after one too many whiskey shots, Ross had confided to his second-in-command that he had personally dubbed them his PLOP Calls. "Pitiful Lack of Progress Calls," he moaned, and then desensitized his frustration with another shot or two.

In the early days of the program, when he answered to Director Hillenkoetter, he almost looked forward to the calls. But that all seemed like another world and another time.

In many ways, it was another world with the arrival of the Cold War and the emergence of the Red Threat. But in many more ways, it all remained the same. Some within the agency had observed that we merely traded things. We traded symbols of hate: from the Swastika to the Hammer and Sickle; we exchanged the German death camps for the Soviet gulags; Fascism for Communism; and the SS for the KGB. We still fought a relentless enemy. He was just a few time zones further east, and yet in many respects, a lot closer to home.

But Ross wasn't complaining. He knew that vicious enemies abroad equaled job security in the intelligence business at home. Despite his many personal flaws, including an expanding ego, and his willingness to ignore due process from time to time, Ross' heart was in the right place...most days.

He harbored no illusions about the threat of nuclear weapons combined with an aggressive, Marxist political ideology willing to use them. He fully intended to use whatever leverage was necessary to gain a strategic advantage for the home team. That driving factor alone made it an easy decision to head up Project SATURN back in 1947, though he had set his sights higher and then been shot down time and time again.

He had witnessed and participated in the meteoric rise and lamentable phasing out of many agency initiatives from Operation Paperclip at the OSS to Project Phoenix to Bluebird and more recently, MKULTRA.

But the time would surely come, he thought on many occasions, when the Western intelligence community would all respect and revere the name of Howard Ross. Project SATURN was his ticket to the big show, and come hell or high water, he was cashing that ticket in.

He stared at the secure phone on his desk. Just minutes ago he was condemning himself by his own admission, confessing apparent incompetency. With phrases consisting of "not at this time, sir," or "not yet, Mr. Director," or "still eluding us, sir," he had reinforced the growing notion that the name of Howard Ross would be relegated to the dustbin of covert history.

The thought was intolerable, that without real progress in the very near future, he would be completely forgotten as the failed director of a failed division that didn't even officially exist. A nobody within a non-agency that achieved no results. He stored a small bottle of whiskey in his briefcase to help celebrate such joyful predictions.

Today was a day to reach into the briefcase.

He had scarcely finished his first swallow when a rapid knock at his office door forced him to halt his celebration. He hid the flask. "Come."

The door opened and his right-hand man rushed in toting a small briefcase. Ross had always said that Neal Schaeffer should have been the quintessential poster boy for West Point. Always smartly and immaculately dressed down to the cufflinks, perfectly shaven, with not a hair out of place. Even his movements and overall rhythm were impressive by-products of years of military precision.

Today was no exception.

Schaeffer spun about, shut the door with care, and eased into a chair in front of his boss' desk. Ross recovered the whiskey, took a quick hit, and locked it away. "I really need some good news, Neal."

Schaeffer leaned forward. "How was Director Dulles today?"

The Chief leaned back and stared through the dusty window blinds. There wasn't much to see except for miles of desert, a few buildings, and the dark, sleek form of a U-2 Reconnaissance aircraft in refuel.

To Ross, those planes represented one of his few major accomplishments at Groom Lake. Under the public guise of high-altitude weather research, and the covert cover of Soviet nuclear analysis, the U-2 fleet had, in truth, been primarily commissioned to study the status of Russian time travel research.

The program was a rare if not unique joint effort between the Air Force and the CIA, but Howard still claimed full credit. Ross knew, however, that his limited credit would gradually evaporate over time.

"Well Neal, to be honest, I would say I've got less than ten months to produce a living, breathing time traveler, or I might be out on Dreamland tarmac pumping Dragon Lady gas in the balmy 120 degree heat of a delightful Nevada summer. And working for tips." He paused. "That's how my call with the Director went."

Ross glanced over at Neal and studied him. Something was up. "We work in intelligence, Agent Schaeffer. You know that it's officially a crying shame when a subordinate knows more than their boss. Spill it."

Neal reached beside his chair and retrieved a compact, black briefcase. He slid the unmarked box across the Chief's desk. He stared at Ross like a boy on Christmas morning waiting for his parent to open his gift.

Ross squinted and examined it from all sides. "I'm not sure I like the expression on your face, Schaeffer." He even looked at the bottom of it. "This case could contain a directed explosive device." Ross grinned at Neal. "You would stand a lot to gain if I were to have an unfortunate accident."

Neal's grin transformed into a poker face. Ross started to slide the briefcase back. "I could make *you* open it," he said.

Schaeffer didn't flinch, and Ross pulled it towards himself once again. "But...where's the fun in that?" The CIA Chief looked up at him a final time. "What is it?"

"FBI field office in Chicago picked this up less than forty-eight hours ago," Neal announced. Ross wasn't impressed. He had always considered the FBI as a nuisance to be tolerated rather than a valuable agency to exchange information with.

Neal released the tiniest of grins. "Trust me, when you see what's inside, you just might want to call Dulles back."

"That'll be the day."

"Today *will be* that day. Trust me. You and I both know that Director Dulles favors tangible, human intelligence over technology any given day."

Ross grumbled. "It's a constant battle."

"Well, that briefcase is right up his alley. It's a game changer."

Ross peered up at him. Neal had never been prone to fish stories, but for a bureaucrat like Ross, exaggeration and hype were the regular currency of the agency. Cold War intelligence briefings were usually long on sizzle and short on steak.

Ross popped the double releases and lifted the lid. Inside was a small, brown leather wallet. He glanced at Neal who was nodding subtly, hands on his chin.

"So, has Project SATURN stooped to pick-pocketing now, Agent Schaeffer?"

Neal didn't respond to the dig.

Ross opened his desk drawer and started to don a thin pair of gloves. "No need, Chief," Neal observed, "it's already been dusted."

Ross reached in delicately and grabbed the supposed game changer. He spread it open, and slid out an unusual, thick plastic card. He turned his desk lamp on and tilted it under the light. His eyes grew wider as he scanned the surface. Ross flipped the card over and then back to the front again.

Neal circled around behind his excited superior and pointed at the wallet. "There's more."

Ross looked up at him, speechless, and then picked through the wallet again. He pulled out a few ten dollar notes and a twenty. He snatched a magnifying glass out of his top drawer and trained it on the bills.

"2011, 2014, 2011, and 2013. Incredible."

Neal moved the briefcase out of the way as Ross spread out the contents of the billfold in an orderly fashion.

Neal leaned forward. "Money, an insurance card, military ID, some other financial cards and a New York driver's license dated 2012."

Ross studied the items, and then scooted back. "Where did you say this was discovered?"

"Chicago. FBI."

Ross gazed up at the ceiling. Everyone at SATURN knew that look very well. It was always followed by work, and usually lots of it.

"I need a list of every agent that came within fifty feet of this wallet," Ross demanded. "Contact the Chicago field office, quarantine everyone on that list until we arrive."

Neal walked back to the front of the desk. "We're still trying to ascertain exactly who initially turned the wallet in."

Ross was irritated. "Why don't we know that already?"

Neal held his hands up. "Hey, Boss, don't flip your wig—it was given to the Feds by one of the local police precincts."

Ross jumped up. "I don't want to hear about one of the local precincts, I want to hear about *which one* of the local precincts, and then about the actual person who turned it in. We need to debrief every single person in the chain of custody."

Neal smiled. "Trust me, Chief, I'm on top of it. Have a little confidence in me, please. We'll have that information by the time our wheels touch down at Glenview Naval Air Station."

There was a pause as Ross, like a chess master, calculated and coordinated his next half-dozen moves.

Neal started for the door. "I'll notify the team, and call the hangar to get your plane ready." He was almost out the door when Ross stopped him.

"Wait."

Neal grabbed the edge of the heavy door and swiveled back in.

Ross may have been an arrogant, impatient dictator at times, but he was good at what he did. There were several reasons why Hillenkoetter handed him Project SATURN, almost on a silver platter. It was during times like these that subordinates learned much by sitting at the feet of the master.

Ross leaned onto his desk and rubbed his face. "Call Washington. I need to collect a probable family list, in New York state, and Illinois, and in that order." He picked up the driver's license. "Get a copy of this signature over to Graphology for analysis. They might be able to give us a general geographic background for our suspect here."

Neal nodded. "Anything else?"

Ross sat down on the edge of his desk. "Consult with our psyche team in Building C. Let them analyze everything; the wallet, the military ID, his photo, signature, even the money. They should be able to give us a probable baseline personality profile."

Neal stepped back up to the desk to collect the evidence. "As you wish, Chief."

Ross paused. "Listen, I know you weren't there at Roswell, Neal."

Schaeffer finished putting everything back into the briefcase, and eyed the Chief. "Sir?"

Howard stood and walked around to the front of the desk. "We made a lot of mistakes. Granted, the department was young. Days old actually. But, that's no excuse. We should have located them."

Neal picked up the briefcase. "Intelligence is an imperfect science, Chief."

Ross snatched the phone handset and glared at Neal. "I won't repeat the lapses in judgment we made with Phillip Nelson. I can guarandamntee you that. Dismissed."

Neal exited and shut the door behind him while his boss dialed. Ross glanced out the window as his face grew a calculated smile that it hadn't worn in several months.

"Linda, get me Director Dulles."

Sunday, May 11, 1947
Journal entry number 164

Not sure what is going on. Grant Forrester, our newest Jumper, is missing, along with his clothes and a few other personal effects.

I'm not sure how to handle this. None of us are.

CHAPTER 29

Denver's eyes popped open as he convulsed and thrashed about like a startled, disoriented beast. *"Jasmine! Jasmine!"* he screamed out in helpless terror. His crazed eyes found it difficult to maintain focus as he struggled to understand his situation. *"Jasmine!"*

What's wrong with my head? What is going on?

He reached up and pressed around on his face and scalp. *Cloth? Bandages?*

And then he felt something else.

Pain.

Sharp, shooting pain.

The back of his head was burning like it had been sliced open with a serrated steak knife. His swollen kneecap was still far beyond tender. He rubbed his face. A few more cuts there as well. His vision started to return as Ellen Finegan rushed into the bedroom. She was just a dark moving shape in his confusion. "What is happening, where am I?" he shouted.

Ellen leaned over him and clenched his arms as he fought her. "Denver. Denver! Hey! Shhhh…Look at me! Look…at…me! It's me, it's Ellen. Ellen Finegan."

He calmed down by degrees, but was still distracted by pain and unfamiliarity. He yelled out, "Where…where's my daughter?"

Ellen leaned across him to stabilize his rage. "Listen…shhh. Listen to me. You're okay. Thank God, you're okay. I'm here."

He didn't find that as comforting as she had probably intended. "Where am I?" he demanded again. "What's going on? What happened?"

A different yet familiar voice boomed through his confusion, "What happened? Death. *Death* is what happened, Mr. Collins."

Denver strained to identify the new shadow walking up to him.

That shape, that hat, a policeman?

"Dead, as in doornail," the male voice declared. The figure pulled up a chair and slid it across the wood floor beside Denver's bed. "Well, at least, you *were* dead," Chief McCloud said. "That is til Nurse Finegan here decided to cheat death ever so slightly in your favor."

Ellen leaned above Denver's face and her beautiful red hair framed her relieved smile. "Welcome back to the land of the living, Mr. Collins."

His eyesight was approaching functional again as he surveyed the small, but cozy bedroom. The wind gently kicked some thin, white curtains around a window off to his left. It appeared to be a beautiful day outside, but inside, his throbbing skull and general aches and pains offered a different forecast. He looked straight up at her. "What, uh, happened?"

Ellen touched his hand. "What's the last thing you remember?"

He closed his eyes. *Last thing?*

His foggy mind tried to repress the horrific sights and sounds of Jasmine, the lightning, the screaming. He remembered the storm, the park, *Jennifer and the Chief!* He shunned those images as well.

It must've been a dream. A cruel dream.

Ellen traded glances with the Chief as she continued rubbing Denver's hand. "Don't you remember anything? Anything at all, Denver?"

McCloud moved closer. "Do you remember the accident in the reactor room?"

Accident! The reactor room accident.

Crisis.

Red lights, warning siren.

Get to the Manual Release Lever! I'll do it for Jasmine!

It all flooded back to him, just not in a coherent manner. It was mere flashes of events at first rather than the actual events themselves. Colors, odors, and emotion. His face contorted as he pieced it all together, eyes squeezed shut.

Ellen spoke softly. "You saved us all, Denver."

The Chief smiled. "And then, to pay you back, Ms. Finegan saved you."

She blushed and slapped McCloud's shoulder.

Denver squinted. "I do remember. I pulled a lever. But, uh, on the way back—"

"On the way back there was an accidental electrical discharge," Ellen added.

"A spark?"

She grinned. "Yes, a spark. It was quite a show actually."

The Chief laughed. "Yeah, quite a show, I'll say! And when the light show was all said and done, the star of the show was lyin' dead on center stage."

Denver blinked several times and gave Ellen a hard stare. "But, I don't understand. I'm, I'm here, right? I'm not dead?"

Ellen started to answer, but McCloud interrupted, "Well, you're not dead *now*, but you *were* dead. I'm a cop, and as the Chief of Police here in Normal, I'm also the Coroner from time to time, Mr. Collins. I know dead when I see dead."

Denver was lost. The Chief plowed on. "No pulse. No breath. You were casket filler, my friend. Well, that is, until Dr. Fraulenstein here decided to zap you back to life."

Ellen dismissed the Chief's hyper-simplified account. "I was just practicing medicine, Chief McCloud, and sometimes in healthcare we have to resort to desperate means for desperate cases."

She gazed down at Denver and lowered her soft hands onto his chest. "Let me guess, you're pretty sore right about...*here*?" He winced and jumped a little.

The Chief roared, "Ha, you jumped a lot higher'n that a few days ago!" Ellen looked over at McCloud, horrified, but the Chief wasn't deterred in the slightest. "Just like jumpin' a dang car battery! Woo boy!"

Ellen offered more dignified version of the story. "The explosion put you into full cardiac arrest. I tried CPR over and over, but it didn't help. Then, I used some electrical leads from a capacitor and—"

"And shocked the heck outta your ticker, pal! Boom baby!" McCloud couldn't seem to contain himself.

Denver probed his sore chest. The medical salve seeped through the gauze.

"I finally got a cardiac rhythm established," Ellen said. "You coughed a few times, opened your eyes once, and then fell into a coma. It was all wait and see."

"And that, my friend," the Chief interjected, "was three days ago. You've been *Siberia* ever since. Out cold."

Denver tapped Ellen on the arm. "Thank you...thanks for not...giving up on me."

Her cheeks flushed and she drew near to his rough face, placing a light fingertip on his nose. "Hey, it was the only noble excuse I could come up with to tear your shirt off and kiss you repeatedly."

McCloud jumped up out of his chair. "Oh, for the luvva Pete! Get a room! *Get a room*, folks!"

Ellen winked at Denver and sauntered away. "Hey Chief," she said, "this *is* my room."

Denver called out to her. "No offense, but I can't seem to remember any of it. I'm sure it was great."

"Oh it was," she said as she disappeared into the next room. "It was."

The Chief lowered his voice. "Flirtin' Finegan, that's what we always call her." He cupped a hand beside his mouth and whispered, "Now you see why I keep her locked up in a basement with a couple of harmless geriatrics."

A less-than-enthused voice from the next room called out, "I heard that."

Denver took a deep breath as he struggled to sit up. The Chief bent over to help. "There ya go! Now, that's the spirit! You'll be good as new in no time flat. No hurry."

Denver grimaced. "Oh, I don't think there's any danger of me hurrying anytime soon, Chief." They worked together and McCloud stuffed some pillows behind him.

"Now, ease on back...there ya go. You're on your butt now, and before you know it, you'll be on your feet."

"Thanks, Chief. Really."

Ellen returned with something piping hot in a cup. "Even in the year 2014, I doubt they have any medicine better than my chicken noodle soup." She paused for a moment. "Well, actually it's *Martha's* chicken noodle soup, with just a little Finegan family finesse thrown in. But drink it slowly. Your system needs to, what is it that Doc always says... oh yeah, reboot."

The Chief cleared the way as Ellen handed Denver her concoction. He took a cautious sip or two when the Chief headed for the door. "When you feel a little stronger, I'll have to bring over a lil' of *my family's* special recipe," McCloud offered. "If ya know what I mean."

Ellen shot him a disgusted look. "Alcohol is a natural depressant, Chief. The last thing his shocked system needs right now."

McCloud chuckled, "Whatever you say, Nurse Finegan. Anywho, I'm headed over to meet with Miss Betty Larson.

Said it was important. But you, Mr. Collins, you need to heal up and get ready."

Denver looked up from another hot and delicious sip, as his appetite returned with a vengeance. "*Ready*? Ready for what?"

The Chief reached the door, and spun about. "School, Mr. Collins."

"You need to get ready for school, son."

Wednesday, May 14, 1947
Journal entry number 165

It has been over 3 days since we have seen Grant Forrester. I don't know what's worse, (a) the guilt that arises from the feeling that we somehow failed him, or (b) the fear of what he may do knowing what he knows.

He knows everything about us, about X, about our plans and research. He knows where we are, when we are from, our names: everything. I guess I had this fear of someone leaving the group stuck in the back of my mind, but I never entertained it seriously. It was an unthinkable contingency, but once again denial must ultimately bow to reality.

A million thoughts race through your mind:
Maybe we should move.
Maybe we should change our names.
Maybe we should focus on finding Grant.
Hire a private investigator.
Maybe we should prepare for the worst.
What if he sells us out?
How long can he stay under the radar?
What if he doesn't want to stay under the radar?
What if he exploits his knowledge and alters the future?

In a way I feel hurt, betrayed, unappreciated. We have worked really hard to lay a foundation for Jumpers-to-be. Out of four, one has now departed. Is this the percentage, the ratio that we will face? A 25% drop-out rate? Is this acceptable? Is this to be expected?

Tough questions, no easy answers.

CHAPTER 30

Police Chief James McCloud was certainly no stranger to private conferences with the town's aggressive newspaper editor. Truth be known, since she took the throne just over three years ago, he actually crossed paths with Betty Larson with surprising regularity. Typically, he walked into her office with his hat in his hand, encouraging her to delay a story here, or to please avoid this or that piece of information.

But she had called the meeting this time.

For various reasons, the Chief avoided dealing with the reporting staff at *The Pantagraph*, an older, bigger rag printed down in Bloomington. It dwarfed the *Journal* in almost every respect, but Betty's daily competitor seemed to ignore their newspaper neighbor to the north. Most of the time.

But in a small town the size of Normal, any incidents, whether mountain or mole hill, involving Chief McCloud or Deputy O'Connell were at worst, page two. Their relationship had stayed civil and professional, or as much as could be hoped for in the tenuous coexistence of law enforcement and media. Both provided a necessary public service, but that's often where their similarity ended.

In its very essence, police work functioned better in the dark, but the press lived for the opportunity to let its little light shine. Nature may abhor a vacuum, but the press abhorred all-things hidden.

Betty attempted to keep one ear open to the concerns of law enforcement. But McCloud couldn't deny that even recently she had plowed forward with stories he had privately pressured her to at least delay, if not disregard altogether.

She didn't do either.

During such times he was tempted to give her a nice thank-you-card parking citation, or repay her kindness with any number of trumped up moving violations.

He never did.

But, he did think about it.

A lot.

Actually, Betty was a vast improvement. McCloud had to endure about sixteen months of misery with the former editor, Gil "the pill" Taylor, following McCloud's appointment as police chief in March of 1952.

Gil was twice as stubborn as he was sanctimonious. He fancied himself a champion of liberty, but most considered him a bastion of ego. After McCloud's second or third unpleasant go-around with Gil Taylor, the editor smirked, "Sometimes the truth hurts."

The Chief fired back. "I guess that explains why you're such a pain in the ass!"

In an exercise requiring great persistence and restraint, Phil Nelson had reminded the Chief to bite his tongue concerning Taylor, and it bled deeply on many occasions. Phil worried, and rightly so, that the tenacious tabloid editor might set his investigative urges upon Nelson Manufacturing, or Chief McCloud, or even Phil himself. It was a distracting source of tension between the Chief and Phil. Shep's penchant for conflict didn't help matters much.

But that was over three years ago.

McCloud let off the gas as he turned onto the rough gravel road just west of Normal. The sun was high and hot, and rolling his window down offered only a token of relief for the chunky policeman as he bounced along the rutted lane.

What does Betty want today? Her phone call sounded… *different.*

He drew alongside a small creek and threw the car into park. *Why outside of town? We've never met way out here. She didn't sound scared, or threatened, or urgent...just different.*

He bent down and fished around inside the glove box. He pulled out a hand-sized flask and took a quick sip. The Chief wasn't proud of his current irregular crutch, but compared to the wasted cesspool he had voluntarily drank himself down into during the early 1990s, he was making a miraculous comeback.

Hiding his habit was a dangerous and tricky juggling act. Officially, Normal was a *dry* community. But just a few blocks to the south, once you crossed Division Street, there were no such prohibitions in Bloomington. He had always felt a bit hypocritical arresting people for booze, so most of them got away with a stern warning. He stashed his own vice and wiped his mouth.

Betty was resting against the wooden rail of a small footbridge as he got out and strolled up. McCloud glanced at the water and back at her. "Working on a front page expose 'bout fish poaching, Miss Larson?"

She put on a wicked grin and turned toward him. "Is that a tacit admission about an on-going investigation, Chief?"

He smiled and leaned on the rail next to her. "Now, you know I can't comment 'bout current police business. But if and when I land a big fish, you are usually the first one to know about it. Sometimes even before I want you to." He looked away. "Small talk aside, Miss Larson, what brings the Chief of Police way out here on a sweltering Monday afternoon?"

She rolled to the side and gazed off into the distance. "Honestly?" She paused. "I wish I knew."

McCloud wrinkled his brow and glanced towards her. "Look. O'Connell took the day off, Betty, so I'm afraid I don't have much time for a guessing game." He gazed down at their reflection in the rippling water below. The Chief knew her well enough to know she would talk when she was good and ready. He could wait.

It didn't take long.

Her voice cracked, "There's... there's something, or at least, I suspect that there's something going on in Normal, or *around* Normal."

He was a bit disappointed with the empty revelation. The Chief spoke with just a hint of laughter. "Well, now, there's always somethin' going on, Betty. That's just normal for Normal...normally."

She didn't appear to be amused as he was and continued to stare. He waited once again.

"As the only full-time reporter in the area, I see and hear a lot of things," she started. "But not just the big things, like car wrecks or birth announcements...no, I also run across other, uh, stories, or things, I, uh..."

She hesitated again and McCloud frowned. "I've interrogated drunk people that made more sense 'n you. *Spit it out*, Betty. What's goin' on?"

She rubbed her hands together. "I have, at the *Journal*, a, uh, a collection. A collection of items...items that are unusual...highly unusual."

His interest level went from mild to piqued instantaneously. He masked his concerned enthusiasm. "Oh, what kind of items, exactly?"

She leaned back and began strolling across the bridge. The Chief wasn't quite prepared for the next sentence that came out of her mouth. "I don't really know how to explain it. Unusual, almost, *futuristic*."

He donned his best policeman's poker face. "I'm sorry, Betty," he offered. "I guess I'm still not following you."

She stopped and spun around. "And I'm not following *me* either!" she lamented. "But I am telling you. These things are almost, like, *impossible*. Like top secret research prototypes or something. I know I must sound crazy."

McCloud took a few steps towards her. "No, not crazy, just confused. Well, I'd be glad to take a look at—"

"No," she blurted. "I mean, not *now*. I'm torn. I feel like reporting it to the authorities—"

The Chief drew closer and shrugged. "Well, I'm not exactly the president, Betty, but I am Chief of Police—"

"Oh, listen—no offense, Chief. But I think this needs to go higher, a lot higher."

He looked back at the creek, searching his mind for options. "I understand, at least I think I do. Uh…I know people," he offered casually. "I know some Feds that could help, maybe help shed some light perhaps on what you should do. I could make some calls."

She peered into his confident eyes and nodded. "Thanks, Chief. Look, I'm sorry to have bothered you, I just—"

"Hey, no apologies necessary, but, who else knows about your little...*collection*?"

She pointed at the quiet brook. "As of right now just you, me, and the fish."

He walked up and put a sympathetic hand on her shoulder. "Now listen. Listen to me good. Don't do *anything* until I get word back from my contacts. I promise, they'll know what to do. They're top-shelf kinda guys. Top-shelf." He grinned.

"I hope so."

"I *know* so. But are the...uh...items *safe*?"

She took a few steps back across the bridge.

"Oh, yeah, they're safe. Literally *safe*."

Sunday, June 8, 1947
Journal entry number 173

It's almost been a month since Grant bailed on us. His departure has had a significant impact on the morale, on the attitude of the group as a whole. Chalk it up to guilt or concern, or a little bit of both, makes no difference. Ken has really taken it hard. He and Grant had a lot in common.

We've needed something positive to rally around ever since. Well, yesterday X may have given us that rallying point. As we work through the dilemmas of physics and the barriers of language, it appears that he is confident that we have reached a major breakthrough.

As best as I can make out, our biggest problem now is power. The potential temporal device he is constructing will require almost unimaginable amounts of energy. A nuclear power plant small enough to fit in half of my garage might do it, but I've looked in all the stores, and even the Sears Roebuck Catalog and I can't find one.

Aside from nukes and the sun, the only source of power that can deliver what we need is lightning. Lightning has a lot going for it.

Think about it:

1. It's pretty common. I think I read somewhere that it strikes the Earth about 100 times per second!
2. It's FREE
3. Extremely powerful

Sounds great. Come to think of it, lightning and earthquakes share many of the same characteristics: pretty common, very powerful, and absolutely free, but there is one major problem:

YOU CAN'T PREDICT THEM ACCURATELY.

There's the rub.

But there is a key difference between earthquakes and lightning: you can't attract an earthquake. But Ben Franklin demonstrated that you can attract electricity in the atmosphere. There are no "earthquake rods," but there are lightning rods. In the movie *Dune* the natives used thumping rods to attract the giant worms and then harnessed their great power. Maybe we can use rods to harness nature's big bolts as well. I will probably have to buy a large pickup truck to haul the equipment.

It's the right time of the year—we have about 6 more weeks of thunderstorm weather in the Great Plains. I always wanted to be a storm chaser, but that was out of pure curiosity, now I may have to be one out of cruel necessity.

CHAPTER 31

Surreal.

That's how a still-recovering Denver Collins described the scene to Leah a few days later.

He surveyed the large conference room at Nelson Manufacturing, taking mental inventory of all twelve of his fellow time Jumpers gathered around a spacious table, with the exception of Chief McCloud. A few of them he had never met, period, and this was certainly the first time he had seen all of them gathered together in one, safe place.

A few of them couldn't help but gawk at Denver as they took long drags on their cigarettes. First off, he was the newest Jumper. Secondly, he was still sporting quite a few bandages and visible injuries. He was the biggest freak in the freak show.

Surreal.

He tried to keep the smile to himself as he contemplated just how crazy this whole arrangement was. He looked around at the improbable mixture: different races, different decades, different vocations, different ages, probably even different religions. It was a motley conglomerate that surely had far more fundamental differences than even the most generous list of similarities.

Ten years, he thought. *This group started over ten years ago. Well, not all of them, but still—this is absolutely amazing.*

He concentrated on the faces least familiar to him.

Now she is new. Must be what—in her middle to late seventies? She looks very proper.

Whoa, that guy stands out. Bald...body builder by the looks of it. A good guy to have your back in a firefight, I imagine. Who else? Move aside, Doc. I don't think I've met her. There. Oh, a young, black girl. Probably early twenties. Cute. Seems nervous. There's that French guy. Patinow or something. Mr. Magoo.

Ellen leaned over and whispered in his ear. "You doing okay?"

He thought for a moment. "About as good as a guy with third degree burns and a gigantic head gash would be doing surrounded by complete and total strangers."

He grinned and she gave him a quick hug. "Don't worry, time will heal all of that. Always does." He had too much male pride to admit to her that the squeeze hurt.

The background chatter died down as a very rushed and flustered Chief McCloud made his grand entrance. He started apologizing even before he was finished tossing his hat onto the table. "Sorry, sorry, folks. Had to make a last minute drive out to the McCallister's. *Again.* Need I say more?"

He hurried across the room and placed his hands on Denver's tender shoulders. "Most of you have had the pleasure of meeting the latest addition to our, uh, family, but, for those who haven't, this is Mr. Denver Wayne Collins."

A sporadic round of applause filled the room. Denver smiled self-consciously and waved. The Chief continued, "Mr. Collins arrived to Normal from the year 2014. He is our second Jumper from the twenty-first century. He is our newest Trailer, even beating Doc by almost ten years."

Another weaker outburst of clapping erupted, and Doc Stonecroft stood and bowed towards Denver across the table. Denver wasn't sure how to react, so he just sat there without making specific eye contact, or at least, avoiding it when possible.

The Chief patted Denver on the back. "As you can see, Denver's had a pretty rough first week here in Normal." McCloud bent over and glanced down at him. "I promise you, Mr. Collins, things will get better for you here, much better. I guarantee it."

Everyone smiled and a few laughed in good fun. Denver just shook his head. He couldn't imagine how it could get worse, so odds were the Chief was right.

"Actually," McCloud said, "even though he's only been here less than a week, this great guy's already impacted this here group; in fact, he has impacted this whole community."

Ellen jumped up. "*Impacted*? How about *saved* the group, and *saved* the community?" A third, louder round of applause exploded, and all stood up.

Awkward, freaking awkward.

A strange, uncomfortable silence followed, and everyone stared at him then each other. He looked around. Clearly he was expected to make some version of an acceptance speech.

"Uh," he began, "I just did what anyone would've done. I'm not a hero. Really. Thanks." He looked around. "Please, sit. Please."

He was thrilled when they did, and the Chief took the spotlight once again. "What I tell ya? What'd I tell ya? One great guy. Well, as he finishes healing up, spend some time with Trailer Collins." He looked down again. "But, I gotta ask, Mr. Collins, do the Red Sox ever break the famous Curse of the Bambino?" The Chief roared and a few joined him. "I'm just kiddin', I'm just kiddin'. Can't be teaching our newest family member to be breaking the Second Accord in the first week!"

By the reaction on his hardened face, the bald body-builder didn't seem to be finding any of the light banter to be amusing in the least. He cleared his throat and cut through the din. "I can't believe you're tellin' baseball jokes, Chief, when there are far more important matters to be discussed tonight!" The chit chat in the room died an instantaneous death. "Can we get on with the *real* business?"

McCloud composed himself and moved back toward his own chair. "As delicate as ever, Mr. Frazier."

"Who cares about being delicate?" Frazier growled. "Our lives are on the line here people."

Denver was stunned.

Lives on the line…did I miss something?

The Chief arrived at his seat but remained standing. "I think everyone has been privately briefed, with possibly the exception of Mr. Collins, about our latest…*situation.*"

"It's not a situation…it's a *threat!*" Frazier shouted, veins pulsating.

Denver could tell that the Chief was exercising extreme restraint, but only out of necessity. McCloud's response was measured and firm. "Regardless if we characterize it as a *situation*, or a *threat*, or a *whatever*, it does not change the fact that we need to collectively discuss and collectively arrive at a solution."

Frazier wasted no time. "There is nothing to discuss. I think we all can see the cold, hard facts here: as long as Betty has those items in her safe, then none of us are!"

Terrance Gaines, the head of maintenance, countered. "Look, Garrett, we don't even know what she really has! It might be nothing."

"Uh, I don't think it takes a rocket scientist, Tee, to figure out that she has enough to get this whole freaking town crawlin' with suits!"

"And once that happens," Shep offered, "it's only a matter of time. The Feds know how to get what they need."

Side conversations and outright accusations began to rebound around the room. The noise and tension rose exponentially. Denver observed that the young African American girl was trying to get everyone's attention. He tapped Ellen and pointed towards her.

Ellen stood up and shouted, "Hey! Hey, listen. Listen." It took far longer than it should have, but the group subdued. "Thank you. Listen, Alexus wants to share something." Ellen sat down and whispered in Denver's ear, "Daniels. Alexus Daniels. She's from 1973. Good kid."

The young woman rose in a timid manner. "There is a chance that the newspaper editor's collection could bring us unwanted Federal attention. I just want to remind everyone that, uh, these kind of witch-hunts don't end so well for people that look like me and Terrance." She stared at everyone with real fear in her eyes. "I don't think America is ready for Dr. King's dream, at least not just yet."

There was a short pause and the Chief spoke up. "Careful with that information, Lexi. *Priors.*"

Alexus acknowledged as she dropped back down. Leah Swan jumped in. "Listen. Lexi is right. And with World War Two and the Korean War, a lot of people don't give Asians like me too many chances either. If they start asking questions and running background checks, it's...it's over. I mean, less than half of us even really *has* a background. Think about it."

Denver studied the shy teenager sitting to Leah's left. *Birthday calculating girl, what was her name...Laura? Lori? Tori. Was it Tori?*

Ellen stunned everyone with a bold pronouncement. "Maybe we should disband, or, or maybe move on to a new town."

Denver caught the tail end of a long, hard stare between Shep and Finegan.

"Conservatively speaking," Doc Stonecroft explained gravely, "it will take weeks to disassemble just the reactor chamber, not to mention the Jump Portal."

For the second time in the short meeting, the chatter ratcheted up to a deafening level. Leah turned to Tori and helped to cover her ears.

The Chief whistled. "Hey, look." He whistled louder. "Nobody is—*hey*! Listen. Nobody is gonna disassemble anything or move anywhere." He paced as if trying to slice through the tension with his physical presence. "We haven't worked all these years, *together* mind you, and got to where we are today, to just throw it all away because of a small town newspaper editor with a box full o' goodies!"

Shep had to rain on his parade. "Those goodies, Chief, could get us all killed or at least hauled off like lab rats in some government facility!"

McCloud spun around. "No one is being shipped anywhere. Nobody's gonna be anybody's lab rat. We just need to do what we've always done, folks: create a plan, then *execute* that plan." He glared at each of them.

Garrett spoke up. "I think execution *is* the plan."

Denver couldn't believe what he had just heard. Actually, he doubted that *anyone* could believe what they had just heard.

"*Excuse me,* Frazier?" the Chief asked. "I hope I'm not following you."

Garrett was defiant. "And why not? What is the life of one woman compared to all of ours?"

"I can't believe this!" Leah exploded. "Are you suggesting that we...that someone *kills* Miss Larson?"

Every eye was fastened on Garrett's unrepentant face.

"Not suggesting, Miss Swan. *Recommending.* Maybe even volunteering."

Leah jumped up and grabbed Tori's arm and fled from the room. Officer Billy chased after them.

Ellen was livid. "What's your problem, Frazier? We don't joke about people's lives! Especially in front of Tori."

"Like she would understand anyway. And who said I was joking?"

Ellen stood and pointed at him. "We don't know *what* she understands, Garrett!"

Dr. Papineau struggled for clarification. "*Excuse moi. Assassiner?*" He drew a finger across his neck with a puzzled look.

Garrett nodded. "Better her than us—it's simple math."

"Murder, Mr. Frazier, is *not* an option," the Chief barked. "*Period*. No discussion. Off the table."

Shep shook his head. "Uh, I don't see too many options *on* the table, Chief."

"There are always options, Mr. Sheppard," offered a platinum-headed, elderly woman three spots to Denver's right. "There are always options—especially when violence masquerades as the only one."

Ellen leaned in once again and whispered, "Grandma Martha. Martha Tomlin. Class act. 1989."

Denver sensed a change sweep over the group. A quiet seriousness descended. *Impressive lady*, Denver thought. Some low-level murmuring eventually returned, but Chief McCloud had one more bomb to drop. "Uh, folks. Folks, there is another complication."

The room fell silent again.

"Denver's identity may be compromised," he said. "He lost his wallet. He told me yesterday that the last time he had it for sure was on the bus to Chicago. It had his driver's license, military ID, and some cash."

Shep threw up his hands. "That's not a *complication*, McCloud. That's...that's one helluva *train wreck*!"

Martha offered more wisdom. "We must operate under the assumption that it will end up in the hands of the authorities, and I am not referring to the boys in blue."

Shep rose from the table and paced the length of the floor. "She's right! The boys in black have it. Guaranteed!"

Denver felt sick. His status had flipped from community hero to local villain in less than fifteen minutes. "I'm...I'm sorry," was all he could say. He wasn't sure if anyone even heard it.

McCloud walked over. "Hey, look, Denver. What's done's done. It wasn't on purpose. Now we need damage control."

"It's hard to control this much damage," Shep retorted.

"He'll need a new name," Frazier proposed. "Maybe even a new look."

Denver found the strength to speak up. "I, uh, I had a beard on my driver's license photo. It was a few years back."

"He should be able to keep his first name," Ellen observed. "It's too difficult to learn a new one and react naturally. Changing the last should be sufficient." Several people nodded.

"Changing names and facial hair is all well and good, but what about Betty Larson's evidence?" Shep demanded. "His wallet may or may not turn up, but her collection definitely will!"

The Chief glanced at Shep. "Well, I bought us some time. She promised not to do anything til I got back with her."

Frazier couldn't resist mocking him. "Well, that settles it, then! All our lives are hanging by one sweet little promise."

"I don't think I like your tone, Mr. Frazier!" McCloud snapped.

Garrett grinned even wider. "Finally! I've been here six months, and now I've found someone who truly understands me."

McCloud stormed across the room as Garrett jumped up. "You need to watch your attitude, Mr. Frazier!"

"I'm not afraid of the badge, McCloud, never have been!"

Stonecroft and Papineau grabbed their coats and exited the conference room. Martha followed them in short order.

Frazier and McCloud stood chest to chest, and seconds from fist to fist.

Denver interrupted the alpha male contest. "There is another option," he said and the postures relaxed. He cleared his throat and leaned forward on the table. "I know it, you know it, we all know it. But no one wants to say it." He paused.

"So the new guy will say it: we have to steal it. We have to steal Betty Larson's evidence. Period."

Monday, July 7, 1947
Journal entry number 182

This may be the lowest point in my life, and I have lived through some dark days, including watching my father waste away with the slow cruelty of Lou Gehrig's Disease. Maryanne had a miscarriage before we were blessed with Kurtis. That was rough. I know that she still suffers to this very day.

But neither of those horrifically tragic events crushed me with the level of guilt like what I have just gone through.

Ken Miller and Larry Etherington are dead.

My two closest friends are gone, and I am effectively alone once more. Intellectually, I KNOW that I need to write about what happened, but emotionally...everything within me refuses to do so. I can't keep food down again, and I shake terribly. The drive home from Roswell was like a surreal nightmare. With the language barrier, I might as well have been as alone as I felt. I don't know, but I think that X is blaming himself for everything. He hasn't said a word or even made an attempt to gesture at me in over 48 hours. I am afraid he may abandon me. And who could blame him?

I will do my level best to explain what happened.

We had been on the road for over three weeks, chasing storms, setting up, tearing down, repeat. It was exhausting. On July 3rd we heard that some bad storms were coming up out of Mexico into the desert Southwest. We got ahead of a big supercell in New Mexico and intercepted it in Roswell the afternoon of July 4th. We set up on a remote ranch outside of town on a hillside.

As the night wore on, it looked promising: lots of lightning, and close. We had just set up the long rods and transfer lines to the temporal device. X had made some last minute adjustments, and activated the Tesla design. I was back by the truck, a good 50 yards away.

And then...it happened.

You swear you hear it before you see it even though you know it is just the opposite. There was a simultaneous flash and blast that will haunt my memories. Instantly, the blast flung me to the ground. After I peeled my face out of the dirt and looked up, I saw an eerie blue glow like St. Elmo's Fire all over the temporal device. There was a strange distortion several feet wide in the center of the machine. X was also getting up and started shouting something unintelligible. The hum from the device muffled everything.

Ken, only a few feet away, started walking toward the device. He reached his hand out and inched up to it. After what seemed like minutes, it was probably only a few seconds his fingers intersected the temporal anomaly. You could tell he was trying to pull his hand back, but it was like his arm was locked in time and space. Larry ran up, yelling, and grabbed him, trying to yank him away. They were both pulled in towards the anomaly and then they began emitting blue light. I could tell they were screaming, but it was like the distortion was trapping their sounds inside an invisible barrier.

The blue fire around the device began to flash and grow increasingly erratic. It appeared that Larry and Ken were sort of stretching out, but you couldn't tell if maybe it was just an illusion, like the way a glass of water distorts an object behind it. I started to move towards them but X ran to block me, protesting with his hands. The hum felt deafening.

Then, eerily, the device flashed with no sound. Zero sound. And then... I woke up. I probably had been unconscious for over half an hour. I was bloodied a bit, the front of my shirt and pants were burnt, and I had a raging headache. The continued flashes of lightning from the passing storm revealed a tragic scene. The device had been nearly obliterated. Twisted smoking metal scattered over the hillside for a hundred yards, random fires burning the scrub and grass.

I found X laying face first in the mud, the back of his clothes fried. I couldn't wake him up, but he was breathing. I dragged him up to the truck, laid him across the front seat, and poured some water on his face. His forehead had a gash.

I stumbled up the hill, and that's when I saw their bodies. I couldn't help but imagine that Larry and Ken had been instantly and mercifully blown to bits as I examined the wreckage. But there they were in almost exactly the same spot where the device had been, but they were...different. Altered.

They still appeared roughly human, but they were smaller and thinner. They could not have been much over 4 feet tall and their arms and legs made them look like bloated children who died of severe malnutrition—except for their heads, which appeared to be almost double in size. I can only imagine that the incomplete time displacement had somehow left them mutated. Their clothing was nowhere to be seen.

I wanted to move their remains, but I saw some headlights in the distance, moving quickly toward our location. I hated to, but I had to leave their bodies. If the vehicle was law enforcement, then we could kiss our futures goodbye. I had a little trouble finding my keys and more trouble getting X up and out of my way. By the time the motor started, the car was pretty close. I shoved my truck into gear and drove back toward town.

I didn't just leave the remains of my friends on that hillside, I'm pretty sure I left a lot of my conscience and humanity there as well.

July 5, 1947

FOR: Captain Sheridan Cavitt, Senior CIC
     Major Jesse A. Marcel, 509th Bomb Group
FROM: Roscoe H. Hillenkoetter, Director, Central
     Intelligence
SUBJECT: Command Transfer

   Howard D. Ross will be arriving at the Roswell
Army Air Field, and under my authorization, Mr.
Ross will be taking the lead in the current
debris field investigation.

   Ensure that the area is secure, detain and
isolate witnesses, and move all recovered debris
into guarded storage at the base. Access to stored
debris is expressly forbidden until Ross assumes
oversight.

   END

   DCI

CHAPTER 32

Is this what passes for coffee in Chicago these days? Weak. Just like the FBI.

Howard Ross set the rejected cup on the far edge of the desk as he poured over a series of large photographs. He snatched a pen and continued to fill several pages in a thick legal pad.

Neal Schaeffer hurried in. "Hey Chief, the last delegation from Norfolk is about ten minutes out."

The CIA boss appeared disinterested in the important update as he raised another photo. Project SATURN staff made it a point to *not be* offended at such times. With Ross it was often par for the course. You just had to learn his game, his style.

Neal hesitated and rocked on his heels. The Chief offered no response, and Schaeffer headed for the door.

Ross seemed to wait until his subordinate was almost in the hallway. "Ten years," he bemoaned.

Schaeffer froze and eased back in. "Chief?"

Ross squinted and leaned forward onto his elbows. "It's been almost ten years." He was in the mood for another CIA history lesson. "You probably didn't know that Magruder had recommended me to Truman during the phase out of the OSS."

Neal smiled. "I was still getting beat up by the upperclassmen at the academy during that transition." He dropped the smile. "I heard it was, uh...*messy*."

Ross set all the photographs down. "Messy? No...cafeterias are messy. Divorces are messy. No, the formation of the agency was a political and logistical nightmare," he rehearsed. "Everyone was grabbing for something, and no one knew for sure if they had anything. Political chaos."

"Well, change is hard, Chief."

Ross didn't even hear him.

"Salvage and liquidation: that was the motto, along with the War Department's lawyers and the State Department's political maneuvering, and the rest is history," Ross mourned. "Souers barely lasted six months, then Vandenberg...a lot of people, many talented people, were overlooked."

"No offense, Boss, but there were a lot of mistakes made by the administration after 1945. Everyone was tired of the war. They just wanted to put it all behind them. It didn't play well politically, either."

Ross droned on. "When the Special Operations division was created, it went to Galloway. I had better experience, he had better connections."

"Don't forget, Chief, you were selected to oversee Project SATURN. That's—"

"*Selected*?" Ross blurted out. "Hillenkoetter tried to *pacify* me with SATURN. Listen—SATURN wasn't an appointment, it was...an *apology*."

Neal stepped back. "You, uh, you can characterize it any way you want, but—"

"Characterizations are not the problem, Neal, *results* are. Next July will be exactly ten years since Roswell." Ross stood and walked around to the front of the desk. "I have precisely eleven months to deliver on SATURN, or the opportunity to rectify the oversights of the past is over. Forever."

There was a long pause, then Neal pointed at Denver's photo. "Once we apprehend Collins, then forget Roswell, forget Nelson," he said. "Project SATURN will potentially become the single most valuable asset in the agency. It's impossible to overestimate the national strategic advantage."

Howard Ross hesitated for a moment, then started nodding. He spoke slow and deliberately. "You mean, it is impossible to overestimate my *personal* strategic advantage."

Ross looked up. "Let's go get this son of a bitch."

July 7, 1947

SECURITY LEVEL: TOP SECRET

FOR: Howard D. Ross
FROM: Roscoe H. Hillenkoetter, Director, Central
    Intelligence
SUBJECT: Project SATURN

Metallurgical and materials studies confirm the
initial assessment of your field crew. Autopsies
involving both specimens recovered from New Mexico
conclusively indicate time displacement. Displaced
Persons remains have been designated DP-1, DP-2.

President Truman has authorized the immediate
creation of a new temporal studies division within the
agency, codenamed: Project SATURN. Locating, isolating,
and interrogating potential living time travelers is now
a national security priority. Your former
responsibilities with the Temporal Sciences Office of
Project Phoenix have been terminated. Dr. Neumann has
been notified.

You have four weeks, commencing 9 July, 1947, to
assemble your team. No information regarding your
activities or investigation is to be shared internally
with Project Phoenix or externally with any other
agency or department. Project SATURN will report
directly to the office of the DCI only.

Regarding Roswell: contain, control, confuse. You are
authorized to disseminate an alternate narrative
implicating flying discs and alien involvement, through
proper channels. Secondarily, release official statements
implicating weather balloon experimentation to account
for all phenomena.

END

DCI/PS

Saturday, August 16, 1947
Journal entry number 188

The crippling pain of the loss of Ken and Larry has only just now begun to subside, but my guilt on the other hand...it is as raw as ever. I had taken these strangers in and they trusted me to help them. But in the end, I hurt them in ways unimaginable. I may have given them temporary hope, but it quickly transformed into permanent failure. In my quest to make the best of times, am I creating the worst of times?

There are so many tired old questions and so many difficult new ones. The Ken Miller and Lawrence Etherington that will be yet born in the future: will it be their same consciousness, the same persons, the same "souls"? How does that work?

Does any of this work?

And then, how can I ever expect anyone else to trust me in the future?

Should they trust me? Am I trying to take on too much?

Should I tell anyone about Ken and Larry? Should I hide it?

If Grant ever returns, he will remember them, so what then?

If I do hide it, would it be to protect the fragile confidence of future Jumpers or merely to protect my own fragile ego and reputation?

I know that in a few decades the Roswell incident will become a hotbed of controversy. Many people will believe that it was about aliens and a government cover up. Actually, it wasn't about *aliens*: it was about *friends*. Not from another world, just from another time.

And now, within our group, if we ever have a group again, ultimately it is my decision if there is to be a cover up. The problem with making complex decisions is that regardless of your own rationalizations of why you are willing to do something, the real reasons may be far deeper, far more personal, and far more selfish. In fact, they can be so deep, personal, and selfish that they are completely hidden from even YOU.

I have no illusions about the clever liar that lives within me.

July 10, 1947

SECURITY LEVEL: TOP SECRET

FOR: Roscoe H. Hillenkoetter, Director, Central
     Intelligence
FROM: Chief Howard D. Ross, Project SATURN
SUBJECT: Roswell

We have completed quarantine and purging of the
Roswell Event location. I have included depositions from
our interrogations of all known witnesses of the event.

All physical materials recovered from the event have
been relocated to Los Alamos by C-54 (First Transport
Unit), but I have reservations about the long-term
security of that facility. In accord with the extreme
sensitivity of Project SATURN, I propose the
establishment of a new, remote base of operations. I am
attaching a draft proposal of locations near Groom Lake,
NV, and Rock Valley, NV, for your consideration.

The list of law enforcement, military personnel, and
local officials exposed to varying degrees of
information is sizable. A debriefing strategy is
currently my utmost priority. Press releases with both
flying disk and weather balloon accounts have been
disseminated and retracted through RAAF Public
Information Officer Walter Haut.

I recommend that General Roger M. Ramey, 8th Air
Force, who was initially notified by Major Jesse A.
Marcel, 509th Bomb Group, be transferred to DC for
debriefing at CIG.

    END

    DCI/PS

CHAPTER 33

Helping Poison Ivy and the Boys (as he called them) to
clean up and repair the reactor chamber in The Basement
was an irritating interruption in Garrett Frazier's work week.

And Terrance Gaines had grown tired of hearing about
it. Tee had counted the complaint at least a dozen times in
the last few hours. He noted that Garrett—who had jumped
only six months prior—always seemed critical of *any* work
performed in the lab below ground. But, to Terrance's credit,
he had also learned the secret about dealing with Frazier:

Listen Without Comment.

It was almost a *Fifth* Accord.

Tee had found that communicating with Frazier was
often a lose-lose proposition. If you ignored Garrett and his
continual complaining, he would get louder and more
annoying. If you listened to his unending grievances, and
then either added to them, or countered them, he would
predictably fly off the handle.

The best policy was *Listen Without Comment*, and today
Terrance followed that policy to the letter. Garrett was in rare
form, even for Garrett.

Terrance stabilized the last badly damaged capacitor
onto the cart and he and Frazier eased the heavy load
through the reactor door. It had been several days since the
disaster, but a disturbing blend of burnt hair, rubber, and an
odd electrical aroma still assaulted the senses. The morning's
cleanup had proceeded without major incident. That is, until
one of the wheels of the cart jammed on a small piece of
shrapnel on the floor.

Terrance could see the sickening cascade, the impending
domino effect, but he could do nothing at all to abate it. Two

of the large capacitors crashed to the floor with a metallic clank that reverberated throughout The Basement.

Papineau lurched from his own work. "*Soyez prudent,* idiots!"

That was all the fuel that a spark named Frazier needed. "Listen, French toast. Don't get on to me when it's your stupid—"

"Gentlemen, gentlemen," Doc Stonecroft mediated. "No need for scandalous verbiage in any language. We all just need to exercise extreme caution."

"Don't you think that's a bit hypocritical, Doc?" inquired Shep as he finished jogging down the last few steps and bounded into the room. He was cradling a new piece of glass, presumably to replace the broken one in the reactor room door. "I mean, don't go preaching to us about exercising extreme caution and all."

Terrance tried to defend the aged scientist. "Doc is right. We all just need to be more careful."

"Yo, Tee! Listen to me good," Shep declared. "When I want your opinion, trust me, you'll be the *last* to know. So drop it!"

Stonecroft motioned toward Shep. "Robert, we need—"

"What we need," Shep interrupted, "is a little inventory of recent events." Shep relocated near the reactor chamber door and pointed at the broken glass. "Let's see. In the past several months, who's been responsible for one hundred percent of the accidents and screw ups around here?"

He glared at the scientists. Papineau shook his head and returned to his work.

"Well, it's safe to say that we haven't had any problems upstairs," Shep said. "Hmm, go figure."

Doc paused for a moment. "Scientific pursuit is not a perfect process, Mr. Sheppard."

"Not a *perfect process*? You're damn right it's not perfect! Your little nuclear playground down here nearly killed a man! Nearly killed us all, actually."

"Ellen saved him," Terrance added.

Shep turned towards him. "You're kinda missing the whole point! He shouldn't have *needed* saving. The mad-scientists-three took us to the brink of a disaster last Friday."

Papineau spoke up. *"Ce n'etait pas notre—"*

Shep silenced him with a raised finger. "I can promise you, the days of the blank research check are *over*."

Doc nodded and placed a trembling hand on his chin. "Your point is well made, my friend. Well made." He glanced up at Shep and adjusted his glasses. "But if I may." A grave solemnity descended across his face. "The perilous path to progress has never been successfully detached from *sacrifice*, Mr. Sheppard. The altars of advancement have rarely been bloodless, but we can hope, we can pray, that our lambs have not, and will not, die in vain."

Doc, having begun his point, walked away, noticeably lost in heavy introspection. "Of all the afflictions mortal man must face, it is the torment of *guilt* that cannot be diminished, neither will it be satisfied."

He halted, misty eyes fixed upon Shep. "Trust me. I have lived with its scourge for nearly as long as you have been breathing, Mr. Sheppard. I do not take it lightly—especially as the scandalous day of my own indiscretion draws nigh." Stonecroft fished out a handkerchief.

"May God above forgive these two hands that have shed innocent blood."

Monday, November 10, 1947
Journal entry number 206

It's a girl!

Actually, a woman. An older woman. Our first. Overall, the score
stands at: Men: 4, Women: 1. Her name is Martha and she is a
graceful, dignified lady. But her arrival to Normal, from all reports, was
anything but dignified. I was helping X in the garage. It was midday,
around 3 p.m. or so yesterday when FlaT happened. We didn't see the
flash, but the thunder (though not as loud as usual) let you know that
something special just happened.

X looked up at me, startled. I motioned and said to him that I
have to go out and look around. He nodded. We are making some
language progress. We usually work on communication during meals (most
words we've learned are related to food. He likes to eat, and is a
decent cook).

I drove all over town, looking in all the usual places. It may not
be like finding a needle in a haystack, but it's not far from it. It
was after 5 p.m., and I figured that it might have been another case
of a jumpless-FlaT (lightning without a Jumper). As I was passing by
the police station, I noticed some unusual activity. I parked the sedan

and went inside, thinking that maybe Chief Brandenburg had heard about some out-of-towner. Someone out of place.

There was a small crowd inside. The Chief was there, three older women I didn't know, another gentleman that was introduced as Doctor somebody, and Barb, the Chief's wife. They were all crowded around an older woman who was sitting in a chair in a nightgown, looking completely lost.

The Chief walked over to me as I stepped in. He said the woman was found about 10 feet off the ground in an oak tree over on Gregory Street. He said that she had no idea how she got there, and that her name was Martha.

My heart and mind raced like crazy. I knew she was a Jumper, but I needed a way to extract her peacefully and convincingly from this predicament. It took all of three seconds. My idea was bold, and based more on desperation than cunning. I think I said a prayer and then rushed up to her, almost pushing a few of them aside. I kneeled down and took her hand.

I called her by her name and then told the group that this was my Aunt (on my mother's side). I said that she had been staying with me for a few days. I motioned for everyone to step away from her for a private consult. They gathered around me and I whispered that she has some mental issues. I told them that I had taken a nap and that when I woke up she was gone. I was even able to fake a few tears and thank them profusely. I broke out of the group and went back to her, gently raising her up. She started to protest, but I calmed her, and started walking her out to the car. Barb followed us (I'm pretty sure I overheard a few "poor dear"s and "bless her little heart"s as we left). I leaned in to Martha and whispered "It's okay, trust me." She was clearly in shock.

The car ride home was horribly awkward, as I had to continuously rotate between driving, calming, and explaining. More calming than anything. I have rarely seen such raw terror in a person's face. That was about 30 hours ago.

This one is all on me, since we lost Ken and Larry...and with the language difference, X can't help at all. I don't think she is a flight risk, but then again, the memories of Grant's sudden disappearance tinges my optimism a bit.

Her name is Martha Tomlin. She is 64 years old and jumped from near my own time zone—1989. She lived in Nashville with her daughter Caroline, she is a widow, and her late husband Calvin died of a heart attack in 1978. She is proper, stately, well-educated, and absolutely terrified. I have to go into town and buy her some things.

Just in case you were wondering, she is a size four and just adores the color blue.

July 12, 1947

SECURITY LEVEL: TOP SECRET

FOR: Roscoe H. Hillenkoetter, Director, Central
    Intelligence
FROM: Chief Howard D. Ross, Project SATURN
SUBJECT: Roswell Complication

We have uncovered that Ms. Pamela Hendrickson, WAC
nurse with the 509th, witnessed both of the recovered
specimens, and was privy to direct information
concerning temporal displacement. She has repeatedly
denied exposure to the information, but two independent
witnesses provided identical details implicating her
knowledge.

She has rank among the remainder of the flight
nursing staff, could leak information to them, and may
have already revealed information. We have debriefed all
medical personnel, and I am in the process of separating
and relocating all nursing staff. To prevent future
access to their information, the personnel records of the
509th will be modified.

Per your authorization, Nurse Hendrickson will be
transferred to Edgewood Arsenal for memory therapy, and
if that proves unsuccessful, her termination. Her eye-
witness testimony and level of access could undermine
Project SATURN.

END

DCI/PS

CHAPTER 34

I'm over thirty-five years old.
I think I'm past my prime when it comes to school.

Denver located a set of doors near the back of the factory. *Ellen said last door on the left.* He took a deep breath. Regardless of his misgivings about returning to school, he imagined that it certainly had to be safer than the reactor room. He grabbed the handle and walked in.

A voice greeted him. "You're tardy."

Denver looked up and caught the hard stare of Leah Swan from across the classroom. She was seated at a small, metal desk and Tori Wilkinson was mesmerized with a book nearby.

One teacher and one underclassman. Great.

He blushed at her complaint and walked up to his new taskmaster. The walls of the classroom were lined with vibrant and expressive paintings of landscapes of all types. There was a large sign just above and behind the desk that read: REMEMBER THE ACCORDS.

Leah repeated herself. "I said, Mr. Collins: you're late."

He reached her desk and donned a mischievous grin. "On the contrary, Miss Swan, considering the fact that I won't even be born until 1979, I would say that I'm at least twenty-three years *early*."

She broke out in a sweet smile and rose to greet him. "*Touche*, Mr. Collins." She turned to her left. "Tori, what do we do when someone walks into a room?"

The dark-haired teen set her book down and stood. She rotated toward Denver. "Hello."

He nodded. "Uh, good morning, Tori."

The contrived exchange was now over and Tori returned to her book. Leah folded her arms and studied her. "Tori and I are working on basic social skills. It's baby steps."

Denver nodded, then strolled over to the wall on his right and examined the paintings, each completely different, but all sharing the same signature: TW. He gazed down at the withdrawn girl, and then back to the colorful artwork. The apparent contradiction was fascinating.

Leah interrupted his musings. "Anyway, how are you feeling? You're looking better, only a few bandages. You looked like the mummy last time I saw you."

He spun about and shrugged. "How am I? Honestly?" She nodded.

"Well," he started, "since I've been in Normal, I've been shot with a tranquilizer gun, incarcerated, apprehended at gun point, I've been both killed and resuscitated by electricity, and now, ten years after I left the military, I'm returning to school in the back of a window factory in 1956. You tell me."

She played along. "Oh, that's all we ever get around here, day in, day out." They both chuckled and she motioned for him to have a seat. "Did the Chief or Ellen brief you about TOC, our little school here, Denver?"

"'Brief' is a good word. How about *very* brief? Ellen told me that all the new arrivals have to be educated, or is it re-educated?"

She nodded. "Yeah, it was decided years ago that we needed a formal initiation process, a structured curriculum to prepare Jumpers for the culture shock of life here in Normal."

He raised his hands. "Well, just to be upfront, I'm a *terrible* test-taker."

She rolled her eyes. "That won't be a problem. I see that Shep has finally given you an ID badge, Mr. Collins."

He looked down and pushed out his chest. "Correction, that's Mr. *Jackson*." He pointed.

She peered closer. "Aha, I see, *Mr. Jackson*. But I'm a bit confused, why the name change?"

He was puzzled. "Don't you remember about my wallet? Oh wait, you left before all that."

She was lost. "All *what*?"

"It's complicated."

She didn't press the matter. "Well, okay, Mr. Collins, or should I say, Mr. *Jackson*, my job is to prepare you to interact with a small-town population from the mid-1950s. Even the slightest error in language, or in the discussion of politics or technology, could destroy our efforts to remain below the radar." She smiled at him. "Speaking of being a bad test-taker, Mr. Jackson, interacting with Locals is one test we simply cannot afford to fail. Even once."

"Makes sense."

"But we also have to be concerned about how we interact with each other as well."

She rose and relocated to the front of her desk, leaning against it. She tilted her own name badge. "If you will look at your ID number—"

He finished her thought. "The last four digits indicate that person's jump year."

"Well done, Mr. Jackson."

He adopted a smug look. "I need to make a confession— I was the head of my class in pre-school." They both laughed.

She moved on. "Yeah, we have to be very careful. We have a rule about not sharing future information with another Jumper from an earlier time. The first few months I was here, the Second Accord used to really give me a headache, always having to pause and filter everything I would say or hear. But trust me—it gets easier."

Denver cocked his head. "So, lemme get this straight, I'm not supposed to tell you that the war of the sexes ended in the year 2012 and that the men won?"

"Both a student *and* a comedian?" She looked to her left. "Looks like we found ourselves a funny one, Tori!" If Tori heard her, she didn't acknowledge it. "You know, we laugh about this, but even seemingly insignificant and trivial information about future events or technology to a Prior could jeopardize all of our futures."

He decided that it was time to get all the lingo straight. "A *Prior*?"

"Oh, sorry, a Prior: that means someone who is from an earlier time than you. Prior, as in time."

"Shouldn't I be writing all of this down somewhere?"

She waved her hand. "Nah, it'll come naturally. Now you, Mr. Jackson, are a *Trailer*. At least to me. Actually, to everyone currently."

He nodded. "I've heard that a few times—it was kinda lost on me."

She leaned in. "Someone from a later time is a Trailer. You see, you follow after a Prior, so you are a Trailer. To give a Prior any information they shouldn't know could cause time ripples once we all get home. Remember—filter—then speak. It's the Second Accord."

He frowned. "Second Accord?"

Leah hesitated and gazed at the ceiling. "I know it seems so overwhelming at first. All the new terms and rules and such." She glanced back at him. "But it's all for our own good, it was put in place by our founder."

Denver looked past her and spotted a picture of Leah with an older gentleman. He pointed. "Is that him?"

She turned and retrieved it. "Yeah. Good ole Nellie," she said with a growing smile. "He was something else. Smart. Kind. I miss him. Every day."

"I'm sorry for asking, but, uh, what happened?"

She handed him the photo and looked away for awhile, blinking hard. She stared down at Tori who had just finished one book and was trading it for another.

Leah lowered her voice. "It, uh—was—he, um, killed himself." She nodded. "About three years ago. Three years ago last month actually. Feels more like three *weeks* ago."

She took a deep breath, long and full. Denver regretted resurrecting such strong, painful memories, but a part of him knew that talking could also be very therapeutic. He was thankful for the many friends that sat up for some late night confession sessions in the months following his last tour of duty in Afghanistan.

It didn't change the past, but it made the present almost bearable.

Regardless of the benefits, he apologized to her. "Look, I didn't mean to start—"

"Hey, no, really. It's okay. I'm a big girl, and, well," she paused, *"you need to know."*

He peered into her eyes. *There's more. There's way more. She's holding something back.*

He pointed at the photo. "Mr. Nelson was only briefly mentioned the other day when I was touring the factory."

Leah rolled her eyes. "Briefly mentioned? Really? Well, I'm shocked he was even mentioned at all."

Denver thought for a moment. "It seemed to be an uncomfortable topic."

"Oh, I'm not surprised. It really isn't talked about...*ever,*" she said, and rather bluntly. Leah leaned up from the desk and walked off. "You know, a lot of what has happened to all of us, with time jumping, and why did we all jump to Normal of all places, and everything, it's just so confusing."

She stopped and turned to him, her voice a bit lower. "But in many ways, Phil's suicide makes even less sense than *any* of that."

Denver wasn't sure what to do or what to say, so he did nothing.

Leah began walking back to the desk. "There were so many questions when it happened, and everything was just—you know—*swept under the rug* all neat and tidy."

Denver grew concerned. "Suicides aren't usually described as neat and tidy."

"See, that's what I mean! It was like, one day everything was fine, or as fine as our crazy situation can be, and then the next," she swallowed, "and then the next, Phil is dead, and no one talks about it. And there were so many things that just didn't add up. It's like the powers that be don't want anyone talking about it."

"Powers?"

She leaned in. "Look, he's a nice guy and all. But, uh..." The distraught teacher stopped. "No. I'm not gonna go there. It's all just supposition." Leah looked over at the photo in his hands. "None of us really had closure...well, at least I *didn't*."

She looked back at him and spoke just above an emotional whisper. "It, uh, it was a closed casket. That made it even harder. You know, it's really hard to say goodbye to a pretty wooden box with pretty flowers all over it."

Denver gazed at the floor. "I, uh, I know. I've been there." He paused, reflecting back. "I've stood beside more red, white, and blue caskets than I care to count. I hate to admit it, but sometimes I can't look at the flag without seeing young widows and little kids without dads. It haunts me."

His thoughts turned to Jasmine (not that she was ever very far from his mind) and he paused.

Leah gazed into his misting eyes and patted his hand. "Hey, look, I didn't mean for this to spiral down into a morbid trip down memory lane—"

He met Leah's compassionate stare and sighed. "Actually, I'm pretty sure I started it. But, it's okay, talking's good. It's good. So, when was the last time that you saw him?"

She looked up, tears forming. "Oh, it was at church earlier that day. It—the suicide—happened on a Sunday night, pretty late. It was the day after Independence Day actually. Ever since, the sound and smell of fireworks makes me ill."

She stared over at Tori and raised her voice back up. "But, whoa, there are way more important things for you to worry about right now. No amount of talking will bring ole Nellie back now, anyway."

Denver pulled the frame closer and studied it. "What's this here, on his neck?" He pointed to a dark smudge.

She leaned over and nodded. "Ah, the famous Nelson Personal Portal." She retrieved the photo and set it back on her desk. "It's a birthmark."

He wondered if she had misspoken. "A Personal Portal?"

Leah chuckled. "Oh, it was a joke with all us Jumpers. It's hard to see from this picture, but Phil's birthmark was roughly triangular. Kinda shaped like our Jump Portal. It was quite large."

She faced him and took a deep breath. "Well, anyway, we have to get down to business, Trailer Jackson. We need to cover politics, money, technology, language, laws, social etiquette, and even relationships."

She glanced up at her overwhelmed student. He smiled back at her. "When's the most important subject of the day?" he asked.

She scrunched her nose. "And just what subject is that?"

His face lit up. *"Recess."*

She wadded a small piece of paper and hurled it at him. "There's no downtime, Mr. Jackson. Too much to know, too much to do, too much to learn and too much to *unlearn*." She leaned across her desk.

"You must think, feel, and act like a man from 1956. It's my job to get you there."

Wednesday, November 12, 1947
Journal entry number 207

Martha is doing better by degrees. She shakes a bit, but I'm not sure if maybe she was like that before she jumped. Her appetite is getting better (she can't afford to lose much weight!). She was very leery of X at first, but that is also on the mend. Her maiden name was Wallingford, and she grew up on a huge farm in Eastern Tennessee (old money).

The one PLUS with Mrs. Tomlin (I feel strange calling her by her first name, she is almost like a grandmother, a matriarchal figure) is that she has already lived through the 1950s. She was born in the 1920s. She won't require too much cultural and temporal orientation. Heck—she could probably teach me a thing or two.

We just achieved a significant anniversary—X has been with us/me for one year now. I'm still shocked that he didn't leave after the Roswell incident.

Another unforeseen difficulty (at least unforeseen at first) arising from the loss of Ken Miller is our sport's gambling income. Without Ken's extensive knowledge of sports, the ability to raise large sums of money quickly is currently stalled. We have plenty, but we have had to replace ALL of the equipment lost in the Roswell explosion. Mrs.

Tomlin will gradually move into Ken's place eventually, but there will be more Jumpers needing homes. Expenses, expenses.

I have made some safe investments, but the stock market is not a quick-turnaround profit center. We will have to be wise.

I did tell Mrs. Tomlin that there have been other Jumpers, but I haven't told Mrs. Tomlin about Ken and Larry's deaths. I'm not looking forward to that conversation.

Ever.

July 14, 1947

SECURITY LEVEL: TOP SECRET

FOR: Chief Howard D. Ross, Project SATURN
FROM: Roscoe H. Hillenkoetter, Director, Central
        Intelligence
SUBJECT: Roswell Event

Per your concern and at my specific direction, the
Roswell Event materials at Los Alamos have been
quarantined under additional security. No one will have
access to the materials until your arrival or per your
authorization.

I have taken your new facility draft proposals to
HST. I feel confident that I was successful in convincing
the White House of the utmost necessity of this
expenditure. I anticipate a green light by week's end,
more than likely the Groom Lake, NV site. Moving
forward, the designation will be Dreamland.

Submit an estimate of lab, office, and staff spaces,
as well as equipment and vehicle requirements. Include a
layout for a long-term incarceration center and an
airfield diagram.

I understand your concern about debriefing of
military and law enforcement, but do not neglect the
greater pursuit of temporally displaced individuals. As
we move forward in time, the leads generated by the
Roswell Event will grow, of necessity, exponentially
colder.

You have authorization regarding Nurse Pamela
Hendrickson, including termination.

        END

        DCI/PS

CHAPTER 35

It may have only been a few ounces of metal.

But it wasn't just any badge. Some men struggled for decades to gain the privilege of even carrying the iconic symbol of the Federal Bureau of Investigation.

But not this man.

In fact, once he left Chicago, he had every intention of flipping the concave piece of gold-plated copper-alloy and turning it into an expensive ashtray.

Howard Ross lingered just outside the noisy auditorium as several suits navigated around him, rushing inside. They were oblivious of the true identity and power of the man they had just brushed past like a homeless stranger.

He glanced down at his fabricated FBI badge, and though it served a useful intelligence purpose in disguising his identity, it mainly served to infuriate him.

It was difficult for an ego-driven leader like Ross to flourish within the invisible confines of the world's most secretive of agencies. For a CIA operative, it was critical that few outsiders knew who you were, and yet the power you wielded oftentimes demanded just the opposite. The psychological contradiction weeded out lesser men, but Ross endured.

He inched up to the door and peered through the window. He hated three things in life and at least two of them were crowds. Through the thick layer of cigarette and cigar smoke that was suspended just overhead, Ross looked with disdain at the hundreds of bureau agents and police officers milling about.

Where is Schaeffer?

He checked his pocket watch. It was show time.

"There you are!" Neal exclaimed, jogging up to him.

"Where have you been?"

Neal smiled. "Uh, looking for *you*, Chief. The stage door is that way." Neal pointed to their far left and handed him a folder. "Come on, let's get you through this. I know how much you just love putting on a spectacle."

Neal escorted his unenthused boss toward the platform entrance. "We've obtained some intelligence on the wallet," Neal offered discreetly.

"Bout damn time."

"Apparently it was turned in by a Greyhound bus driver."

Ross slowed down. "And just why aren't we talking to him right now instead of this—*circus*?"

"Patience, great one. Patience. We haven't located the route or the driver just yet, but we're close. And right now, your adoring fans await."

Neal opened the door for him in military fashion. "After you, FBI Special Agent Ross."

Howard held up the folder as he passed through and flipped Neal off privately. Schaeffer just winked at him. "Go get 'em, Boss. I'm right behind you."

Ross ascended the platform in a dignified gait, and approached the podium. He tapped the microphone a few times, and the room began to settle down to a manageable roar. He leaned in and set the folder down. "Good morning, gentlemen." A quick squeal of feedback made him lean away.

He restarted, "Good morning." The chatter evaporated. "I am Special Agent Ross. The urgency of the operation and the immediacy of our window of opportunity has brought us together today. We are looking for this man." Ross nodded and a huge image of a bearded face filled the portable screen on the opposite end of the stage.

"Due to matters of extreme sensitivity related to the national security interests of the United States, we are seeking this man," he paused for effect. "*Denver Wayne Collins.*"

Ross may not have liked crowds, but he sure knew how to work one. He glanced back at Schaeffer, who was tucked just behind the main curtain. Neal was nodding and smiling. Ross continued with a grave stare. "This fugitive is considered extremely dangerous, and possibly armed with advanced weapons." He hesitated again. "But you may not, under any circumstances, use deadly force. He must be taken alive."

He glanced down at the officer sitting next to the slide projector. The image changed to a detailed composite sketch.

"This is a possible rendering of Mr. Collins clean shaven. Once identified, Denver Collins, and all known associates, are to be immediately taken into protective and solitary custody." He stepped back and coughed. "He is not to be questioned, interrogated, photographed, or recorded by any person at any time until I arrive with my team."

He motioned with his hand. A map of Northern Illinois filled the screen with a red line, reminiscent of a bulls-eye, encircling Chicago. Ross took a sip of water (Neal had added just a splash of lemon, the way Ross liked it).

"You will sweep every city, every town, within a hundred-fifty-mile radius of the Chicago city limits. Notify and recruit all local law enforcement and distribute copies of his photograph and physical description. However, do not alert the press." He glared out across the auditorium and spoke with firm precision. "No press. Any leaks will be...*career ending.* I hope I am clear."

Ross pulled the microphone out of its holder and stepped out from behind the safety of the large podium, trailing the cable behind. He looked down for a moment, always the showman. "I cannot overemphasize the value of his capture to the safety and security of the United States of America."

He nodded once more and the face of Denver reappeared, far larger than life. Ross sauntered over to it, his distinct shadow falling upon the screen.

Neal laughed as he mumbled under his breath, "Just had to get yourself on that screen somehow, eh, Chief?"

Ross continued, "When you eat, I want you to see the face of Denver Collins in your soup bowl. When you sleep, I want you to dream about him all night long. When you make love to your wife, I want you to see the face of Denver Wayne Collins staring back at you."

A low, disgusted rumble rippled through the all-male crowd.

"I want your every desire, your every waking thought to be the arrest of Denver Wayne Collins."

Thursday, November 13, 1947
Journal entry number 208

I was re-reading yesterday's journal entry about Martha Tomlin. I don't know why this didn't occur to me earlier. The ramifications and implications are mind numbing, migraine-inducing. Huge.

Mrs. Tomlin was born in 1925. That means that there are TWO Martha Tomlin's living in the world right now! There is (1) my Martha here in Normal, Illinois, and (2) her younger self in Eastern Tennessee, or rather, wherever she was/is in 1947.

How can this be? What does this mean?

Is it possible that she could MEET HERSELF?

Is that safe? What would happen?

How could anyone know for sure?

What would that do to the time-stream if your non-Jumper self met your Jumper-self?

I haven't said anything to her about it. Maybe she has already thought about it. This could happen again; we could have more Jumpers arrive who have younger versions of themselves somewhere out there. It is so strange to think that I, Phillip Allen Nelson, will be born in about 18 months. What would it be like to see yourself through the hospital nursery window? To attend your own actual birth day? It is perhaps dangerous enough to go anywhere near your own parents or grandparents, but to go near yourself...wow. Interesting but potentially disastrous. I need to formulate a new ACCORD to prevent a time-catastrophe.

The First Accord: Walk Without Footprints
The Second Accord: Filter the Future
The Third Accord: Prevent Personal Profit

The Fourth Accord: Avoid Meeting Yourself

I am planning to put together a comprehensive Jumper training program eventually. There is so much information that needs to be categorized and sequenced.

July 15, 1947

SECURITY LEVEL: TOP SECRET

FOR: Roscoe H. Hillenkoetter, Director, Central
      Intelligence
FROM: Chief Howard D. Ross, Project SATURN
SUBJECT: Roswell Situation Report

We have correlated a Ford truck that was seen
leaving the ranch near the site of the Event with a Ford
truck that had been at a motel in Roswell the evening of
3 July, 1947. The motel owner said there were four men in
the truck, and that the back of the vehicle had something
large covered with a tarp. Our ranch witness (William
Woody) affirmed that there were only two men fleeing in
the front of the truck on 4 July, 1947.

In this possible scenario, the two specimens recovered
are the other two men. The motel room was paid for by a
male, dark-haired, medium build, late thirties with an
unusual birthmark on his neck. A thorough sweep of the
room revealed no compelling physical leads.

According to the autopsy report, one of the specimens
had blond hair, and the other was nearly bald. No
birthmark on the neck of either specimen.

The room was signed for by one Phillip Nelson.

END

DCI/PS

CHAPTER 36

"The tricky part is the timing," Shep said as he studied a calendar spread out in the middle of the table. Several Jumpers studied him with interest as he rolled up his sleeves, and rubbed his hand across a full-day's stubble. "If we steal it too soon, it will obviously turn Betty's suspicion to you, McCloud, since she said that you were the only one who knew about it."

The Chief agreed without hesitation, but a different issue was troubling him. He leaned in and tapped several times on the table. "Actually there's two tricky parts." He stared over at Shep. "You're absolutely right—one's the timing, but the other—the other's motive deception."

"I'm not following you, Jim," Ellen admitted. A more recovered Denver looked over at her and shrugged.

McCloud sank into his chair, ideas and plans stirring within him. "We gotta steal her collection, yes, but it has to look like we weren't tryin' to steal her collection." He gazed around the room, wide-eyed. "It has to look like somethin' else."

Ellen jumped in. "Okay, gotcha, like a regular burglary that, that just happened to get the other goodies."

McCloud pointed at her. "*Bingo*. If we can do that, then we got it made in the shade. Now we just need the actual burglars."

Officer O'Connell piped up. "Hey, if you're looking for volunteers, Chief, you know I'm on board. Count me in."

Shep seized the opportunity to unload on him. "Are you crazy, O'Connell? Can you imagine what would happen if this ever got linked back to you? A *police officer*? Might as well just call the Feds right now!"

Frazier added insult to injury. "Dumb idea, Billy. Really lame."

The Chief advanced toward the enthusiastic but inexperienced officer. "Shep's right, Billy. No way, it's way too risky. It needs to be Jumpers that have the least amount to lose and the least amount of ties back to this group."

McCloud's recommendation left little to the imagination.

Denver's two eyes met five other pairs. "Wait a minute," he chuckled. "Are you honestly suggesting that I break into the local newspaper and rob it?"

McCloud stepped towards him. "Not suggesting, Mr. Collins. *Volunteering*. You're perfect for the job! You're practically unknown in these parts, and your knowledge of us and our group is—is not much."

"But that doesn't mean that I'm an experienced thief," he protested, "even if it is for a worthy cause. And the new name's *Jackson*, not Collins. Didn't everyone get the memo? Remember me—lost wallet boy?"

Denver turned to Ellen, his voice expressing his desperation. "Ellen, tell them—I'm still recovering from death. That takes a while, right?"

She angled in her seat and stared him up and down. "I think you're fine, both medically, and personally. And I do mean *fine*."

The Chief stepped between them. "Don't worry. You won't be alone, Mr. *Jackson*. How's the recon going, Mr. Frazier?"

Garrett stood and towered above the table. "I can tell you how many seconds it takes for our beloved reporter to go from her desk to her sedan, including the time it takes for her to lock the office door, and she always checks it twice."

Several people traded confused glances as McCloud explained. "I asked Frazier to start monitoring Betty's movements since our big meetin' a few days ago."

Denver put his head in his hands. "Well, I sure hope you know what you're doing, Frazier, 'cause I'm a bit new to the whole breaking-and-entering thing." Denver sat up. "We did our fair share of searches in the war, but that was house to house, three guys, big guns, and we didn't care who knew about it."

The Chief smiled broadly. "Oh, don't worry, Mr. Jackson, you're gonna get plenty of practice."

Ellen started laughing and leaned back. "Oh, this I gotta see!"

"And *see* you will, Miss Finegan." McCloud put a firm hand on her shoulder. "You're gonna be one of their first victims!"

Ellen spun about. "Whoa, I may spend too much time with a short French physicist, but *excuse moi?*"

McCloud strolled back to his chair. "Well, it would be too obvious if only the *Normal Journal* was robbed in an isolated criminal event." He pointed at the two would-be-thieves. "Denver and Frazier are going to do a whole string of small break-ins. Motive deception is the name o' the game."

"So, let me get this straight," Denver said as he articulated the absurdity of the proposal. "The *Chief of Police*, the man charged with the safety and security of the entire community, he is planning a whole series of robberies, right in his own home town, which includes breaking into the homes of some of his *closest* friends, using two time travelers, in order to confuse a newspaper editor and abscond with a mysterious box of goodies?" Denver took a much needed breath and surveyed the room. "That...*that* is your plan?"

The Chief rocked back on his heels and smiled like a proud father of triplets. "*Yep.*"

Thursday, January 15, 1948
Journal entry number 229

Jumper Number 6 blasted into our lives yesterday, and I do mean blasted. The lightning flash and shockwaves of thunder put all the rest of the FLaTs to shame. He was another late night/early morning apocalyptic arrival. Michael Ritenour went from June of 2006 (wow—the next millennium!) to January of 1948 in less than one second, at 1:30 a.m. on Wednesday, January 14th.

His grand entrance unintentionally created the perfect diversion. When I threw on a bathrobe and walked outside, I could see every light on in Normal. Ten minutes later, as I drove around town, there were still dozens of people out and about. He was just one among many.

In this culture of near-Cold War anxiety, I imagine most people assumed that we were under attack by the Commies. I'm afraid that the distrust that will be fomented by a McCarthy-type "Red" paranoia could hurt us Jumpers. I don't think that Senator McCarthy will start his witch hunt for another year or so, but after that—watch out. People will start to worry about all "newcomers." Average folks will see Communists behind every tree, and Russian-sympathizers under every rock.

Back to Michael. To make a long story short, I played a hunch that I've been harboring for a while now. If I found myself suddenly transported to a strange town, with no idea what happened, I would probably seek out law enforcement. So, after driving around and realizing that the number of people outside was going to make this impossible, I parked in front of the Normal police station. Sure enough, about 45 minutes later, Michael Ritenour sauntered up to the (locked) door, with a small electronic device in his hand. I walked up and said, "Let me guess, this ain't the right WHERE, and this ain't the right WHEN?" It took a bit, but I won him over, at least enough to head to the house.

He is tall, dark headed, and 29 years old. He is divorced, with two kids, and jumped from a suburb of Boston. He has a manufacturing background. It's still a bit early to judge (every time-traveler has to get through some degree of what I call "Jump Shock" or "Time Trauma"), but he is somewhat guarded in his personality. More of a closed book than me, for sure. Hard to read. But I've only known him for less than 2 days.

Mrs. Tomlin, on the other hand, has begun to relax a little and open up. We have sat and talked for hours about her experiences growing up, especially in this time period. She was the one who first brought up the "two Marthas" problem. She said that her 22 year-old other self is living in Ohio right now with her husband Calvin. She can't talk about him or her daughter Caroline without misting up quite a bit.

She longs to go see her husband, even from a distance, but she also knows the real and abiding dangers of that game of emotional and temporal roulette. Until we know differently, the Fourth Accord must be enforced with all our might.

Oh, I almost forgot (after re-reading this)—the device in Michael's hand is called a cellphone. It's like a portable telephone, a glorified walkie-talkie. I wanted to know more, but even I must follow the Second Accord.

July 22, 1947

SECURITY LEVEL: TOP SECRET

FOR: Chief Howard D. Ross, Project SATURN
FROM: Roscoe H. Hillenkoetter, Director, Central
      Intelligence
SUBJECT: Project SATURN

I just received authorization from HST regarding the
Dreamland facility at Groom Lake, NV. Construction will
commence on or about August 4. Temporary housing and
storage will be installed in Phase I and Roswell Event
materials should be relocated from Los Alamos
immediately thereafter.

We are compiling a master list of all US residents
matching the name of Phillip Nelson in the age range
specified. You are authorized to utilize the FBI in the
dragnet, but all interrogations must come through your
department. Project SATURN personnel have been issued
cover credentials through the Criminal Investigative
Division of the Bureau.

END

DCI/PS

CHAPTER 37

I really miss power steering.
And a good CD player.
And air conditioning.

Denver brought the dark red coupe to a jolting stop and signaled a couple of muddy kids waiting to get to the other side. He could make out a pair of grateful smiles through the crusty dirt. They wasted no time crossing. Denver glanced into the rear view mirror and examined the one remaining bandage on his forehead.

Leah pointed ahead. "Quit looking at yourself. You look fine, pretty boy. Now, make a left at the next street."

"Hey, don't get onto me. I've seen plenty of gals putting on lipstick while talking on their cellphones, and all while driving. A few of them might've even been smoking."

Leah looked over at him. "Talking on their what?"

"Ms. Swan, you are so *1991.* I'm trying to enforce the Second Accord." He slowed and turned left. "I meant to ask earlier…where is Tori today?"

"Oh, I took her over to Martha's place. Go straight," she said. "Martha is just great with her."

"Is she, you know, *slow?*"

Leah faced him. "Technically, she has autism. It's really rare in girls. I learned a lot about it from Doc. You know, us *1991-types* are still in the medical dark ages." She winked.

"But, wasn't he breaking the Second Accord by sharing that with you?"

"Fair question," she replied. "But since it was kind of a medical emergency, we made an exception. My world knew about autism, we just were immature and lumped it all together with a lot of other disorders. It's way more complicated than that. It covers a huge spectrum of issues."

She motioned. "Make a right. It's difficult to generalize about autism, but there are—*strategies* that can help. For one thing, avoid using exaggerated expressions."

"*Like?*"

"Like saying something like 'I will just shoot myself if I ever have to do that again', or 'go jump in a lake', you know, non-literal expressions."

He smiled. "Well, I have noticed that you eat like a bird."

"Yep. Those kinds of expressions require a more complex level of processing, and many people with autism have real difficulty separating fact from fiction. But that's just one thing, I mean, some struggle to even communicate at all, or struggle to just convey normal emotions."

"I have a nephew like that. He is, kinda, in his own world. We can't seem to break through the shell. No one can. Even specialists. Pretty sad."

"Sounds like he is at the severe end of the spectrum. Does he scream a lot, and hate loud noises?"

He nodded.

"It's heartbreaking, I'm sure," she replied.

"Well, speaking of heart—you've got a pretty big one in my book," Denver said. "I think it's really great how you look after Tori, and all. I mean, she's not your responsibility."

Leah grew quiet for a moment, and gazed out her window. "She is not a burden, Mr. Jackson. She's a *gift*. She's an amazing person, with so much to offer, so much to share. We just have to help her let it out. She's a butterfly that needs a little more time than the rest of us to break free."

Denver couldn't have been more impressed. "You have a rare gift, Ms. Swan. A rare gift, indeed. Even in the twenty-first century, we don't see too many folks like you."

"Think about your daughter, Jasmine," Leah began. "If she were lost, and surrounded by strangers, what would you be willing to give to make sure that someone good and kind took her in and treated her well?"

He didn't have to think very hard. "I would give everything I had."

Leah smiled. "*Exactly*. I try to remember that when I look at Tori. She means the world to somebody, and I need to be that person that they are praying for."

He shook his head. "Like I said, you are one special person."

"Just trying to take care of the least of these, Mr. Jackson. You, uh, you can park anywhere uptown, but not too close to the diner."

Denver found a few open spots with generous amounts of shade beneath a hulking, lopsided oak tree. He imagined that it would've taken a lightning bolt or severe ice storm to have crippled the towering giant. He killed the engine and deposited the keys into her waiting hand.

"Thanks," she said. "Ready for your first official public test?"

He blushed a little and tapped on the shiny steering wheel. "C'mon Leah, do you really have to chaperone me while I eat lunch?"

She wagged a delicate finger at him. "Protocols are protocols, Trailer Jackson. No new Jumpers are allowed to be unsupervised in public for their first thirty days."

He rolled his eyes. "I know all that."

"Well then, you also need to know that it's not *lunch*, it's usually called *dinner*. Midday meals in the Midwest are called *dinner*, well, most of the time."

Denver was uneasy. This whole arrangement was just— *wrong*, like being watched by your parents on a first date. "So, what, are you going to get out a notebook and grade me or something? Lemme guess, observe and report?"

"Observe and *rescue*," she corrected.

"*Rescue*?" He couldn't believe that she was serious.

She was.

Leah squinted at him. "Mr. Jackson, who is the current candidate for president on the Democratic ticket?"

Denver's eyes shot around and he rubbed his forehead. "Wait, hold on—I know this, it's—"

"Too slow." She pursed her lips. "Too slow. Slip ups like this can be disastrous, Denver."

He blushed and took a deep breath.

"I observe," she said, "and if you get into trouble...I, uh, *rescue*. Give me a few minutes lead, then come in the restaurant. Sit near me, but don't look at me or talk to me. Do you have your money?"

He dug into his shirt pocket. "Ten vintage bucks."

She double checked the cash and pointed at his wedding ring. "Have you thought any more about what we talked about?" she asked. "About your *ring*?"

He stuffed the money away and held his hand up, twisting the golden band.

She put her hand on his shoulder. "Not wearing it doesn't mean that you don't love someone." She looked into his distant eyes. "It's just that it...it *complicates* things around here. It will create questions about where your wife is and such. If we don't have to deal with those questions, it would be better."

It was a strange warfare that raged inside of this displaced soldier. In his logical mind, he absolutely knew that Leah was right. But every time he even tried to slide the ring off, something deep inside groaned. He tried to drown out the shame with a flood of his own rationalizations.

It's not that big a deal. It's just a piece of metal. A lot of professions can't even wear rings. It's a safety or health issue. It's okay. It's what's in your heart that matters, not what's on your finger.

Denver settled the decision in his head, though his chest was still languishing. He slid the precious token off of his finger (it was only the third time he had ever done so since they were married) and stowed it away in his pants pocket.

Leah rubbed his arm and leaned closer. "I'll see you inside, Mr. Jackson." She checked her makeup in the visor, and hopped out, but then grabbed the door frame and smiled at him.

"Oh, yeah," she said, "the answer is Stevenson. Adlai Stevenson."

Wednesday, January 21, 1948
Journal entry number 231

    I have finally begun crafting a formal curriculum for our "New Jumper" training program. I am thrilled that my background as a high school teacher can finally come into play. My TOC (Temporal Orientation Classes) will start with the Big 4 (the Four Accords). After that I am breaking it down into:

    1. Recent History—our history, more than anything else, shapes who we are. There is a lot of history that hasn't happened, yet we will have Jumpers whose lives are molded by un-happened history. No Vietnam War, no Korean War, no Civil Rights movement, no Moon landing, no hippies, no satellites, and no Kennedy assassination.

    2. Politics—orienting Jumpers to the current leadership landscape, from the White House to the local courthouse. Also, it's not the 50 United States...there are only 48 states now. Hawaii and Alaska come into statehood in the late 1950s. That's a tough one to remember. Also Interstates—there won't be a Federal Interstate system until the mid to late 1950s. And America doesn't even have zip codes yet. Apparently that's still a long way off (Mrs. Tomlin is great for these subtle details).

3. Entertainment—that's sports, movies, television, music. Television is still brand new (we won't even see color TV for about 6 or 7 years, I think) and is not really a household staple yet. We have to be careful about TV and television terms, like rerun, soap opera (I think they have these on radio though), cable TV, etc. Movies (if you forget radio) are a huge part of the culture. Current movie stars are THE stars, more so than musicians and singers.

The problem is that most of the Jumpers will have heard of most of the big stars and even some of the musicians, but we have to be careful about WHAT movies and WHAT songs that we associate with them (especially Elvis—we are almost 10 years too early for him).

No Godzilla, no Star Wars, no Beatles, no Michael Jackson, Disney-yes, Disneyland-no, no Six Million Dollar Man, no Charlie's Angels, no Gilligan's Island, and no Brady Bunch. Ouch.

4. Technology—there are no microwave ovens, no CELLPHONES (thanks Michael), no color TVs, no home computers, no space program, no calculators, no seatbelts, the word "digital" isn't even in common use yet. Also, most people do not have washing machines or dryers. But I'm very thankful that window-unit air conditioners were recently invented though!

5. Language—nothing can get a person into trouble quicker than their tongue. As the sage observed: "Thy speech betrayeth thee."

Language has both a positive aspect and a negative aspect. On the negative side, Jumpers have words, phrases, and quotes that don't exist yet in the late 1940s, and therefore must be SUBTRACTED. On the positive side, there are words and phrases that must be ADDED to their conversational lingo to make them authentic.

Of course there are other areas to learn such as social etiquette, acceptable behaviors, and such. Many of these will come organically, not formally. And then there are more personal, sensitive issues—like relationships. Should a Jumper go on a date with a Local? The entire goal of our Jumper community is to stay below the radar until we find the technological breakthrough to send us all back home.

Should we get involved with a Local, as a boyfriend, girlfriend, or husband/wife? Isn't that too risky and selfish—knowing we are going to be leaving? If we get too involved, and then leave (disappear), won't that create problems/questions and therefore violate The First Accord? Won't relationships leave too many well-established footprints?

A Jumper too entangled may NOT WANT to return. I can't even imagine what kind of a problem that would create with the future time-stream!

Oh well, enough school...time for a recess.

CHAPTER 38

The broken bell at the diner did its level best to jingle when Denver entered, but the pitiful result didn't even rouse a solitary glance from the floor. Of course, Denver felt every eye upon him from every possible angle. An irrational sensitivity plagued him, followed by a case of crippling self-consciousness. As his dad would've said, he "felt as guilty as a whore in church." Denver never noticed that no one noticed him.

A lot busier than the last time. Smells great. Let's see, where is Leah—oh, there. Act casual, Collins.

He meandered over to the bar and plopped down a few seats over on Leah's left side. He spotted her subtle nodding out of the corner of his right eye.

So far so good. Piece of cake.

Denver lifted the famous trifold paper menu, disappointed that this one didn't have any cleverly simulated coffee stains. He laughed at himself. It had been well over a week since he first sat here, but in many ways it seemed like mere moments ago.

The kitchen doors burst wide open and waitress Katie Long backed out with a large tray covered in steaming dishes. Denver was distracted by the mouthwatering menu options and didn't notice her at all. But once she spun about, regardless of his misguided sensitivity, there was only one pair of eyes following his every move.

He felt confident of his eventual order a minute or so later, and folded the menu, risking a quick glance over at Leah. She had nearly dumped her entire purse out on the counter, hunting for something. Their eyes met for less than an instant, and he turned away.

The door jingled pathetically and two older farmers decked out in denim overalls and caps strolled in and sat down immediately on Denver's left. The closest one removed his dusty hat (revealing a mop of dustier hair) and acknowledged Denver with a hearty grin. "Afternoon."

Denver overthought his own reply for a few moments. "Good afternoon."

Gotta be smoother, quicker Collins.

Katie had found the way back from her big delivery and passed in front of the two newest arrivals, flipping and filling their coffee cups. "I better get some big tips this afternoon, boys, or I might just accidentally tell your wives where you had dinner today!"

The gentlemen chuckled and one of them spoke up. "The womenfolk are out at Twin Grove, visiting my sister."

Katie put on a pitiful face. "And they left y'all to fend for your little ole selves?" She smiled wide with her deep red lips. "Shoulda married me. I would've taken better care of you than that."

"Speakin' of matrimony," the one furthest from Denver noted, "when're you gonna settle down and get hitched, Katie?"

Denver busied himself with the menu again, acting like he wasn't listening in on the authentic 1956 conversation. She glanced at him. "Just waiting for the right man to jump into my life," she said. "And hopefully a man from the city. I may be a farmer's daughter, but I sure don't wanna be a farmer's wife. *No offense, boys.*"

She winked and they all three laughed. Katie took a few steps over and looked up at Denver. "Well, welcome back, bus boy."

Leah glanced over, but Denver struggled to play it down. "Bus boy? What? Oh, yeah, the bus."

She poured some coffee. "Is your life still...*complicated*?"

He knew that Leah was parsing every syllable with all the cunning of a prosecuting attorney. It wasn't a very pleasant thought. "Uh, always. That's me, complicated," he said. "You have a good memory, uh, *Katie*."

She put a hand on her hip. "You forget that I am a waitress, and a waitress never forgets the biggest tipper in probably the entire history of tipping!"

Leah rotated towards him on the bar stool.

Strike one, Denver thought.

Leah's body language screamed what her mouth didn't. If this had been a driver's exam, Denver knew he had just blown a red light. His mind scrambled for an appropriate response. "What can I say, just in a generous mood I guess."

Beverly slipped up behind Katie after refilling Leah's coffee. She whispered discreetly, "Careful, trouble, trouble."

Katie shifted her weight and gave Bev both a not-so-subtle bump and a dirty look as well. She snatched her order pad. "So, uh, are you here to stay this time or just passing through?"

He floundered right out of the gate as if he had lost the ability to simply communicate. *You are staying Collins. Say it.* He cleared his throat. "Well, uh...I uh, I am, staying, for a while. A while. I think."

Strike two.

"How does the other guy look?" she asked.

He froze. *Other guy? What is she talking about?*

He shrugged. "I'm sorry, the *other* guy?"

She pointed at his facial injuries. "The other guy. Did you get in a fight? Was it over a girl?"

Respond Collins. Now. "Oh, no, no, nothing like that. I, uh, see what happened was, I, it—"

Strike three.

Leah reached for her purse and squarely smacked her coffee cup. It flipped across the counter and exploded in white shards on the well-worn tile floor. "Oh!" she cried out, jumping up, "Oh, I am so sorry!" The hot coffee ran like a dark river and dripped everywhere.

Katie sprang into cleaning action like a pro, damming up the runaway spill with a large dishtowel she whipped up out of nowhere.

"Don't you worry, ma'am, happens all the time," Katie calmly assured. "I'll clean this up and getcha a fresh cup."

"On it," Beverly chimed in as she sailed around the corner.

"Thanks, I am really sorry," Leah blushed. "I guess I wasn't paying attention."

Katie snagged a dry towel and hurried out to wipe down Leah's bar stool. "No problem. No problem." She slapped the seat with her hand. "Dry, good as new, and a fresh cup."

Leah looked over as Katie departed with a filthy rag and Bev arrived with a clean mop. Denver mouthed the words *THANK YOU*. She acknowledged him with graceful subtlety and sat back down.

Denver peeled his half-soggy menu up off the sticky counter.

Well, that explains the coffee stains.

October 29, 1947

SECURITY LEVEL: TOP SECRET

FOR: Roscoe H. Hillenkoetter, Director, Central
    Intelligence
FROM: Chief Howard D. Ross, Project SATURN
SUBJECT: Phase I - Dreamland update

Phase I of the Dreamland facility has been completed.
Temporary living quarters, incarceration center, storage,
and currently-adequate airfield have been established,
along with basic utilities.

All Roswell Incident materials have been
successfully relocated to Dreamland.

Phase II, which will encompass permanent housing,
office, research, and incarceration centers, should be
completed on or around 27 March, 1948.

Phase III, which primarily centers on upgrading the
temporary airfield, hangar, and communication facilities,
is slated for completion on or around 3 June, 1948.

END

DCI/PS

Monday, May 2, 1949
Journal entry number 375

Something hit me as I was driving around Normal and South Normal (that's what the Locals like to call Bloomington—it really gets the Bloomington folks bent out of shape!). It may be the answer to many of our problems. As I drove around I saw a lot of family businesses. I mean, if you think about it, up until fairly recently in human history, just about everyone worked in the family business, whether farming, or carpentry, or fishing or whatever.

As a matter of fact, many people's last names were associated with the family business, i.e. the Smiths were a family of prominent blacksmiths, the Bakers were known for breads and pastries, the Carpenters...well, you get the picture. I realized that our group of Jumpers, we are just like a family. We need our own cottage industry. This would solve quite a few difficulties right now:

1. Jumpers need something to do (but not for money, we don't really need money). People in the community without a job are suspicious.

2. Jumpers need to limit their exposure to the Locals. Having one place that most of us work at would cut down on unnecessary interaction.

3. We need a central place of training and schooling for new Jumpers. Meeting in people's homes too regularly can look suspicious.

4. A business would allow us to order and receive equipment that we need (for research) without raising any eyebrows or any appearance of impropriety (Too many big shipments to a house can be a red flag).

5. We need a cover story for our time displacement research.

With all of this in mind, I proposed to the group that I think we need to build some type of business, like a small factory somewhere just outside of town. This would fulfill all of these requirements. I can imagine a manufacturing facility upstairs (ground level), and a research lab downstairs (underground). It was very well received. We just need to pick a type of product that we can make which will allow us to order the raw materials and machines we need for downstairs, but make it look like it is for the upstairs.

A few weeks ago NATO was officially formed. The Cold War cometh quickly. On a different note, it has now been two years since Jumper Number 4, Grant Forrester, disappeared. Not a word. In a way, no news is good news.

He knows where we are. I hope that is a comfort for him, even though it is a source of great concern and liability to me.

Wednesday, August 3, 1949
Journal entry number 412

We broke ground today for the factory. Mayor Vorhees was there, as well as a few of the city aldermen. We are continuing to keep all of our actions as low-key as possible in this town of several thousand people. In terms of 1949 cities, it is above-average size here in the Midwest, but it is still small enough for most people to know just about everything that goes on. That is the problem.

Hopefully the factory will allow most of the Jumpers to work together, which has the side benefit of limiting their exposure to the outside world. Once the building is done (contractor estimated March 1950), we plan to build our new research lab underground. The Cold War hysteria surrounding nuclear annihilation (most people say atomic warfare) will cause bomb shelters to become popular among the well-off. It will be an easy sell to get the dirt excavated and the concrete poured. No one will think a thing about it.

To celebrate this momentous occasion, all of us Jumpers went to Steak 'n Shake at the corner of Main and West Virginia. I'm pretty sure this is where the chain started. This may be the first time that all of the Jumper community was in one place at one time (in public).

I gladly paid...ticket came in under $5.

CHAPTER 39

"The upstairs is pretty much the same," Ellen called out over her shoulder, as she led newspaper editor Betty Larson around her freshly vandalized home. "Not as bad as the downstairs, but the same kind of mess."

Betty knelt and snapped a few low-angle photographs. Drawers were jerked out and flipped over, personal items strewn all over the floor, a real residential disaster.

It was picture perfect.

She slid a thin pencil out of her mouth and jotted a few observations. "The Chief said that they broke in your *back* door?"

"That's right," Ellen lamented as she hopped over a dumped drawer and nodded towards the kitchen. "Just about knocked it off its hinges."

More photos. A few more notes. Betty looked up from the pad. "What do you think is the value of the stolen items?"

Ellen halted and rubbed her forehead. "Oh, I don't know...it's just now sinking in. Uh, maybe a hundred dollars?"

Betty began writing feverishly as Ellen continued, "It was some jewelry, silverware from my grandmother. A little cash. It's not the monetary value; it's the sentimental value."

"Oh, I know...absolutely." Betty did her best to balance the need for the story, and the need to be sensitive. One of her journalism professors observed that a reporter had the curious dilemma of both exploiting and consoling people at nearly the same time.

She put her notes away. "And thank the Lord you weren't home. No tellin' what that bastard might've done to you!"

Ellen put her hands on the side of her face, and a tear leaked through. She brushed it off her cheek and into her red hair. "I don't like to even think about it. You hear about stuff like this on the radio, up in Chicago, but—"

Betty couldn't resist capturing a quick emotional photo. She always felt that such frozen moments in time represented the pinnacle of her profession, the blending of hard facts and broken humans.

"Unfortunately, it's the same story as the break-in at Martha Tomlin's place three days ago," she said. "Back door kicked in, a few expensive items, some cash." Betty took another long look around. "Well, I'm sure the Chief is doing everything he can."

As Betty carefully navigated her way back to her car, Ellen smiled and mumbled, "Who, the Chief?" She paused.

"Oh, he's involved alright...very involved."

Thursday, Feb. 9, 1950
Journal entry number 452

Ahead of schedule and better than expected! The contractor "turned over the keys" to the factory today. The "Nelson Manufacturing" sign should arrive early next week to finish it off and make it official. Shep has ordered several pallets of parts, supplies, and raw materials in conjunction with Ritenour's guidance, and nearly all of the machinery has been ordered, some of it has already arrived and has remained crated.

We should be building residential windows within the next few weeks. Leah and Martha are busy setting up the office and accounting and a little decor. Stonecroft and X continue to draw up the plans for the underground research lab. I have been toying around with a pet name for it. I was thinking about calling it: The Basement (I don't have a future in Marketing or Advertising).

There is such optimism in the air. It has been a long time coming. With a more secure temporal studies lab hidden from prying eyes fifteen feet underground, we can put our efforts into high gear. I really feel like we are on the edge of a major breakthrough.

Once again we all celebrated at the corner of Main and West Virginia.

CHAPTER 40

His first public test as a man from 1956 was over.

Denver was privately relieved.

As he headed out the diner door, there was little doubt in his mind that he had failed miserably. He hurried out onto the sidewalk, and politely held the door wide for an elderly lady with a young, blond-haired boy in tow. The well-behaved youngster, not quite half Denver's height, looked up into his eyes.

Right then—something snapped.

A swirling array of sounds, sights, and emotions shredded Denver's mind like so much shrapnel. It was pain, and screaming, a child, voices, confusion. His hand slipped off the metal frame of the door, and he stumbled towards Leah's car, grasping the bridge of his nose. He blinked repeatedly, leaning off-balance like a doomed ship and growing nauseous.

Several irregular steps later, the bizarre episode subsided, at least the overwhelming intensity of it all. He halted, took a slow breath, and looked back at the diner.

What is going on?

Leah intercepted him. "Hey, why didn't you tell us?" she demanded.

He still hadn't cleared his mind to the level of a meaningful conversation. "Uh, tell, you...what?"

"Why didn't you tell us, about the fact you had *contact* with that waitress back there last week! And lemme guess. You paid with your money. *Future* money?"

He spun about, a bit lost, but recovering. "I'm, I'm sorry...it was before I, uh, I knew, about all of this." He lurched over. The vomit was rising much quicker than good responses. He swallowed hard.

Leah bent towards his face, which had lost all of its color. "Hey, whoa, sorry. Listen...you okay?"

"Well...yeah, I think so." Another swallow. "I, uh, just had a little episode back there. I'm fine. It's nothing. Really."

"Episode? What do you mean?"

He raised back up, squinting into the sun, and rubbed his face. This was going to be hard to explain. "I, um, have these—flashes," he said.

"Flashes?"

"Or…quick thoughts, like overpowering images will shoot through my mind. Usually violent. Seem to involve children. Sometimes night terrors, too."

Leah guided him towards some shade. "Are they random, or do they have triggers?"

"Dunno. I've had it for a long time. Unpredictable."

She put her hand on his shoulder. "I'm not a doctor, but you told me that you saw fighting overseas. A lot of violence. These flashbacks, you know, lots of guys that came home from Vietnam had them—especially soldiers that witnessed children being harmed. The stories I've heard are enough to give me nightmares." She locked empathetic eyes with him. "Maybe the painful memories you've tried to repress are kinda leaking through."

He nodded. "Yeah, you're probably right. That must be it."

It wasn't it.

He lied.

He didn't really intend to. It just jumped out of his mouth like a verbal reflex. It wasn't true, but at worst, it was probably a third degree falsehood.

He didn't tell her that he had been crippled by these disturbing experiences long before the war in Afghanistan, long before the attacks of September eleventh, and long before he even got his driver's permit.

But Leah got it half right.

Denver knew that this wasn't leftover trauma from the war somehow percolating up into his consciousness. No, this was something far earlier, and something far more personal. He suspected that these paralyzing incursions were the echoes of experiences that were refusing to be shackled any longer.

And they were getting worse.

As they strolled back to the car, Katie's eyes may have escaped their notice through the dusty window, but the entire fiasco did not escape hers. Katie watched the two patrons interact at the car then she popped open a small pad and scribbled down notes. Her pulse quickened and a fascinating new excitement rose within her.

She strained to read the woman's license plate. For an instant Katie imagined herself as an investigative journalist: lurking, listening, learning.

She had already worked out a rudimentary headline— MYSTERY MONEY MAN INVADES NORMAL.

She leaned against the cool glass, reveling in her new fantasy job. But fantasies are impossible to sustain.

A customer called out. She pursed her lips and flipped the pad shut. Katie hollered over her shoulder, "Coming."

Back to reality, girl.

August 11, 1950

SECURITY LEVEL: TOP SECRET

FOR: Roscoe H. Hillenkoetter, Director, Central
     Intelligence
     Dr. Willard Machle, Asst. Director, OSI
FROM: Chief Howard D. Ross, Project SATURN
SUBJECT: Project BLUEBIRD

Dr. Edwards reports that Subproject 1 studies by the
Medical Intelligence Unit at Edgewood Arsenal regarding
chemical psychological enhancers has been completed.
Initial results are attached.

I would offer that the value of this technique for
information extraction from time displaced subjects
cannot be overestimated.

Requesting permission to expand BLUEBIRD
significantly per Subproject 2 & 3 objectives. Subproject
2, which primarily focuses on memory annulment/
replacement, is essential for final debriefing of staff
involved with interrogation of time displaced subjects.

Please advise.

END

DCI/PS

Tuesday, March 21, 1950
Journal entry number 466

Spring is here and the dirt work is underway for The Basement (our "bomb shelter"). The plans are for 3 underground rooms: a conference room, a power room, and a time-displacement chamber (largest room). Oh, and a bathroom, so really four rooms. We are letting the contractor do almost all of the concrete work, but Doc Stonecroft said that we will need to finish the "time" chamber ourselves. Something about the walls need to be curved for wave reflection/refraction/something.

I'll just be glad to get all that equipment out of my garage and barn. An empty garage will be a sign of progress. A few weeks ago the Soviets finally publicly admitted that they have successfully detonated an atomic bomb. Now the Cold War will really begin to heat up.

I remember watching those black and white atomic safety videos and reading about the nuclear-paranoia of the early 1950s. But reading about it and living it are two completely different things. There are times you just want to grab people by the shoulders and tell them it's gonna be okay, especially the children. They are so afraid.

But you can't. Fear shaped an entire generation, and that generation shaped our future.

CHAPTER 41

Struggling with a loose socket on a stubborn nut was not exactly Ellen Finegan's first choice this morning, but Doc and Papineau rarely asked her to do much physical work. So either out of respect for them, or pride for herself, she pushed forward with minimal success.

She stretched back and wiped her damp forehead. It was during times like these that she really missed her dad. Not that she had ever really spent much time with Lieutenant Commander George Wyatt Finegan, though.

The double burden of being a Navy brat and an officer's kid forced a childhood and lifestyle upon Ellen Marie (that's what he called her) that no *normal* kid would have ever chosen. In the military, success is nearly always linked to sacrifice, and the family is typically the first thing offered on the proverbial altar.

The Finegan's certainly fared no better.

In any respect, Ellen and her mother Marie, were the real Finegan family. George Wyatt (as her mother called him) was more miss than hit, a familiar face at all things Navy, but typically a stranger in his own home.

When she was small, Ellen just imagined that all daddies were like hers. As they moved throughout the world, from promotion to promotion and base to base, she never really had time to get to know very many other kids, let alone time to gauge the patterns of normal fatherhood.

The uncharacteristic nature of her experience didn't really strike close to home until her freshman year in high school. George Wyatt had been reassigned to the U.S. Naval Air Station in Kodiak, Alaska, in early 1950. Tensions in the Pacific theater rose on a hair-trigger as the Korean Peninsula became the center of global political and military maneuvering.

Alaska, still nearly ten years from being a U.S. State, was certainly no paradise on Earth in 1950, but his latest assignment brought something new to the Finegan household: *off-base* housing. Ellen Marie had always existed within the rigid confines of a military residence, perpetually surrounded by other transient brats.

But Alaska had more to offer her than merely a long winter and weeks without normal daylight. The disconnected Alaskan territory allowed Ellen to connect with real kids: regular kids with real and regular dads.

High school was a strangely bittersweet period for Ellen. It was the first time in her life she ever had a best friend who was really *there* for her, yet also the dawn of the realization that her own father wasn't.

She still loved him though.

Deeply.

In Ellen's mind she fancied herself as a daddy's girl, though she inwardly took the blame for his sporadic influence. There was certainly no way to avoid the hidden suspicion that a big, important Navy man like Lieutenant Commander George Wyatt Finegan would have naturally wanted a *son*.

Maybe Ellen was supposed to be an *Allen*? She had always wondered that, and the fact that her grandpa's name was Allen, only fueled that painful fear.

In the irregular times that her father was home for more than three hours, she smothered him, showcasing her accomplishments, begging for validation. It was a trend she would never break free of, throwing herself at powerful men (or any man), seeking affection at any cost. It made for relationships that took off like a rocket, and went down like the Titanic. Two failed marriages in less than seven years proved it all too well. With George Wyatt's ignoble example, she didn't expect much from a man, and she usually got it.

But today, regardless if she was supposed to be an Allen or an Ellen—regardless if he wasn't there in the past—*today*, Ellen Marie wanted Daddy to help her with this jammed little bolt! She gave it another shot, and it mocked her once again.

Of course, not that he even *could* be there.

It had been just over three years since Ellen Marie had lost her part-time father. A failed take-off in a Fairchild R4Q-2 Packet on July 17, 1953, had violently extinguished the lives of over twenty brave men, including George Wyatt Finegan.

The father who was rarely there would now never be there again.

Being a time Jumper meant a lot of different things to different people, but for Ellen it meant losing her father *twice*. When she first jumped in 1951, she begged Phil Nelson for just one more chance to go and spend even five minutes with her father before the fatal plane crash.

Just five minutes.

Intellectually she assented that he was absolutely right in denying her request, but there were moments she secretly hated him for it. Over time, though, she grew to respect his tougher decisions. As he did for others, the larger than life Phil Nelson became a second father to her. Little did she know that she would tragically lose both her surrogate and biological father in the same year, in the same month, and only a few short weeks apart.

Ellen shoved all the undermining memories aside and gave it another big Finegan try.

Shep's booming voice echoed through the Jump Portal Chamber, breaking her concentration. "Time for a break?"

She dropped the sweaty wrench and didn't even look up. "I'm busy."

He walked down the metal mesh walkway and lowered a steaming cup of coffee by her face. "Even pretty girls need a break every now and then."

At first she decided to ignore him, but changed her mind. "But what about old men? Don't *they* get a break every now and then?"

"Now what's *that* supposed to mean?"

She twisted around and locked fiery eyes with him. "You know *exactly* what that means! I heard about your own personal little meltdown the other day, Robert. And you joined with Garrett Frazier, of all people!" She jumped up and wiped her hands. "Doc and Emile deserve your *respect*, not your *threats*! And if my sources are correct, apparently you also included me in your little tirade?" She began to march off.

He paused for a moment. "That's old news, Ellen. Plus, you and I both know it needed to be said!"

She spun around and took a deliberate step towards him. "What I *know*, Robert, is that we have experienced incredible progress down here over the past year, and all three of us have busted our asses to make it happen! We need *support* not sarcasm."

He stepped over and clutched her by the shoulders. "No," he affirmed, pulling her in close. "What you need, Ellen, is to slow down a bit. You're so busy chasing something out *there*, that you're missing what's right *here*," he looked into her eyes, "right in front of you."

She jerked away and stared dispassionately at the Jump Portal. He tried to reclaim her attention. "Hey, what's wrong with you? What's changed?"

She looked away. "Nothing. Nothing's changed. It's just...it's just that, we're close. I can feel it, we're *real close* to making this thing work!"

He maneuvered between her and the portal. "And I think that you and I are close, close to making *us* work."

She wasn't about to encourage him. "I...I think we need to, kinda, cool it for a while."

Robert Sheppard was stunned.

He studied Ellen's unyielding face, and then scrambled for a plausible explanation.

Things were great—what's changed? What's happened?

He started to protest, but his pride refused to let him beg. Shep turned on his heels and headed for the door.

Just outside the chamber, Stonecroft was explaining something—no doubt deep and mathematical—to a curious Denver Collins. Shep studied their newest arrival. He halted and spun. "I think that we both know what's changed, Ellen."

He hesitated. "The only thing that *has* changed."

Friday, May 12, 1950
Journal entry number 479

The sound and the feeling never gets old.

And now, with a small army of Jumpers to help find our newest additions, the recovery-window is getting pretty small. For Officer James McCloud, he went from LOST to LOCATED in about 12 minutes yesterday, around 1 p.m. local time.

Unfortunately for him, he was found by Leah. Out of respect for him, I will just say that those two now share an unforgettable memory. Let the record show he was not...at his best.

People around town are starting to really take note of the lightning and the thunder associated with FLaT. There has only been solid overcast a few times when it happened, to at least make the flash and boom seem somewhat reasonable. The word on the street is that it is due to some top secret government weapon or testing facility nearby.

As Jumpers we certainly aren't opposed to a little public suspicion like that. It is rare that the government serves a positive purpose, so we'll take this one with a smile. There is a lot of suspicion running rampant in society anyway. A few weeks ago President Truman tried to make the case to the American public that Communists had not infiltrated our country. Incredible. He doesn't even know that the US has been "infiltrated" by Jumpers from across time—how could he know if there are Communists from across the sea?

I digress.

I like this new trailer already. He's a 50-year-old policeman from Atlanta, and he jumped from 1996, a full 10 years into my future. He looks like a rotund drill sergeant, but that's where the similarity ends, apparently. He has taken his jump better than most and is very friendly, like someone you have already known for a long time.

Doc Stonecroft and Michael Ritnenour are still our most "advanced" trailers, but McCloud's arrival stirs again the subtle temptation to find small ways to gain future information while the Jumper is fresh and green—before they find out the rules.

It's easy to make laws—it's a bit tougher to live by them.

CHAPTER 42

There were persistent grumblings that CIA Agent Neal Schaeffer practiced the chain-of-command principle with an unnecessary religious fervor.

Some would say even to a fault.

But the young West Point graduate would respectfully disagree. As second in command, it was ingrained within him that his most sacred duty was the necessity of filtering everything before it gets anywhere near the *first* in command.

And Neal did what he was trained to do.

With a powerful and connected superior like Howard Ross, Schaeffer insisted that all intelligence flew across his own radar first—and with good reason. Ross had a well-established habit of chasing every fragment of intel, regardless of insignificance. This had been especially true over the last few years, as his desperation for a breakthrough often trumped better judgment.

Ross always lived in the light of his 4:30 p.m. Monday update calls with the Director of Central Intelligence.

Always.

The natural consequence of the Monday conference call simply translated into hectic weekends preparing for it.

Within a few weeks after Ross had recruited Neal from the PRS division of the Secret Service in late 1949, Schaeffer began weaning Ross away from his micro-management leadership dysfunction.

On more than one occasion, Ross had made Schaeffer feel like a temporary intern rather than the first assistant to one of the most important divisions within the agency. With Neal, it wasn't so much about protecting his own ego, rather it was about increasing efficiency within the organization. He took early measures at subtle but consistent course corrections. Everyone at Project SATURN noticed, with perhaps the singular exception of Ross, and everyone appreciated the transformation.

Ross' own workload diminished so gradually that some noted that he even became almost tolerable to be around again. In spite of the positive change, most SATURN agents still avoided Ross at all costs though. Too many off-hand comments became discussion points. Discussion points had an odd way of becoming policy, and policy had a strange way of increasing everyone's already over-taxed workload.

The discovery of the Collins' wallet threatened to break the spirits of even the most dedicated within SATURN. The Chicago initiative put the entire organization on mandatory eighteen-hour shifts, with a slim chance of having two days off in a row until at least Thanksgiving, over three months out.

Ross had an odd fascination in reminding everyone about it, and he did it multiple times per day. His new favorite mantra was: "If you wanna have a life again, find me Denver Wayne Collins."

And it was Neal Schaeffer, far more than anything else, that made those kind of days even bearable.

Agent Schaeffer's new temporary office just off Lake Michigan was a swarm of activity. There were so many suits rotating through that it more closely resembled an office party than a full-tilt investigation. His desk was wallpapered with a series of maps and littered with several cups of coffee in various states of fill (with at least four hopelessly over-stuffed ashtrays). One of the coffee cups had been officially commandeered as a *fifth* ashtray.

Neal hung up his phone just as a young agent pushed up to him through the considerable crowd with a clipboard. Neal scanned the top two pages and grabbed a pen, signing each one. "Thanks, William." The young man navigated a swift exit as Schaeffer's desk phone began buzzing, probably for the fiftieth time since he had lost count.

He snatched it and tucked the handset onto his shoulder. "Schaeffer." He lifted a map up and inspected it for a few moments. His eyes grew wider and he dropped the document.

"*Where*? Are you sure?"

July 22, 1951

SECURITY LEVEL: TOP SECRET

FOR: General Walter Bedell Smith, Director, Central
     Intelligence
FROM: Chief Howard D. Ross, Project SATURN
SUBJECT: Media Concerns

In light of recent national media attention to
agency activities, and the leaks uncovered by VENONA, I
propose an intelligence program to monitor and
manipulate news reporting in the US and even abroad.

By carefully selecting key media gatekeepers, we can
supply them with filtered information to guide national
and international attitudes/awareness. Like
mockingbirds, they can be groomed to repeat narratives
favorable to various initiatives.

This will especially come into play regarding Project
SATURN. If leaks or investigative journalism turns up
compromising information, this operation could identify,
redirect, or redact such reporting.

END

DCI/PS

CHAPTER 43

Neal shoved into Ross' office, lacking the decorum and professionalism he was typically famous for. With surprising dexterity he squeezed past at least half a dozen suits to get access to the Chief. Ross was in mid-sentence with two FBI agents as Schaeffer spoke into his ear. "We just received new intel on the wallet."

Ross immediately stopped talking and faced him. Neal dropped his voice low, breathing a bit heavy. "It was found on a Greyhound that runs from Oklahoma City to Chicago."

"On 66?"

Neal nodded, and Ross wasted no time, bulldozing several folders off his desktop, revealing a well-marked map underneath. They both leaned in and studied it, focusing on Northern Illinois.

Ross cleared his throat and clapped a few times. The room calmed down. "Gentlemen, gentlemen, we need to reallocate resources. We have a new region of concentration."

Everyone in the office moved forward, crowding around his desk. He grabbed a red grease pencil and traced an oval along Route 66 from Chicago south down toward Normal.

He gazed up. "South of Chicago on 66. All other locations are null and void. This noose just got a lot tighter! Make the calls, c'mon, let's go people!"

Within seconds, Ross and Schaeffer were left alone in a room infused with old smoke and new excitement. Neal was still smiling. Ross didn't look at him.

"*Speak.*"

"Oh, yeah, and I thought you'd like to know, we found the driver that turned it in."

Now Ross turned to him. "*And...?*"

"*And* he'll be here tomorrow afternoon."

"Why not *this* afternoon?"

Neal pointed down at Arkansas. "He's on the road, still several hours out of Oklahoma City. We've got a flight ready for him late tomorrow morning. I have people positioned at the terminal already."

Ross dropped into his seat abruptly and began scratching out questions for the interrogation. In his tenure at the OSS, Ross was affectionately dubbed Howard the Hammer. It wasn't an exaggeration. He could break anyone.

Now that Ross was in the zone, Neal had become an unnecessary piece of furniture. He was almost used to it. "Oh, you're welcome," Neal mumbled as he retreated out the door. He had convinced himself that the absent "thank you" was surely just another unfortunate oversight.

Then again, many things were unspoken when Howard Ross was involved.

Friday, June 9, 1950
Journal entry number 481

Things are going really well in the factory "upstairs" (The
Basement is mainly on the north side, not directly under the facility,
connected by a hidden staircase). Shep has moved into the role of
plant manager. Leah is our receptionist and is in charge of our
books/accounts payable/receivable. Mike takes care of shipping/receiving,
and works on the floor with Shep, Tamara, and myself. Martha
provides wise advice from time to time, but is retired and keeps to
herself. She misses her only living child Caroline (at least living in
1989), and speaks of her often, but I don't think Momma Martha
expects to ever get back home.

Our newest addition to the family, James McCloud, has been
with us about a month now. Leah says he is doing very well in his
re-education. With about 4 years of experience, we have really honed a
program and curriculum that can prepare a Jumper for life in the
1950s (as much as possible).

McCloud's background in law enforcement has given me some
ideas, some pretty radical ideas, actually. Riley Brandenburg, our current
Police Chief, has been serving Normal far beyond his usefulness. He
was probably past his prime before Pearl Harbor was bombed, with all
due respect. I think my friendship with Mayor Vorhees, coupled with

a few financial donations to community improvement could open some doors for a special appointment.

It could be very advantageous to have a Jumper in a position of power in the local community. Most of us need to stay below the radar, but we still need eyes and ears out there.

On a less local but yet more somber note, we are only days away from the official beginning of hostilities in what will be called the Korean War. As a Jumper, you lie awake at night and think about all the phone calls you would make to the president, and all the advice you would give.

Some people are quick to think that knowing the future would be a blessing. There are several people here in Normal, Illinois, that would beg to differ.

CHAPTER 44

A heaping dish of fried chicken and mashed potatoes pushed past the main door into The Basement.

"A delectable dinner is served, my dear Stonecroft," Ellen said sweetly in a spot-on imitation of her beloved colleague. Dr. Papineau followed closely behind hauling two more plates.

Ellen scanned the area as she set the meal on the table. "Doc?"

The delightful researcher was nowhere to be seen. She glanced over as Emile checked inside the bathroom. He leaned back and shook his head. The reactor chamber door was clearly shut, but the entrance to the Jump Portal was somewhat ajar.

"The aroma should be getting to you by now," she teased as she ventured into Doc's only remaining hiding place. Dr. Papineau was peering through the dark window of the reactor chamber when Ellen's scream echoed through The Basement.

"Doc! No, Doc!"

Emile scrambled to reach her, knocking a metal chair over in his haste. He rounded the doorway and caught sight of Ellen kneeling on the metal mesh walkway next to Doc's motionless form sprawled out on the floor.

"Stonecroft *mon ami! Ce qui s'est passé?*" he cried out.

Ellen frantically checked for vitals and began patting Doc on the shoulder. She glanced over at Emile, her eyes flooded with tears. "He, uh, he is alive."

She paused, reflecting on the language barrier. She smiled weakly. "He is okay. Okay." Ellen leaned across the wrinkled face of the unconscious researcher. "Doc, Doc— wake up, Doc. Doc Stonecroft. Hello?" She wiped her eyes as a single hot tear fell onto his cheek, and it began to run down the side of his face.

Emile rubbed Doc's hand repeatedly. *"Mon ami. Mon ami?"*

Stonecroft's fingers quivered, and then twitched several times. Ellen spotted the movement and patted his shoulder again. "That's it, hey Stonecroft, come on, dinner is getting cold."

She scanned his face for any sign of consciousness when Doc began blinking rapidly. He raised his right hand and felt around on his face for his missing glasses.

Ellen leaned down and gave him a quick hug in her excited relief. "Don't you ever scare me like that again, Doc Stonecroft."

He reached up and patted her on the back, still obviously disoriented. She leaned back, and with Emile's help raised Doc to a seated position. Ellen fetched his mangled eyeglasses and handed them to the shaken but good-spirited colleague.

"Oh, dear," he groaned as he took them from her. "Yes, I believe that you will find that the reports of my death have been greatly exaggerated." He felt the damaged frames. "But I am not so certain about the reports of my spectacles."

Ellen looked him up and down. "Are you hurt?"

He chuckled. "Oh, I am quite alright. At least, I think so." He looked at her. "But you are the medical professional, Miss Finegan. I will have to defer to your expertise and judgment."

She did a further exam, rubbing his arms and legs and checking his pulse again. "How do you feel?"

"None the worse for wear, I assure you my dear friend. A little shaken, as you might suppose." He paused for a moment, then smiled. "Fortunately, I think my back broke my fall."

Emile looked at Doc and then at Ellen. "*Bon?*"

Ellen smiled and nodded. "*Bon.* He's good. *Bon.*" She got right in Doc's face. "Do you think you can stand?"

He raised his bushy eyebrows and joked. "Why? Are my legs presently detached?"

"Well, at least your sense of humor isn't damaged. Come on, up you go."

They tenderly raised him back to his feet and assisted the aged scientist as he shuffled to a chair back in the lab. The bent frame on his eyeglasses occupied his attention while Ellen pulled up a chair beside him. "So what happened?" she asked. "Do you remember anything?"

He slid his glasses back on and grinned widely at the concerned redhead. "Remember? My dear Miss Finegan," he laughed, "on the contrary, I doubt I shall ever forget!"

Dr. Papineau pointed at the Portal Chamber with great excitement. "*La Port été activé?*"

Doc processed for a moment and his face lit up. "*Oui, oui!* Oh, yes. It was active alright, Emile. Quite active. Wonderful!"

Ellen felt a bit left out. "What are you talking about...*what* was active?"

Doc faced the table and slid a piece of paper toward himself. He pulled a pen from his front pocket and held it out to her. "Pray tell, what is the most famous equation in the world, Nurse Finegan?"

She hesitated for a second and took the pen, accepting the challenge. She wrote E=mc^2 in large print on the paper.

Emile beamed. "*La théorie du relativité d'Einstein.*"

Doc nodded. "Yes, Emile, precisely. But in all of our years of research, it wasn't until *today* that I finally realized the fatal flaw."

Ellen's face contorted. "Wait—*Einstein*, Albert Einstein was *wrong?*"

Doc roared with surprise. "No, no, no. Not Einstein, Nurse Finegan. Mass, *mass* was the flaw."

Papineau was also baffled. "*Masse?*"

Doc retrieved the pen from her and circled the letter M on the sheet.

"*Mass*," he declared triumphantly. He underlined the letter E. "We have been seeking to generate the amount of energy, for the mass of a person, a human being."

He stared into their blank but interested faces. "Now, at this stage in our progress, that is far too aggressive, too lofty of a target. Maybe soon, my dear friends, but, alas, *our reach still exceeds our grasp.*" He glanced up into her puzzled face.

He leaned closer. "*Browning.*" She still appeared to be on the outside of an inside joke. "Robert Browning. From *Men and Women—*"

"Yes, yes—poetry and mathematics aside, Doc," Ellen demanded as she stood up, happy but frustrated. "*What did you do?*"

He sank back, adjusting his glasses that were refusing to cooperate and stared off into the distance.

"It's not what I *did*, Miss Finegan. It's what I think that we are about to *see*. It will change *everything*."

Thursday, February 8, 1951
Journal entry number 535

I was actually out of town in Chicago with Michael and Doc Stonecroft looking at some equipment, and we all missed the fun. Yesterday, back in Normal, they said the morning sky got much brighter for a brief instant and the thunder rolled. This FLaT brought us one Terrance Gaines. (We have had a few jumpless-FLaTs recently.)

Shep and Leah found him wandering uptown. Terrance is an African-American in his mid-30s, and he arrived in 1951 from 1983. Normal is not very ethnically diverse, and when one combines that with his non-period clothing—he was easily identified.

I've only spent a short while with Terrance. He is pretty shaken, and he is not afraid to cry, which is odd at first blush. He's athletically built and his emotional state doesn't seem to fit your expectation when you see him. But he has a wife and 3 kids back in 1983, and he is suffering a horrible dose of "time trauma." Terrance is a veteran, and has mechanical and machine repair experience from his time in the Navy.

I am particularly concerned about the status of race relations in the Midwest in 1951. The Civil Rights Movement hasn't officially begun yet. I am trying to prepare Terrance for culture shock (as we had to do with Tamara), and I have continued to warn Shep about his offensive language and racial attitudes. Shep seems interested in updating our technology, but has no interest in updating his own outdated, racist mindset.

It seems that we will relive the Cold War, and the Race War—both born of fear and mistrust.

CHAPTER 45

"His name is Gerald Williamson, thirty-nine years old," Neal Schaeffer offered as Howard Ross stepped up to the viewing window bordering the interrogation room.

On the flip side of the one-way glass a balding bus driver waited in a tiny chair. He was perched in the most uncomfortable position and fidgeting excessively. Sweat poured from his wrinkled forehead, and his drenched handkerchief was already too soaked to provide any actual relief. The driver studied the reel-to-reel recorder at the end of the table and then looked down at his own trembling hands.

Ross gawked at him like a zoo exhibit. Neal had always sensed that his boss took a twisted interest in watching anxiety destroy a person. It was all part of the break-down process, Ross had said: a brief period of silent, foreboding isolation, strengthened by the mounting tension of waiting for that door to open.

Ross told Neal on more than one occasion that getting information out of a suspect was very much like digestion. "First," he said, "before you can extract the information out of them, you have to chew them up, kinda break 'em down a bit. Like using your teeth to crush food. That," he declared with a smile, "that is what the solitary waiting period is for. Never skip that important step. If you rush it, it's like not chewing your food enough: you won't get out of it what you are looking for."

Howard Ross glanced down and flipped open the folder Neal had shoved into his hands moments before. "Where's he from?"

"Champaign," Neal replied.

Ross looked up with a hard stare. Neal noticed and elaborated. "The *city*, not the beverage."

The driver stood up for a moment and took a few nervous steps, passing right by the glass, inches from them. Neal could almost smell the man's fear.

"I want a team on site to search his residence," Ross announced. "He had the wallet, he might have more."

"Uh, slight problem—we don't have a warrant."

His boss didn't seem impressed. "Get one if you think we need it. I don't."

Neal squirmed. "Just a little thing called the Fourth Amendment?"

Ross shrugged. "The Constitution, Agent Schaeffer, is the supreme law of the land, is it not? Of the people, by the people, for the people?"

Neal nodded. "No argument here, Chief."

"The Constitution protects the people, and *we* protect the Constitution." Neal's mind raced, but Ross didn't give him time to comment. "What good is the law of the land, Neal, if there is no land?" Ross paused.

Neal knew the Chief had no intention of further defending the merits of his legal position. Schaeffer predicted that Ross would conveniently change the subject.

He did.

"Where is the bus right now?" Ross asked.

Neal looked at his watch. "Should be arriving at the lot in about three hours."

"Make sure that no FBI agents touch it, just our people."

"Already taken care of. I assigned Kincy."

"TDS Film?"

"On site and ready."

Ross started to say something but then stopped. He paused, gazing at his victim. "This won't take long."

Neal looked at Ross' pitiful prey.

Nope, it won't take long at all.

Ross threw open the door as they burst into the stuffy interrogation room. The driver nearly jumped out of his chair and coughed.

Always a grand entrance isn't it Boss? Neal shut the door behind them being careful to make as little as sound as possible. He knew he was breaking protocol, and that he would probably pay for it later.

Ross circled around his victim and towered silently above him—his arms folded. Mr. Williamson swallowed hard, and apparently avoided all direct eye contact.

Ross signaled Neal, who stepped over and activated the tape recorder. Ross flipped open the folder again and marched to the other side of the small table. "Good afternoon, Mr. Williamson."

The driver nodded. "Uh, yes, good afternoon, Sir."

Ross paused before he sat down, locking eyes with him. "How is, uh, your wife Samantha, and your sons Daniel and Thomas?"

Come on, Boss, really? Ross had a one-size-fits-all interrogation style, which Neal knew consisted of fear, intimidation, repeat.

The poor man clasped his hands and struggled to answer. "Um, well, Sir, she is—I mean, they are fine. Just fine, Sir."

Ross sat, keeping his unblinking eyes on the driver. He angled back and lit up a cigarette.

Neal intervened. "Mr. Williamson, I want to assure you, that you are not in trouble in any way, shape, or form." Ross shot his assistant a cold stare, but Neal continued in spite of it. "We just have some questions for you, and we need the complete and honest truth. That's all. No more, no less."

The driver nodded. "Oh, yes, sure. Sure."

Ross took a long hit on the cigarette, flaring up a hellish glow on its tip. "What exactly happened on your bus the day you found the wallet in question?" Streams of white smoke snaked out of his nostrils.

The driver rubbed his hands together. "It, uh, was, uh, very strange, Sir. It was a Friday, Friday August the tenth. I was, we were, northbound on 66, about twenty minutes out of my first Chicago stop."

Ross leaned forward, transfixed, and Neal wrote careful notes, occasionally looking up to offer Ross' victim a friendly face. (With Neal and Ross, it wasn't a "good cop/bad cop" routine. It was more "good cop/you better freakin' tell me everything I want to know or I will destroy your life and the life of everyone you care about, cop.")

"*What* strange thing happened?" Ross pressed, even though his lips seemed motionless.

"I was, we were, pulled over, Sir."

Neal almost dropped his pencil, and Ross leaned forward, releasing a sideways blast of smoke. "*Who* pulled you over, Mr. Williamson?"

"Well, Sir, the police, of course. Um, two policemen."

Neal and Ross traded taut glances. Both of Ross' elbows rested on the table. "What kind of markings did you see on the police car? Did you get a good look at it? What city?"

The driver looked up and around, searching his memory. "It was a dark sedan, uh, no markings that I can remember, Sir. But there was a police light and a siren."

Neal glanced up from his paperwork. "Did you get a good look at the license plate, Mr. Williamson?"

"No Sir. It's a large bus. You don't see much out back, Sir."

If Ross was fascinated, his face was far too disciplined to reveal it. "What happened next?"

The driver relaxed, but only slightly. "As I said, two policemen, one on either side of the bus, came around and started yelling, yelling out a name. Some guy got up, I guess it was him, and walked off the bus—no struggle or anything. Strange."

Neal's heart began to race. He was perpetually amazed at how Ross remained stoic at such critical times. Howard smashed his cigarette into an ashtray. "Do you remember what they yelled? What name?" He paused. "It's *important*."

The driver leaned back, and mopped his brow a few times. Neal offered him a dry cloth.

"Thanks," he said.

Ross pressed, "A *name*, Mr. Williamson."

"Uh, it was, uh, Collins. Collins, Sir."

Neal had to fake a cough to cover his excitement. Ross' face appeared cooler than blue steel. "Are you sure?"

"Uh, yes, Sir. Absolutely." The driver looked over at Neal. "When I found the wallet, later, I looked for identification. I saw the name again, a Denver Collins, Sir."

Ross jumped up. "You searched through someone else's private property, Mr. Williamson?"

The driver sunk down like an abused child, panicking. "Look, no, I, uh, didn't steal anything or anything improper, Sir."

Ross was unrelenting. "What did you see in the wallet?"

"Uh, nothing, nothing really, Sir, just a strange driver's license—"

"*And—*"

"And, uh, some, some, cash, and, uh, that's just about, about it—Sir."

Ross hurried over to him. "What else?"

The man was on the verge of tears. "Nothing, Sir, nothing, just the license, and the, uh, the money, Sir."

The CIA Chief glared down at him. Neal recalled Ross' formula: fear, intimidation, repeat. *Here comes the repeat*, he thought.

Ross bent towards him, face to face. "Are you lying to me, son?"

The bus driver couldn't sink any lower. "No, no, Sir."

Ross froze, unflinching, no doubt to enhance the crushing effect. He lit a fresh cigarette in slow, deliberate motions. "Describe the two officers. Anything unusual—mannerisms, tattoos, anything?"

The driver relaxed visibly as Ross walked back to his chair. "Uh, it was hard to see much, Sir. They were wearing hats, and sunglasses. I don't recall seeing anything on their uniforms."

Neal interjected, "Any idea on their ages, even just a ballpark?"

Williamson strained, "Uh, one was probably, I'm not sure, maybe late fifties? The other, maybe late twenties, early thirties?"

Neal didn't look up. "Any accents, such as a foreigner might have?"

The driver shrugged. "Older one had a bit of a Southern drawl, I think, Sir. Nothing un-American."

Neal jotted some things down. He looked over. "What about build? Height and weight?"

"Uh, that's hard to say, uh, they were down on the ground, I'm, uh, a bus driver is up pretty high."

"I understand," Neal replied. "Was either one of them above average or below average height or weight?"

"Uh, well, older one was a bit heavy, a little overweight, maybe. Um, younger one about average, a little slender."

Ross resumed control. "Their uniforms—city cops, or Illinois State Police? Blue or brown?"

"Uh, blue. Yeah, city cops."

Ross released a veil of smoke. "What else did they say, the two policemen?"

Williamson paused. "Uh, not much. They, uh, thanked Mr. Collins for getting off the bus, and uh, then the older cop told me to get the bus out of there."

"That's all?"

"Uh, yes Sir. To the best of my memory. I was a little scared, kind of, like now. Sorry, Sir."

Ross straightened up. "Did it seem like they knew each other?"

The driver was at a loss. "Uh, Sir," he began, "I'm not sure I completely understand—"

"Did it seem like the policemen and Mr. Collins had any kind of prior relationship? Did they seem familiar with one another in any way?"

He shook his head. "Uh, they, uh, knew his name, that was it."

Neal stood up halfway and slid three photos across the table to the driver—snapshots of two random men and one of Denver Collins. Neal sat back down and looked at the driver. "Are any of these the man that got off your bus that day?"

The Greyhound driver picked up each one and studied them, quickly dismissing the first two. He held on to Denver's for a while. His hands were shaking as he set it down and pointed. "It all happened so fast, but, uh, it, I mean, he looks like the guy." He rubbed his chin. "I don't remember the beard though."

Ross made a subtle signal. Neal opened a folder and pulled out the artist's sketch of a clean-shaven Denver Collins. He spun it around and held it up for the driver.

Mr. Williamson began nodding. "Yes, yes, Sir. That looks like him."

Neal stashed the drawing away, and Ross continued. "Did Mr. Collins—the *gentleman*—say or do anything else that you can remember?"

The driver paused. "No, not that I can recall. The cops, they, uh, they did all the talking."

"Do you remember if Mr. Collins was alone on the bus?" Neal asked. "Was he sitting by anyone, did he talk to anyone? Any associates?"

"I'd, uh, be lying if I said I knew anything about that, Sir. Unless there's a fight or a medical emergency, I usually don't notice too much. Sorry."

"How about clothing? Do you remember what Mr. Collins was wearing?"

"Uh, jeans? And a plaid button up, I think, Sir. Maybe blue?"

"How did the two policemen act?" Ross asked. "Did it seem serious, or tense?"

The driver wiped his forehead again. "Serious? Yessir, it was serious! They, uh, had their guns drawn and everything, Sir." He stopped for a moment, recollecting. "When he got off the bus, they, uh, put him on his knees, guns to his head. Scared most of the passengers, that's for sure."

For the first time in the interview Neal saw Ross react in surprise. No doubt that part of the story must have interested Ross greatly. He probed deeper. "Did you see anything in your rear view mirror after you pulled away? Did you see or hear any gunshots?"

He shook his head.

Ross was relieved. "Did they ever pass you? In the police car?"

"No, I, uh, never saw them again."

"Do you have any recollection, even just an educated guess, just where Mr. Collins may have boarded your bus?"

Mr. Williamson threw his hands up, and shook his head. "No, Sir. I'm sorry. I mean, dozens, sometimes over a hundred people come and go every day. You get kinda numb to it all. Been doing this for over eight years, Sir."

Neal slid a map over to his boss. Ross walked over and displayed it the driver. "Can you show me, using this map, exactly where you were pulled over?"

He could…and he did.

Friday, October 26, 1951
Journal entry number 561

It's funny how stereotypes seem to be reinforced by life.

Her name is Ellen Finegan. She came into our community of Jumpers late afternoon yesterday. She was discovered unconscious and laying in the back of a truck by Michael and McCloud.

We revived her at Mrs. Tomlin's place. Everyone left the room except for Martha as Ellen was starting to come around. We thought it would not be as shocking. Martha's grace and wisdom once again prevailed nicely.

Ellen is 39 years old, and she jumped from 1968. She is our first actual medical professional, a nurse (RN). I think she might be a good addition to the research team in The Basement. Doc and X could use some help, and her knowledge of the human body and medical science could aid our research efforts.

Yes, she is Irish, yes she is a redhead (an attractive one at that), but I have no idea (yet) if she is a hothead. Speaking of redheads, my all-time favorite sitcom *I Love Lucy* started airing a little over a week ago. Gotta love Lucille Ball.

June 4, 1952

SECURITY LEVEL: TOP SECRET

FOR: General Walter Bedell Smith
      Director, Central Intelligence
FROM: Chief Howard D. Ross, Project SATURN
SUBJECT: High Altitude Aerial Reconnaissance
         Photography

Researchers here at Dreamland have developed a
specialized film emulsion (TDS Film) and development
process that identifies the presence of temporally
displaced materials. When tested on the materials
recovered at Roswell, including DP-1 and DP-2, the
results were above 94% reliable.

Utilizing high altitude balloon-camera tests, and
large format versions of the film, remote detection of
Temporal Displacement Signatures through TDS Film
techniques has been successfully demonstrated at
altitudes up to 80,000 feet. This technology can be
leveraged to provide intelligence regarding the
locations and progress of suspected Soviet temporal
research facilities, and to facilitate the apprehension
of domestic targets.

I propose the development of high altitude (>70,000
ft.) surveillance aircraft that could be used to
facilitate the imaging of the Soviet Union using TDS
Film. Current Pentagon projections indicate that Soviet
radar technology is limited to <65,000 feet, and Mig
interceptors to <50,000 ft.

To maintain the extreme secrecy of this operation,
the overt mission of the program could be Soviet nuclear
reconnaissance or even high altitude weather studies.
Either of these serves as both a necessary function and
plausible cover story. Cameras for both nuclear
installation ("weather") photography and TDS Film could
be mounted in the aircraft.

END

DCI/PS

CHAPTER 46

Looks are deceiving.

Especially in 1956.

He surveyed the average dirt shoulder, of this average highway, on this average August day, and tried to imagine the *not-so-average* event that had played out here just a few weeks before. Neal Schaeffer exited the dark sedan and took a prolonged breath before donning his sunglasses.

For a newcomer to the intelligence community, this tiny dusty patch had been solemnly transformed into hallowed ground. Just traveling here was akin to a religious pilgrimage for many Project SATURN operatives.

He peered over at Ross who was still hunkered down inside the car, barking out a litany of orders on the wireless.

Neal recalled his boss' experiences, indulging in a fair amount of jealousy in the process. Ross had been *there* in 1947. He had trod that sacred stretch of ranchland north of Roswell.

Ross had stood where time travelers had stood.

He had handled, like relics, the equipment that time travelers had handled. Ross had touched the two bodies of the mutated time travelers that were found lying in the wreckage of the holy event.

But that was in 1947, a full two years before Neal was ordained into the order.

Schaeffer had only *seen* these things from a distance in the secure storage units at Dreamland. Neal had never even personally traveled to Roswell yet. On one occasion, though, in July of 1952 he had been privileged to see the recovered time traveler bodies. It was during a five-year audit and review of the status of the items recovered from the Roswell event. Working in special suits at a balmy minus fifty degrees

Fahrenheit in a cryogenic chamber, Neal watched a team of doctors and techs examine the horribly disfigured men. Neal had seen dozens of photos of DP-1 and DP-2 over the years, but it wasn't the temperature that sent a cold chill up his spine that day.

But now, four years later, wearing a much more comfortable suit in a much more comfortable environment Neal was at ground zero of the most significant event since Roswell.

It felt good.

"It's about time," Ross complained as two more vehicles pulled onto the dusty expanse. Several agents exited, and less than a minute later, all were huddled around Ross.

"I realize that this site has gone cold, gentlemen," he began, "but there may be some evidence lingering. Let's scan a fifty yard radius from my location." He paused for effect. "Nothing, and I mean *not one thing*, should be considered insignificant." He clapped. "Let's go—meter's running!"

In a loosely choreographed dance, the team fanned out, donning gloves, retrieving equipment, and documenting every step of the way with cameras and clipboards.

Ross cupped his hands for one last charge. "I want full coverage of the area with TDS Film."

He walked south along the edge of Route 66 and Neal jogged up to him. A few cars crept by, passengers gawking.

"He said they were headed north and were pulled over by two cops right here," Ross rehearsed. "Right *here*." He stopped moving and ripped off his sunglasses, looking up and down the road. Another car passed on the far side. Ross continued to think out loud. "Two *policemen*." He glanced over at Neal. "Now, what were two boys in blue doing way out here, and why were they after our poor Mr. Collins?"

Neal was pouring over a map he had just unfolded. "The policemen may have been just a cover, Chief. Like we've discussed in the past, there could be...*other* interested parties. Domestic and...*foreign*."

Ross squinted as Neal elaborated on the international ramifications. "Someone knew a high value target was on the bus. Easiest way to extract him? Impersonate law enforcement. Small footprint operation, remote location, low casualties. Could've been a foreign job."

Ross worked through it verbally. "We must assume they were at odds, or why the big performance? And why *city* cops? Shoulda been state police way out here on the highway."

"There are so many possibilities, Chief. I don't know. Did they want him alive or dead? They could've killed him here—out in the middle of nowhere—then threw the body in the trunk." Schaeffer paused, as an idea began percolating. "And then, there's the wallet."

Ross frowned and stepped closer. "What? What about the wallet?"

Neal eased into it, his wheels beginning to turn like a steam train gaining traction. "Well, what if, and just hear me out," he paused. "What if, we were *meant* to find it?"

Ross was incredulous. "A *plant*?"

He nodded.

"But...but *why*? What possible benefit or, or strategic advantage could that offer? And your execution theory— who would kill someone they knew was a time traveler?"

Neal processed for a moment. "Perhaps *another* time traveler?"

Ross motioned for Neal to continue. Neal allowed the scenario to mature in his mind. "It could be time travelers from two different future governments or factions engaging each other across space and time."

Ross shook his head. "Wait—wait—you got all that from two policemen, a nervous bus driver, and a lost wallet?"

"Just throwing out ideas, Chief," Neal shrugged. "*Possible* scenarios. It is what I was trained for. You came to me, remember?"

Neal returned to studying the map, but out of the corner of his eye he saw Ross continuing to study him. The CIA Chief looked away and took a few steps. "Do you miss the old days at the White House, the days before I...*rescued* you?"

Neal chuckled as he folded the map, and they began walking. "By the *old days* I assume you mean the endless hours of assault scenario preparation and simulation at the PRS?" He grinned like a school boy. "No, no, I don't miss that part of the Secret Service, trust me."

He paused for a moment. "I used to literally dream about every possible way to kill a president. Weapons, explosives, vehicles, food, sound waves, diseases, moles, airborne toxins, accidental electrocution, drowning, even insect stings and, and...*suicide*."

Ross spun on his heels, eyebrows raised. "Suicide? *Seriously*?"

Neal waved his hand. "Oh, yeah, absolutely. It's a bit of a long term strategy, I'll give you that, involving psychological manipulation and negative reinforcement across multiple stimuli, but, yeah...suicide, it was considered. I mean, as a remote but possible potential threat." He paused again and lowered his voice as another agent walked by.

"We were concerned that the, uh, emotional complications from Hiroshima and Nagasaki could, you know, take their toll on Truman."

Ross shook his head. "He did what had to be done, plain and simple."

"Says the man who didn't kill over two hundred thousand people by simply writing the words: *release when ready*."

Ross began walking again, signaling to Neal that he was not currently interested in a debate concerning morally justifiable atrocities. "You know, with your extensive knowledge of presidential assassination techniques," Ross said, "the boys in D.C. better be glad you're one of the good guys."

Neal stayed in place, lost in thought. He glanced up. "Oh, and I almost forgot...my *personal* favorite."

"Wait—don't tell me you actually had a *favorite* way to kill the president? Really?"

Neal stepped up to him with a wicked smile. "Jealous first ladies."

A little excitement erupted about fifteen yards due south of their position. Ross rolled his eyes as they both hurried over. "Like they say, hell hath no fury."

Three SATURN agents were huddled around some *Object of Interest* in the dirt. Ross broke into the tight group. "Whaccha got, boys?"

One of the operatives bent down and pointed at a piece of yellowish metal pushed into the rocky soil. Another agent squeezed in and snapped several photos. Neal retrieved some tweezers and knelt to extract it. He rose slowly and held up the squashed piece of brass. "Two-seventy Winchester bullet casing."

Ross studied it for a few moments then spread his arms out.

"Alright boys, let's scan the immediate area and look for blood, or the bullet, or both. Let's go."

Thursday, May 8, 1952
Journal entry number 630

Earlier today, Mayor Vorhees officially appointed James McCloud as the new police chief, replacing Chief Brandenburg. I think that this will gain us a huge advantage in having a Jumper in a position of power. Especially when new Jumpers arrive, we have already seen that disoriented people tend to look for law enforcement.

To celebrate this important milestone, we headed over to the corner of Main and West Virginia (as usual). I drank two shakes. I need to be careful about my weight. Whenever I get "back home" it would be strange if I suddenly weighed 20lbs more!

On another note, I am a little concerned with McCloud's growing friendship with Robert Sheppard. If there is a problem in the Jumper community, Shep is always somewhere near the center of the issue. I encouraged Shep to be plant manager—thinking that the workload would help to corral some of his negative energy. I was hoping the amount of managerial responsibility would keep him too busy to cause problems.

I greatly underestimated his capacity for conflict.

CHAPTER 47

It had been over two years since Howard Ross had endured this circus lifestyle: in and out of cities, in and out of hotels, and in and out of relationships.

He flipped on the light switch and deposited his dark suit coat onto a chair in his plush, twelfth story, Chicago accommodations. As he loosened his collar, he stared across the spacious bedroom of his temporary hotel home. He couldn't deny that even though it was much, much smaller, it was still a cut or two above his home at Dreamland back in Nevada.

Nice hotels are nice for vacations or road trips, he had always said. But Ross maintained an assertion that even the poshest of accommodations rarely retained their charm much beyond ten days.

And he knew that this gig in Chicago could conceivably transform weeks into months, and all too easily.

In the early days of his appointment with Project SATURN, Ross was an intelligence gypsy—traveling from town to town, exploiting what opportunities it afforded and then moving on to the next target. The relentless pursuit of Phillip Nelson consumed Ross and the new division within the agency. It was an elaborate and exhausting juggling act at times.

Ross was tasked, not only with the primary objective of apprehending a time traveler, but also with the managerial responsibilities of overseeing the construction of the Dreamland facility adjacent to Groom Lake.

Adding to that crushing load, the Director of Central Intelligence had even charged Ross with oversight on temporal counter-intelligence. The workload and resources necessary to fulfill this aspect of his commission had remained fairly manageable for the first few years. Stalin's tentacles may have penetrated deep into the Manhattan Project, but, as far as the CIA knew, to the KGB and GRU, SATURN was still just a large planet with rings.

Then...*everything* changed.

Ross remembered well how the Venona Project analysts at Arlington Hall had cracked several Russian communiques mentioning Project SATURN in the spring of 1949. The sad irony was that the agency had been so successful concealing its own existence that even the government analysts cracking the Soviet codes didn't know what SATURN was.

The Venona revelation led to the first great purge in the young division, and few had escaped the heartless scalpel of suspicion. In the ensuing vacuum of a painful departmental recovery, Ross chanced upon Secret Service SAIC, Neal Schaeffer, at the president's winter retreat in Key West, Florida.

Truman favored both the warmer coastal climate and the warmer political climate at the Little White House, and Christmas 1949 was no exception. Ross, who was aiding DCI Hillenkoetter for a series of briefings with the president, was instantly impressed with Schaeffer's West Point discipline and formidable skill set.

Ross, toting a martini, drew alongside Neal while he was watching a particularly fierce beach volleyball game. Ross took a sip and made a presumptuous offer. "How would you like to go to work for a man with *real* power?"

Now seven years, two CIA Directors, and one president later, Ross may have shed some of his arrogance, but none of his persistence.

He sauntered across the Chicago hotel room while firing up a smoke, and pulled back the double curtains a bit. Ross leaned into the spotless window, as a police car with lights flashing went screaming by, far, far, below in the night. He took a prolonged, deep drag on his cigarette and its glowing embers painted his crimson reflection in the glass before him. The past decade had etched visible reminders of not enough sleep and more than enough booze upon his chiseled face.

But appearances didn't matter much to Howard Ross.

He wore his wrinkles like marks of seniority, like proud stripes on a well-worn uniform. He wasn't intimidated in the slightest by youth or youthful ambition. He was an older, wiser man at the helm of an older, wiser intelligence apparatus.

Phil Nelson may have evaded a younger, less experienced iteration of Project SATURN, but Denver Wayne Collins was now facing a fully mature and ruthlessly efficient covert machine.

Ross' introspection was put on hold as his hotel room phone began ringing. He released the drapes, blew out a lungful of smoke, and detoured around the bed.

"Hello?"

A deep and modified voice made him nearly drop his cigarette, or what was left of it.

"Hello, Howard. *Miss me?*"

It can't be. But how? How did they find me here?

Ross' eyes darted about as he yanked on the phone cord, desperate to create slack in the line. "How can I miss you?" He snatched up the base and turned out the lights, hustling back over toward the window. He peered out through the gap in the curtains, fishing for clues. "We've never met, or have we?"

Howard frantically scanned up and down the street, scouting payphones, lighted windows across the street, anything, anyone. There was no sign of the caller as the voice continued. "It's almost the first of the month, Howard. It's time for another...*installment.*"

He jumped to the other side of the window in a frenzied attempt to isolate even a hint of a lead.

"An installment?" Ross said. "Oh, so that's what they call *blackmail* these days?"

The voice was unrelenting. "Go to the corner of Clark and Madison at exactly two a.m."

Ross scrambled for his pocket watch: *12:38 a.m.*

"There is a phone booth there. Bring the money, and I will call you and give you payment instructions."

Stalling had never worked before, but Ross still vied for more time while he put the watch away. "But, I can't, I have to be—"

The line went dead.

He pulled the handset away from his face and glared at it for a few moments. Despite his blindsided rage, he wasn't all that surprised.

Ross hung up the phone and hit the lights as he rushed over to his half-opened closet. He bent down and retrieved a small briefcase buried deep within. He tossed the black box onto the bed and used a small key to unlock it, popping the latches. He raised the lid and glanced down at rows and rows of fresh, flat, and banded ten dollar bills. He slid a large envelope out of the top flap, and reluctantly began shoving bundles in.

They were forcing him to pay, time and time again.

One day he would return the favor.

June 17, 1952

SECURITY LEVEL: TOP SECRET

FOR: Chief Howard D. Ross, Project SATURN
FROM: General Walter Bedell Smith
      Director, Central Intelligence
SUBJECT: TDS Film

I have been briefed on the results of your TDS Film
research, and I have considered your proposal of
overhead Soviet reconnaissance.

A dialog has been initiated with Defense Secretary
Lovett concerning a high altitude Soviet nuclear
reconnaissance program. My early impressions of these
discussions is that there is some resistance within the
Pentagon about authorizing the CIA to handle "military
matters." Of course, my interactions did not include our
intentions of utilizing TDS Film, which, if implemented,
must remain a program within our agency.

If there is a growing consensus to move forward with
this initiative, and the Pentagon asserts control (Air
Force), I may be forced to brief Truman, or his successor
concerning TDS Film. He can provide an Executive Order
securing agency oversight. There may be counter-
intelligence value in creating the appearance that the
source of this initiative is the White House. Regardless,
if authorized, this will be a hellish political battle.

I am not in the mood for another ulcer.

END

PS/DCI

July 28, 1952

SECURITY LEVEL: TOP SECRET

FOR: Chief Howard D. Ross, Project SATURN
FROM: General Walter Bedell Smith
      Director, Central Intelligence
SUBJECT: High Altitude Reconnaissance Program

The creation of a fleet of high altitude
reconnaissance aircraft for evaluating the
status/progress of the Soviet Temporal Displacement
Program has been authorized.

Under the aegis of Soviet nuclear threat analysis,
the Air Force, utilizing Wright Air Development Command
(WADC) has been tasked with the development of the
aircraft for the program. To minimize the threat of
discovery of this initiative, most of the aircraft
funding will pass through the agency, shielding the Air
Force from a traceable paper trail. Unfortunately,
budgets, motivation levels, resources, and timetables have
all been drained by the continuing war in Korea.

Estimates for the modification of existing aircraft
or the creation of a new design range from 9 months to 2
years. It appears, Howard, that we must now show the same
patience that Moscow demonstrates in its pursuit of our
eventual destruction. As you well know, I, unfortunately,
have firsthand experience in this assessment of the
intractable Communists.

This initiative has been codenamed: Project AQUATONE.
To maintain secrecy and control, I would envision
further modification of the airstrips and hangars at
Dreamland to accommodate these high altitude aircraft,
but it looks like we will have plenty of time for those
preparations.

In addition, since the program will be in concert
with the Air Force, a new designation for Dreamland must
be inaugurated to protect the integrity of Project
SATURN. When referencing all activities related to
AQUATONE, use the location designation: Paradise Ranch.

END

PS/DCI

CHAPTER 48

Frazier killed the headlights the moment they pulled into the uptown alley. Denver noticed that the brilliant harvest moon made headlights unnecessary anyway. His stomach tightened to a painful knot. The thought of being alone with Frazier down a small alley in a town over fifty years from home wasn't exactly comforting.

Stay focused on the mission, Collins.

Denver had made it his life's goal to avoid getting caught up in any part of anyone's rumor mill. But, as Normal's newest Jumper, it seemed everyone was quick to drag him there anyway. These various factions probably saw each arrival as a fresh opportunity to further stack the deck, to build their own club, or maybe to secure yet another vote. There were fascinating and highly speculative tidbits floating around about several of the Jumpers.

But none juicier than those surrounding Garrett Frazier.

Not that he didn't deserve most of the gossip, Denver mused. Garrett's tactless unsocial skills and violent tendencies provided continual fuel for the eager fires of suspicion.

He was the sort of character whose actual past may have dwarfed the monster quickened by malicious mouths. Three days ago, Ellen confided to Denver that it was entirely probable that Frazier had jumped from prison. The thought had never even occurred to Denver that someone might have actually been *glad* to have jumped.

To a hopeless, incarcerated felon, a temporal rift could be the ultimate prison break—not only freedom gained, but a clean slate to boot.

He glanced over at Garrett's distinctive features, etched by the intense but colorless light as they closed in on the rear of the *Journal.* Garrett definitely fit the physical profile, but

Denver had served with dozens of guys who were bigger, looked meaner, and yet whose only crime was perhaps stealing a girl's heart.

Denver struggled to keep those suspicions at bay, but every time Garrett opened his mouth, he seemed determined to service the stereotype.

They rolled to a stop directly behind the back door to the newspaper office. Once the engine died, it was unnaturally quiet and Denver was pretty sure he could hear his own throbbing heartbeat.

Calm down, Collins. Come on, the chief of police set you up to do this! What's the worst thing that could happen?

Garrett cracked his door and slid out, slipping on a pair of black gloves to complete his dark outfit. He reached into the backseat and snatched a bag of tools and looked over at his nervous accomplice. "Ready, Collins?"

Denver was honest. "Nope, but let's get this over with."

They made the short trek to the back entrance without making any more sound than a few soft footfalls. Denver played the lookout while Garrett made quick work of the door. He glanced up at Denver, who made a final survey of the situation. He nodded as Frazier then shoved a small pry bar into the soft wood frame. One firm push and it was all over.

Garrett made it look all too easy, and disturbingly—all too *familiar*.

They popped their flashlights on as they eased in and Denver shut the door gingerly behind them. Garrett paused. "There are blinds on the front windows—kill your light and go shut 'em."

Denver went dark and dutifully headed up the narrow hall towards the foyer. It reminded him of countless late night missions in Afghanistan—only this time he was without the aid of monochrome night vision headgear and he was without the threat of potential death. The moonlight pouring in through the front glass provided all the illumination he needed. He stayed low and gazed out into the uneventful downtown area.

Nice and quiet. Let's keep it that way.

The reluctant thief moved sideways and grabbed the cord to the left window. With a small tug he first released and then gradually dropped the blinds. He repeated the process twice more, and retreated to find Frazier.

Denver spotted a dancing pool of light in Betty's office and crept up behind Garrett. "Done," he reported.

Frazier spoke without interrupting his own search. "Good. Look behind the front counter for the cash drawer, and I'll locate the safe. Once we find what we need, we can trash the place a bit."

Denver nodded under the cover of darkness and stole his way back towards the foyer for his second objective. He crouched behind the counter and flicked his light on, scanning the loosely organized shelves.

Cash box. Where are you?

He noticed a stack of receipts and examined them, more or less.

Must be close.

He moved another stack of papers and an old, wooden box with a small lock came into view.

Bingo.

He slid the dictionary-sized container across the shelf-paper and relocated it on the floor directly in front of him. Seconds later the thin metal clasp was no match for a small pry bar and the lid popped loose. As Denver lifted it he was greeted by neat little rows of ones, several fives, and a couple of tens, plus scores of coins.

Just over the wall to Denver's left, Frazier's prize—on the other hand—would not give itself up quite so easily. He searched all of the filing cabinet drawers, moved all of the furniture, and scanned under the big desk.

He stood and aimed his flashlight at the wall behind her office chair. A large painting came into view and he moved closer. He placed the flashlight on the desk and lifted the bottom edge of the frame, sliding his free hand along wall behind it.

He retrieved the light and panned it off to his right. Another wall, more artwork. He stepped up to it and lifted the edge, shining the narrow beam into the gap. Something glimmered and Garrett lifted the frame off its hooks. He couldn't help but smile as the wall safe became exposed.

"Well, hello there, beautiful."

He lowered the painting off to his left, and fetched a medium sized pry bar. Starting in the corners, he began to dig several holes in the plaster around the perimeter. He grabbed a larger bar, and shoved it in a hole below, rocking it up and down, seeking to loosen his prize.

Denver returned triumphantly with the cash box and displayed the contents. "Extra. Extra. *Spend* all about it."

Frazier glanced down as a little sweat fell. "Sweet. Now, set that down, and gimme a hand. Pry the other side."

Denver obeyed and grabbed his own bar, sliding it into another gap. He began applying pressure as Frazier wooed the metal box from the tight cubby hole. With some reluctance the safe finally surrendered in a waterfall of plaster and dust. The two men guided the surprisingly heavy, reinforced enclosure down to the floor. Garrett paused and studied it for a few seconds, examining it from different angles.

Denver looked over at him. "Should we try to open it here?"

"We *have* to open it here," Garrett replied. "If the items aren't in here, we have to keep looking. We can't leave til we got the goods. We get one shot. One."

"How do we open it?"

Frazier laughed. "You don't *open* a safe, Mr. Collins, you *crack* it."

Fair enough, Denver thought. He whispered, "So crack it—like a crab leg?"

Garrett reached back into his bag. "Oh, I bet you never used one of *these* on a crab leg." He lugged out a bulky power drill and handed the cord to Denver. "Plug it in over there."

Frazier motioned over his shoulder. "This will be a bit noisy. Keep a lookout at the front window."

Denver snuck away as Garrett dug a small cloth sheet out of his satchel and spread it out. With considerable difficulty, he lifted and set the safe dead center on the cloth, face up. He looked around and borrowed a small pillow from a nearby chair. Frazier examined the locking mechanism for a moment, and then positioned the drill bit precisely. He held the pillow over the drill and pulled the trigger.

Although he knew it would come, Denver still jumped when the drill began its unnerving screech. It was still quite loud, even though muffled by the pillow. He turned back toward the window and peered along the empty street through the blinds.

The drilling stopped. Frazier called out in a loud whisper. "Still clear?"

"Yeah, yeah...all clear," came the reply.

The violent drilling started up again with a vengeance. Ten seconds later it stopped again.

Denver called out. "Everything okay?"

The reply was calm and cool. "Perfect. Starting hole number two. Still clear?"

"Clear."

Frazier shoved the pillow down and grabbed the trigger, leaning his considerable weight into the process. The bit and the safe protested with unnerving wails amidst the grinding.

Denver began to smell the hot aftermath and pungent, dark smoke that drifted over the short wall.

Without warning the drill broke through and Garrett released the trigger. He wiggled it rhythmically to extract the red hot bit, and then laid the drill off to the side. He positioned the flashlight and peered inside the smoking holes. He blew hard. A few tiny, twisted metal shards ricocheted off his face.

Frazier picked up a stout hammer and a long metal punch. He inserted it into a drill hole and angled the rod with careful precision. He began tapping it several times. There was a pause, he re-angled the rod, and repeated the process.

Denver took a final survey of the street and stole his way back to watch the much quieter action. He dropped beside Garrett. "What're you doing now?

Garrett scrunched his face and moved the metal punch. "I'm bending, or at least, *attempting* to bend the cams out of the way to release the bolt."

Denver was fascinated. "How do you know what to do? And what tools to bring? Was it Doc, or the Chief?"

Frazier didn't even miss a beat. "Life, Mr. Collins. *Life* taught me. Hold these." He transferred the punch and hammer as he bent over and investigated his handiwork. Denver looked down at the cloth spread across the floor.

"What's up with the bed sheet?" he asked. "Gonna take a nap?"

Frazier retrieved his tools again as Denver pointed his own flashlight upon the work area. "The sheet," Garrett began, "collects and holds the metal shavings from the drilling. If we did this on the bare floor—"

"We would leave evidence that someone drilled the safe."

"*Correct*, Mr. Collins." He finally looked up at Denver. "Regular thieves would've just yanked the damn safe and opened it somewhere else, to save time."

Denver paused for a few thoughtful moments, having discovered the wisdom of the plan. "But if the thieves opened it *here*, that would mean they were probably looking for something in particular, instead of a generic robbery. Brilliant, absolutely *brilliant*, Frazier."

Garrett leaned in and strained to see in the darkness. "Hold your applause til *after* we have the items, Mr. Collins. More light."

Frazier raised the punch again and struck it a few more times. He discarded the tools and clutched the release handle on the safe door. He worked it back and forth with some restraint, until something popped deep inside.

Denver glanced up. "That sounded promising."

"Well," Garrett grinned, "we're either about to cross the finish line..."

"Or return to the starting blocks," Denver added. "Will it open?"

Frazier twisted the handle and tugged. He looked up. "It will." Together they pivoted the safe down into a normal, upright position.

Denver apologized. "Well, sorry, we both know the rules, *Mr. 1974*. The Second Accord must be honored."

Frazier growled as he stood. "Look, I don't need to be schooled, especially by you." He turned around and looked back over his shoulder. "And if I leave the room, it's because

I'm choosing to leave." He plodded off. "I've never been a big fan of rules."

Really Garrett? I never would've guessed.

Denver thought about his orders as he watched Frazier disappear around the corner. Doc, Shep, and the Chief had unanimously agreed. As the most senior Trailer—so to speak—they decreed that Denver alone should look at Betty's items.

No one knew for sure what type of futuristic items she had found. They argued that even simple knowledge of advanced technology to the wrong person could jeopardize their future in any one of several complex and unforeseeable ways.

The safe door swung open easily enough, and he inserted his hand into the dark chasm. He smiled and his heart raced somewhat as he pulled back a small wooden box, and set it on top of the iron chest. He double checked for anything else he might have missed.

Nothing.

Denver wasn't quite sure if he subscribed to their gloom and doom forecast about the newspaper editor's little collection—though he would never verbally admit it.

Not yet, at least.

The idea that a tiny event could ripple outward and replace aspects of the future was not even at the level of a theory in his own deliberations at this point.

But the others believed it, or, at the very least feared it. Denver had been trying to be a model Jumper. He had memorized the Four Accords. He probably could have written a one-page paper about each of them, but his current perspective was strangely not in accord with the Accords.

He was yet in the early stages of *survival* mode, only a smidge past *denial* mode. Many of the salient points of being a good citizen of the Jumper community were lost on a hopelessly out of place man seeking to find his place.

He glanced down.

This ain't Pandora's Box, guys, come on.

Still, a burning knot grew in the pit of his stomach and a certain strange apprehension built up inside the skeptical thief. Denver spun the box about on the floor and toyed with the token lock for a few seconds. He grabbed a small tool and snapped the lid open without much trouble.

He raised the cover and bathed the interior in a pool of light.

Nice collection. A digital watch with a black plastic band, shiny red flip phone...battery's dead, go figure...a thumb drive, a small flashlight, and a five dollar bill.

Denver picked up the cash and looked at the date, 2013. He remembered his first diner visit, and looked at all four corners—one was almost completely torn off.

That's gotta be my money. But how did the newspaper editor get it?

The temptation crossed his mind of simply removing the offensive money from the box. A flood of rationalizations broke over him. No one would know. Plus, he was already in enough hot water with the powers that be regarding his lost wallet.

He started to put it in his pocket, when Garrett's irritated voice from the hallway broke the silence. "You done yet?"

Denver reconsidered his little cover-up and shoved the money back into the box and closed the lid. He deposited it all back into the safe. "All clear!"

Ike Sanders was accustomed to rising before the chickens, but half past one in the morning was too darn early, even for him. A "sorry to wake you" phone call from his brother—who was in the middle of a barnyard emergency—prompted the impromptu, red-eye express through Normal.

Ike was always aggravated that the best path with the least amount of miles, also entailed the most amount of traffic signs. And, of course, right through the center of town.

But at this ungodly hour, he considered stop signs as little more than scarlet and white landmarks (actually, a few of them were still yellow and black, but those were outside the city limits). Ike rolled past them, confident that the Chief and Officer Billy were exactly where he should be right now.

Of course, Ike was being a bit of a hypocrite to his own philosophy that anyone out and about in the middle of the night was just up to no good.

He had no idea how right he was this night in Normal.

"On three," Garrett declared out of breath, as he and Denver prepared to lift the safe over the bumper and then down into the trunk of the car. They locked eyes with each other.

"One…two…*three*." The metal box scraped the edge of the vehicle, but the operation was a success.

Garrett looked up as he shut the trunk. "I, uh, I will get the tools and the bed sheet and all out of her office. Why don't you go back up front and start roughing the place up somewhat?"

Denver nodded, popped his flashlight on, and made his way back up to the foyer. He started overturning a few chairs and scattered some papers from the countertop all across the tile floor.

Ike had just blown through another uptown stop sign when a flash of light caught his eye inside the *Journal*. He began slowing down, far more than he had for any intersection thus far, and struggled to identify the source of light.

Denver came out from behind the counter just in time to see the pair of headlights not quite twenty-five yards away.

"*Car! Car!*" he yelled out in a panic-stricken but controlled shout. He dove hard to the floor and covered his flashlight. Garrett rolled behind a wall in the back as well.

Denver's ears could track the loose muffler as the truck rolled by, but the pounding of his own heart was almost as loud. He peeked out and followed the beams rippling across the venetian blinds. He was thrilled when he finally saw the white headlights change to red taillights, and then to no lights at all.

Frazier called out. "All clear?"

Denver raised up on all fours and crept up to the left window. He pinched the bottom corner of the blinds and lifted them, ever so slightly. The dirt-covered pickup truck was making a left turn at the end of the square.

Denver leaned back and released the blinds. "All clear."

Ike rounded the uptown corner and killed his lights, coming to a lazy stop along the curb. He glanced out the window back towards the *Journal*. He knew he had a duty to help his family, but he couldn't shake the feeling that he also had a civic duty of investigation.

Pastor Guilliams may not have been the most inspiring preacher (according to Ike) but he had continually reminded the congregation about being your brother's keeper.

Now without a doubt, Ike's *physical* brother needed him. But Ike couldn't shake the echoes of Pastor Guilliams' fiery admonition that a brother is anyone in need.

And tonight, it sure looked like the *Journal* was in need, to some degree. Either out of obligation or indignation, Ike yielded to that still, small voice. A distressed cow would have to wait a few minutes more.

He shut the engine off, but the motor had a mind of its own, rattling and choking and sputtering as if in the throes of death. He patted the dash. "Come on girl, go to sleep."

With a furious shake the truck went silent. Ike had been meaning to rebuild the carburetor for at least the last five years, but that repair job somehow never seemed to be convenient. He resolved that if the truck ever started backfiring, maybe then he would get serious about it.

Maybe.

After pulling his keys out and stashing them in their usual home above his visor, Ike climbed out. He wasn't a spring chicken, but decades of farm work had molded him into a powerful yet lanky middle-aged man. He dug around in the bed of the truck hunting for his tire iron. The handy weapon was found beneath a couple of cinder blocks, and the duty-bound citizen took off towards the newspaper office.

Ike wondered what the people in the town would think if they saw him passing in and out of the shadows uptown at this time of night, lugging a lethal metal bar. Most knew he was inclined to neither liquor nor violence, so that would rule out two possible scandalous scenarios.

But it didn't really matter, no one noticed the movements of the farmer-turned-vigilante.

He closed in on the *Journal*, slowing down just several yards away. He was hugging the inside of the sidewalk when he witnessed another small flash of light through the closest window. Ike's pulse quickened and he inched up to the edge of the brick building. He rolled to his right and peered through the glass, witnessing a stranger knock a large picture off of the far wall.

Ike dropped back for a moment, then bent forward again, spotting the tell-tale flashlight beam of a second intruder in the hallway. He took a deep breath and leaned his conflicted head back against the bricks.

Ike wasn't entirely sure if Pastor Guilliams would approve of him whacking someone with a tire iron in the name of being a good Samaritan, but he was fixing to do just that. He felt especially justified since there had been a rash of these break-ins in a town whose biggest crime problem of late had been a string of window eggings over by the University.

He tightened his already tight grip on the bar and ducked down below the window sill, gliding toward the front door.

Denver finished casting a few more papers on the floor, and paused to survey his professional vandalism. He smiled and called out. "I think I'm done up—"

He may have finished the sentence, but no one— including Denver—could possibly have heard it above the tremendous explosion of glass, wood, metal, and flesh that imploded into the foyer. A shower of shrapnel hit Denver in the back as he yanked his head around just in time to see the farmer lunging at him.

Denver narrowly avoided the first blow from the metal rod when it crashed down on the tile floor. In the fury of confusion he still managed to scream. *"Run! Run!"*

Frazier snatched up the bed sheet and his remaining tools, charging like an NFL lineman out the back, protecting his face the whole way.

Back in the foyer, the farmer went tumbling down with the force of his own failed swing, and Denver took the opportunity to jump up and flee. He took two steps and fell victim to his own vandalism, slipping on a pile of papers and slammed face-first into the floor. The farmer recovered and towered over him, as Denver struggled like a flailing turtle to roll over onto his back.

Ike raised the bar of justice above his own head. "Two things I can't abide, son...a liar, and a *thief!*"

Denver shielded his face with his arms, but it was a hopeless case of far too little, far too late. With the force of a golfer's swing the tire iron accelerated toward his head.

Mercifully, he didn't feel the powerful crack.

August 9, 1955

SECURITY LEVEL: TOP SECRET

FOR: Allen W. Dulles, Director, Central Intelligence
     DDCI, General Charles Pearre Cabell
FROM: Chief Howard D. Ross, Project SATURN
SUBJECT: AQUATONE

What began as a radical concept on our conference
room table just over three years ago is now flying in the
skies above Paradise Ranch.

Yesterday, the first U-2A (Article 341) took full
flight from the enhanced runways here at the Ranch.
Bissell was pleased with the performance of the aircraft
and the early test data, cruising at just over 32,000
feet. Camera installation and test filming will commence
on or about 1 September, 1955.

Implementation of TDS Film to study the progress of
the Russian temporal program should be operational on or
about 1 December, 1955.

Kelly Johnson has indicated that the remaining 21
aircraft will be delivered over the next 16 months.

     END

     DCI/PS

CHAPTER 49

Being both a newspaper reporter *and* a newspaper editor, often resulted in many irregular experiences and in many irregular hours. But it had been some time since a big, breaking story had jerked Betty Larson out of a comfortable and deep sleep.

There had been several instances when she had passed on a late night event, preferring to cover it fresh first thing the very next morning. Here motto was: if it can wait, then I can sleep.

But when a police officer called just before two in the morning and revealed that the *Journal* had just been robbed, she was out the door and in her car within three and a half minutes.

As she headed into town, Betty thought back to the very first time she had received a late night call (she called them "bedside invitations") to cover a breaking and fluid situation. Like tonight, the call was also late on a Sunday. It was near the end of the first week of July just over three years ago, and Betty had only recently stepped into the position as editor at the *Journal*.

She had been putting in at least sixteen-hour days during the difficult transition at the small town paper. When she wasn't at the office going through filing cabinets, making calls, and writing stories, she was at home going through file folders, making calls, and writing stories.

In those days *food*, *friends*, and *fun* were merely three words in the dictionary she had only a passing familiarity with.

But on Sunday, July 5, 1953, Betty Larson was thoroughly exhausted, having worked well over eighty hours that week. With lingering fireworks sounding off in the distance, she crashed onto her bed, face first, clothing on, at 9:10 p.m. Her sweet and well-deserved coma-like state was barely two-hours old when the phone rang. Betty never even heard the first four rings, but the fifth through the twelfth led to a gradual regaining of consciousness.

She may have been dead to the world, but the policeman on the other end spoke of another type of death altogether.

It was a suicide.

And a strange suicide at that—that is, if any suicide could be considered *normal*.

A respected member of the community had—according to police reports—inexplicably blown his head off at his place of business. It was a tragic and horribly sad story all wrapped up in a bit of a mystery. There were so many unanswered questions, but the urgency of her new position, piled on top of her complete lack of editorial and emotional energy, brought the investigative piece to a forgotten standstill.

Phil Nelson's death would make page one that following edition, but the follow-up that should have followed-up— well, *it never did*.

Thoughts and fears filled her mind as Betty came around the corner and pulled up beside the Chief's squad car in front of the *Journal*. Her hand covered her mouth when she first glimpsed the gaping hole that was once her front entry.

The Chief was patiently standing vigil on the sidewalk next to Ike as she stepped out of her car. McCloud nodded as they walked towards her. "Evenin' Betty. You remember Ike Sanders?"

She was still in shock. "What? Oh, I'm sorry, yes, yes, hello, Mr. Sanders. Chief."

McCloud gestured towards the shattered door. She shook her head, peering in. "What, what happened?"

The Chief grinned. "I'll tell ya what happened—looks like Ike here saved the day."

She turned to the farmer. "Officer O'Connell told me that, uh, that you stopped the burglar. Thank you. Really. Thank you."

"Actually, Ike stopped *one* of the *burglars*," the Chief corrected, adding considerable emphasis to the last syllable.

"*Burglars?*" Betty asked.

The Chief nodded. "*Burglars.* There were at least two of them rascals. Billy's out on patrol right now, keeping an eye out for anything unusual."

She glanced inside at the complete mess. "So, uh, so what exactly happened Ike?"

The blushing farmer cleared his throat. "Well, my brother called about half-past-one this mornin' and said one of his cows was in distress—she was calving. He was afraid to lose 'em both, so I jumped in my truck and was heading to his ranch when I saw lights moving inside yer place." He pointed off into the distance. "I parked round yonder, grabbed a tire iron and, and—"

"And busted through the door and caught one of the robbers," McCloud explained. "Laid 'em out cold, actually."

The editor was speechless. The Chief looked up at her. "Wanna see 'em?"

Betty froze, but McCloud laughed. "Oh, don't worry, he's takin' a nice nap right now. A good long nap."

He led her over to the rear of his police car and opened the back door, revealing an unconscious form. The male perpetrator was lying on his back, hands securely cuffed.

She studied his bruised face in the dim light. "Who is he?"

The Chief closed the door gently. "We don't know, *yet.* He didn't have any ID on 'em. And Ike didn't get a good look at the other one, or other *ones.*"

She turned around to head into the office and patted the farmer on the shoulder. "Thanks, Ike. Really. This town owes you."

"Just helpin' out a neighbor, Ma'am. What the good book says." He smiled and then looked over at McCloud. "Chief, if I'm done here, I need to get over to Dillon's. Probably too late, but—"

"Sure, Ike, sure. Billy can swing by tomorrow to get your official statement. See ya, and thanks."

Betty picked her way carefully across the shattered threshold with McCloud trailing right behind. She stared down as each step crunched and popped beneath her.

McCloud apologized. "Sorry, Betty. We didn't want to touch or clean anything up til after you'd had a chance to see what the Five Finger Discount Boys had done."

She nodded. "That's quite alright, Chief." She stepped behind the counter and slid her hand around on the shelves.

"What's wrong?" the Chief asked.

"It's gone," she answered, bending down and scanning the area. "The, uh, cash box. My cash box. It's gone."

He walked up to her, his heavy frame crunching quite a bit louder the entire way. "Any idea how much?"

She rose, wiping her hands. "Ball-parking it, I would say thirty-five dollars, maybe forty?"

He gave a low whistle. "That's a nice little chunk of change."

She nodded and then the Chief followed her up the short hall to her office. Betty gasped as she stepped through the doorway. McCloud came up alongside the distraught editor and stared at the gaping hole in the opposite wall.

Betty's eyes darted around, looking for the safe, or any remnants of its contents. The Chief tried to lighten the mood. "Lemme guess, you have an aggressive termite problem?"

She moved forward cautiously, examining everything. "No, I wish it were, Chief." Betty glanced behind her desk. "It, uh, it looks like they got my safe, too."

He eased into the center of the office. "Anything of value in there?"

She paused and stared at the hole for quite a while, lost in thought. "Maybe. Maybe," she mumbled. "At least five bucks worth anyway."

He turned towards her. "Excuse me?"

She bit her lower lip. "Oh, nothing."

Betty rummaged through her desk drawers, not really sure if she would even notice if anything was actually missing amidst the clutter and her own confusion.

McCloud bent down and retrieved few curly metal shavings, obviously leftovers from the drilling. Betty stood up and noticed. "Find something, Chief?"

He covered them quickly. "Well, I thought so, but it was nothing." He rose and hid the shavings in his pocket with all the skill of a practiced magician.

Betty navigated out from behind her desk, and he spun around and pointed towards the rear end of the hall. "They gained entrance through the back door. It's been forced open."

She glanced around the corner and noted, "Just like the other robberies."

The Chief agreed, but not too eagerly as he moved out. "Sure looks like it was all the same people. And we got one of 'em," he said.

Betty wandered back into the messy foyer and leaned on the counter.

"Billy's gonna camp out here tonight," the Chief called out. "At least til we can get Bode down here first thing in the morning to get your doors fixed and secure."

"Bode?"

He smiled. "Bode, Bodenschatz, Hank Bodenschatz."

"Oh, yes—thanks, Chief. Really."

He caught up with her by the front windows as she raised the blinds. "It's what we do, Betty, remember—we are your public servants."

They crunched their way back out onto the sidewalk, and the bewildered editor breathed a sigh as she gazed at the wreckage through the windows. McCloud strolled over to his car to check on Denver. "Listen Betty," he said. "There's nothin' you can do tonight. Go home and grab some shuteye. We'll sort through everything in the mornin'."

She couldn't resist the wisdom of his guidance, but still protested. "Easier said than done, Chief. I doubt I'll sleep a wink tonight."

"Well, at least *try*." McCloud glanced in on Denver one more time. "I'm gonna haul Mystery Man here to the station and put 'em on ice. If he's up to it, he'll face Judge Seyer tomorrow afternoon, Tuesday at the latest. Don't worry, we'll get 'em to sing."

Betty almost started to laugh at the simple irony of her situation. "You know, Chief, a newspaper office is supposed to *print* the news, not *be* the news."

"Well, I'm sure your competition down at *The Pantagraph* are gonna be facin' a real conundrum tomorrow," he said.

"How's that?" she responded, squinting a little.

"Well, they can't hardly ignore covering somethin' as big as a business robbery up here in Normal." He grinned. "But I reckon it will just about make 'em go ape at the thought of givin' you free advertising!"

"This certainly isn't the kind of publicity one would wish for, Chief."

He smiled at her and stepped away from the car. "Ah, it's not that bad. I'm in the news all the time." He looked around and whispered. "I think the editor likes me."

She chuckled and waved her hand at him. "I'll see you in the morning, Chief."

"Yes you will, Ms. Larson...yes, you will."

CHAPTER 50

1:56 a.m.

Howard Ross returned his watch to the interior pocket of his long, dark overcoat. With the minor exception of the occasional drunk stumbling away from a bar to his left, he appeared to be a lone, dark figure on the streets of Chicago.

It was surprisingly quiet as he hovered near the payphone. The only sounds were the muffled, intermittent jukebox singles that drifted in and out of the nearby tavern door along with the winos.

He found it odd that a city of such ethnic diversity and famous for cultural and civic corruption could sleep in such apparent harmony. Of course, he knew it was merely an illusion, a thin veneer.

Like his overcoat, the darkness concealed layers upon layers of secrets. And tonight, just as many other nights stretching into the past, he was willing to pay a nameless, faceless voice to keep it that way.

The payphone began ringing, like a siren call threatening to expose him in the night. Ross yanked it off the hook.

"I'm glad to see you're dressed for the occasion," the voice began. "It can be brisk this time of the year in the windy city, Howard."

For a powerful man who concealed many of his nation's deepest secrets, Ross felt naked and exposed. He spun around, identifying every possible vantage point on his location.

Where? Who?

He clutched the receiver and growled. "You won't need a jacket where I'm gonna send you, you little *sonofabitch*, when, and I do mean, *when*, I find you!"

"Whoa—harsh language there, Howard," the caller taunted. "Even for a big shot CIA-man like yourself. Of course, harsh words are not your *biggest* problem, Howard. I would say that these compromising photos that I am holding are a much *bigger* problem."

There was a pause.

"So, I would choose my words a bit more carefully."

Ross made some effort to contain his rage. "I think I've paid you enough over the last few years to use just about any kinda language I want!"

He could hear the blackmailer smiling. "Paid *enough*? Well, well, Howard, that all depends on what these pictures are worth to you, I suppose."

Ross had played this game too many times before. "So, where's the drop?" he asked.

Unfortunately, the caller at the other end of the line was obviously still enjoying the banter. "Is the address of Director Dulles still Washington 25, Howard?"

"Where is the drop?" he demanded as an inebriated couple passed by him, singing the entire way.

There was an infuriating pause. "She is very pretty. I'll give you that, Howard. It's a shame you didn't look deeper than her face, though. You of all people should know that the truth is always buried somewhere below the surface story."

Ross wouldn't be baited.

"A big, important G-man like yourself, you should have known that she was just as red as her lipstick, Howard."

Ross relaxed his tone. "The drop?"

"And just how do you get any rest these days...I mean, knowing that you were sleeping with the enemy?"

There was an uncomfortable pause. Ross glanced around, fidgeting with the packet of money stuffed in his coat. "I'm still waiting," he said.

"Was she anyone's whore or just *your* whore, Howard?" No response. "Either way—I'm sure she wasn't paid nearly enough."

"The drop."

"Twenty feet from where you are standing—there is a storm drain on the edge of the street. Do you see it?"

Howard turned about and spotted the tell-tale metal plate. "Yeah, I see it."

"Throw your money down the drain."

The phone went dead. Ross stared at the handset. "I couldn't have said it better myself." He slammed it on the hook and walked away, glancing up and down the quiet and empty street.

He stopped next to the storm drain and made a final check in all directions. Ross knelt, as if to tie his shoes, and surveyed the area yet again. He reached into his coat and tossed the thick bundle—and a good chunk of his self-respect—down into the hole.

Ross drew out a cigarette and cupped his hands, lighting it. He made one last survey of the serene yet deceitful scene. He rushed over to his sedan, and moments later, was gone—another thirty days of fragile silence bought and paid for.

The engine noise of Ross' hurried getaway had just begun to fade when the door to the nearby bar opened once more.

Neal Schaeffer stepped out of the lingering smoke and strolled toward the drain.

CHAPTER 51

The incessant knocking at his front door grew louder by the moment. Robert Sheppard roused from sleep, and leaned over, struggling to find and pull the lamp chain. The light popped on, blinding him momentarily as he squinted to read the clock. The knocking continued.

2:41 a.m.

He threw the covers back.

Even more knocking.

"Alright. *Alright!*" he growled as both feet hit the cool, hardwood floor and he stumbled through the darkness toward the living room. There was a final round of loud pounding just as he cracked the front door.

"It's me," McCloud said. "We need to talk—*now.*"

"Terrific," Shep muttered as he unhooked the safety chain. McCloud pushed past him in a rush.

"Let me guess," a groggy Shep said, "they didn't find Betty's collection?" He yawned. "You know, you could've waited til tomorrow morning to give me an update."

The Chief turned around. "We have a situation."

Shep yawned again. "Yes, we have a situation. We *always* have a situation." He strolled past McCloud to start a pot of coffee. "Our whole existence in this town, at this time is a situation, McCloud. What's new?"

The Chief hesitated. "Denver Collins got arrested tonight."

Shep stopped cold at the coffeepot. He paused for a moment then looked up at McCloud. "Ok...uh, *arrested?* Hmmm. By who? County, State—Bloomington?"

"By me."

Shep stared back at the coffeepot. "Look, Chief, I really hope you're having fun with this little late night joke, but—"

"It's no joke, Shep," the Chief said. "I don't know if you have ever met Ike Sanders, but he happened to see our boys inside the *Journal*. He stopped Denver and laid 'em out cold with a crowbar."

Shep stared at the floor. "And Frazier?"

"Frazier's fine, he got out with the goods. Ike didn't see his face."

"They found her collection?"

"Yes. It was in the safe."

Shep kept his head down as he wandered back into the living room. "And, uh, what else happened?"

"I had to call Betty in."

Shep snapped his head up. "You did *what*?"

The Chief was resolute. "I called in Larson. Like they say, it's important to keep your friends close, and your enemies way, way closer."

Shep stepped up to him. "Oh, and let me guess. She saw Denver, too?"

The Chief nodded. "Of course! But it doesn't matter—she would have seen 'em the next day, anyway."

"Yes, yes it *does* matter!" Shep blurted out. He paced for a moment. "It could've bought us some time, time to figure out a better exit strategy, McCloud!"

The Chief started to rebut him, but held his peace.

Shep shook his head and put his fingers on his temples. "This absolutely *can't be happening*! How could you let this happen?"

McCloud didn't budge.

Shep snapped his head up and glared at McCloud. "Your mismanagement of this whole—*crisis*, is jeopardizing everything we have worked toward, McCloud!"

The Chief fired back. "Whoa, I don't remember *you* comin' up with any great ideas to deal with this situation,

Shep! You and I both know if we try to cover this thing up, it'll blow up in our face!"

Shep lost control. "What in the devil's hell is your problem, McCloud? It has *already* blown up in our faces!" He stormed off across the room, looking out the window. "And it continues to blow up in our faces!"

Shep rubbed his chin. "The way I see it, there are two huge problems: the first is that walking disaster area known as Denver Collins." He spun around, walking up to McCloud. "The second is just how blind you are to what truly needs to be done with him!"

"What're you talking about?"

Shep moved closer. "There is only one way to even *begin* to fix this mess. Denver Collins is a walking, talking liability! Can you imagine what would happen if this went to court, if, if he had to go before a *judge?* The Feds probably have his wallet, McCloud! He is way too hot. He needs to be removed from the equation. *Permanently.*"

Shep started to turn away, but McCloud grabbed his shoulders and spun him around. "Forget it, Sheppard! You ain't draggin' me down that twisted road. You're way outta line!"

Shep shoved the Chief's hands off of his shoulders. "Don't lecture *me* about tough but necessary moral choices, Police Chief James McCloud!" He circled around him. "Because every single, accusing finger you raise up to point at me is already *dripping* with blood. No, forget dripping— no, no, it's—*gushing!*" Shep looked up with feigned ignorance. "Or, my good friend, have you already *forgotten?*"

"We did what had to be done. And remember, it wasn't even my idea."

"No," Shep said as he continued circling. "No, it wasn't your idea, but you helped in the execution."

"We did what was best for the survival of the group!"

Shep smiled. "And I'm only saying that, three years later, we just need to do it once again."

CHAPTER 52

Sometimes it is far better to be completely wrong than anywhere close to being right.

And tonight, for Betty Larson, it was one of those times.

She had predicted that she wouldn't be able to sleep, and when Betty rolled over at just past four a.m. to check the clock—she cursed her own fulfilled prophecy.

At other times she would invoke the medicinal properties of a good novel to woo herself towards oblivion, but the break-in at the *Journal*, and the loss of her unusual collection mocked any known sleep remedies.

Disgusted, she sat up and turned on the bedroom light. Betty envied that select group of blessed people who had hobbies and interests they could engage in to pass the hours at nearly any hour.

For Betty Larson, *work* had always been her hobby, *and* her husband, *and* her home. It's not like she hadn't tried to diversify and multiply her interests. Betty had even made a few running starts at relationships over the years but with minor amounts of success and generous portions of disappointment.

At first she always imagined that each implosion was all on them. But eventually, her journalistic knack for the truth fixed the blame much closer to home.

The editor convinced herself that she had become a victim of her own profession. Betty dismissed her inability to get close to people as stemming from a reporter's ultimate virtue: *objectivity*.

She maintained that every journalist worth their salt knows that to get involved with a story is to potentially corrupt a story. In like manner, somewhat unconsciously,

Betty imagined that getting involved with people brought similar—perhaps even inevitable—transgressions.

But tonight, with her dizzying array of concerns, Betty needed a distraction. She needed something else as a focal point. The emotional consequence of the robbery, of having her private affairs ripped open and violated, was that Betty longed for those things that remained. It was time to be reoriented to that which is real, to that which is secure.

She slid out of bed and knelt beside it, almost in an attitude of prayer. Her right hand slid beneath the white bed skirt, searching for something for a few moments. She latched hold and eased a ragged shoe box out into the open and laid it on the bed.

Perhaps as a nervous reflex, she turned her head, scanning the room for any witnesses.

She was alone of course.

Betty lifted the cardboard lid and set it aside. She leaned forward and gazed into the humble container. She was relieved. Everything in her second stash was still there, including a Sony Walkman tape player, a well-worn *Bee Gees Saturday Night Fever* cassette tape, a ten-dollar bill minted in 1974, and a handful of color-faded photos.

She dug around and fished out one of the Polaroids and pulled it close, studying the picture. It had a teenage girl in a red graduation gown clutching a diploma with a beaming, well-dressed man standing beside her. Betty's eyes dropped down to the words along the bottom, handwritten in black ink: GRADUATION 1966.

She looked up—ideas and explanations tormenting the tired reporter. She knew, she positively *knew* that something not normal was happening in Normal. She didn't put much stock in intuition or premonition, but she felt that she was so close to an answer. Incidences and coincidences seemed to be converging of late—but to what end?

It was maddening.

Losing the cash would definitely hurt in the short term, but financial loss was not forefront in her mind at the moment.

I can't believe they took my safe!

She rose off her knees and walked over to the sole bedroom window and gazed toward the scattered lights of town.

They took my safe! What are the odds?

She froze for a moment, paralyzed by her own question. *The odds. Yes—what are the odds?*

She played with the catch on the window release.

But who could've known what was in the safe? She continued to mess with the lock.

Nobody knew. Well, nobody except for someone completely trustworthy.

She stopped toying with the window and looked toward the middle of town. Betty had always been driven by curiosity, by questions, and some questions grew into obsessions. It was yet another curse of being a journalist. At that very moment she felt the odd thrill of a new obsession emerging, and there was nothing she could do to stop it, nor did she want to.

She stared at her shoebox collection over on the bed. *Is the robbery related to these items? But how? Why?*

She faced the window again, leaning against the sill, her heart pounding faster. *Wait. Maybe, just maybe those aren't the right questions,* she thought.

Forget the how and the why for just a moment, Betty.

She stared into the night. Betty recollected watching Chief McCloud open the door of his squad car, as if in slow motion. She recalled, in brief flashes, the bruised face of a nameless man spread across the seat.

The Mystery Man.

Forget the how and the why, girl, she contemplated. *Focus on the who. The who.*

She raced over to her dresser and grabbed a notebook and pen. There were so many points and possibilities, like dots on a page.

It's time to connect them.

Friday, July 3, 1953
Journal entry number 743

There will be fireworks...and that has me concerned. When I was growing up in Pueblo, the excitement about the 4th of July was almost on par with Christmas morning. But I am not excited about this one.

A few days ago I walked into the middle of a conversation in The Basement that I am confident that I was not supposed to hear. In fact, after a little investigation, my fears were confirmed. My worst fears actually.

I have irrefutable evidence that some of our group are planning to break the Third Accord. They are making plans to exploit our technology and use it for purposes that could alter the future in unforeseeable ways.

Terrible ways.

I am going to privately confront them right after the holiday. We have come too far. We have all sacrificed so much, far too much to let something like this happen now. I have never had more hope and educated optimism about our future.

It kills me to think that some would be willing to do this.

CHAPTER 53

It was the very essence of a contradiction.

The late afternoon sun poured golden beams through his window, transforming the swirling dust into brilliant, dancing shafts that played across the floor.

But he didn't notice.

In fact, he never noticed.

It was difficult to even imagine him outside of the rusty wheelchair that was his pathetic throne. Its occupant was a shell of a man—whose hair, beard, and emotionless gaze made it impossible to accurately discern his age. He faced the incoming rays, apparently transfixed by the view, yet his cold form had probably not been truly warmed in years.

The heavy, metal door that separated his lonely existence from a callous hallway opened in a short arc. A sensuous voice called out to him. "Good afternoon, Mr. Thompson."

There was nary a change in his stupor to indicate his awareness of her presence or even of her voice. Nurse Beussink closed the door with both hands and walked up beside her newest patient. She attempted to gaze into his distant eyes. "Gordon?"

Predictably, there was no response.

She knelt beside him, caressing his bare right arm, and leaned in close. "Gordon. I want you to know...*I believe you.*"

Then it happened, not all at once, but it happened.

His head began moving—it was almost imperceptible at first—and he turned to face her, but tortuously slow, like a glacier.

She was thrilled. "Yes...yes, you understand. Don't you?" His clouded eyes darted around to some degree and she took it as a good sign. Nurse Beussink slid her hand down into her side pocket and produced a syringe of dark, orange fluid.

She focused her gaze on the tip and a small, glistening drop emerged. She smiled with satisfaction. Her eyes studied the door for a moment, and then she plunged the needle into his arm. As for the pain, his catatonic expression masked it well, if he even felt it at all.

She watched with interest as his left eye blinked in an erratic fashion and his lips began quivering. She leaned in, catching raspy attempts at incoherent words, merely fragments of thoughts borne of a fragmented mind.

Nurse Beussink grabbed a noisy metal chair and scooted right up to him and sat down. She retrieved a notepad and a pen. "It's okay, Mr. Thompson. Go slow. Now, what was that?"

His body started to vibrate. Then it shook, as he struggled to speak. Words began forming, words actually in order. "I...I'm...I'm...not, not—"

She cocked her beautiful head a bit. "You're not *what*, Mr. Thompson?"

The trembling invalid strained to complete his thought. She was waiting. "You're not what?" she asked again.

His eyes appeared to be staring at hers. "Not...cr—crazy."

She licked her deep red lips and nodded, rubbing his shoulder. "I know, I know you're not crazy. I *believe* you."

He squeezed his eyes shut, as if to relish the moment. Tears welled up and began to cascade down his wrinkled cheeks as he opened heavy eyelids again. She brushed the tiny droplets away and studied his face with feigned compassion. His countenance continued to brighten. It was as if his tears were washing away years of abuse, neglect, and isolation.

Now she couldn't be certain, but Nurse Beussink thought that she had detected a hint of a smile.

She placed her soft, manicured hands on either side of his rugged face and tilted it to match hers. The nurse opened her eyes wide and smiled even wider. "Listen to me, Gordon. Listen to me."

He managed to lock misty eyes with hers. She nodded with a rehearsed subtlety. "Tell me, Gordon. What year are you from?"

He began blinking, apparently processing her request. She nodded again with a politician's grin. "Tell me *when*, Gordon."

He gazed down at her lips as his own began moving. "Fffr—from—from." He paused and strained.

"That's it, yes, what year, Gordon?"

He hesitated once more and then leaned forward. "Ffr—from—nnn—nine—nineteen."

"Yes, nineteen. Nineteen *what*, Gordon?"

"Ni—nineteen—eigh—eighty—seven. Nineteen—eighty seven."

The nurse's mesmerizing blue eyes grew wide with excitement, an excitement that had been waiting patiently for years. She caressed his arm, her own tears welling up, and moved close to his trembling face. "Tell me, Gordon—do you know Mr. Nelson? Have you heard of Mr. Nelson?" She scanned his eyes for even a shred of confirmation.

Her heart sank as the broken man started to nod off, his heavy head drooping onto his chest. She scrambled to reload her syringe, her own tears making it difficult to focus as she attempted to pierce the narrow opening on the bottle.

He was fading fast.

The nurse slapped his arm. "Hey, hey, now—Mr. Thompson, hey! Stay with me." She raised the needle and shoved it into his atrophied shoulder.

"Hey, come on, now—Mr. Thompson? Don't you go to sleep—we still have lots to talk about. Hey. Hey!"

His head didn't move, but the pathetic patient started mumbling once again. She slid out of her chair without delay and knelt before him, looking up into his tired face. His eyes were half open, and a thin line of drool was beginning to dangle from his quivering mouth.

She reached into a pocket and held up her shiny silver ring. The red gemstone seemed to glow in the narrow beams of sunlight. With grace she rotated it before his eyes, hoping to give him a point of reference, a focal point.

"Look at this pretty ring, Gordon. Isn't it beautiful? It was a gift from my mother."

His eyes crossed a few times and blinked, but eventually locked onto the piece of jewelry.

"There, there. That's better. Now, Gordon," she said, "can you pretty please tell me if you know Mr. Nelson?"

His eyes opened wide and his head rolled to one side.

"Nelson," she requested. "Do you know Mr. Nelson?"

His head bobbed a bit and he clamped his eyes shut. The trail of drool dripped down to his shaggy beard.

As she wiped up the spittle he spoke, and spoke with an increasing clarity.

"Nelson," he said. "Phil—Phillip. *Phillip* Nelson."

CHAPTER 54

The sun had risen in all of its late August fury. All in all, it appeared to be a typical Monday morning in Normal, Illinois.

But, of course, it wasn't typical.

There hadn't been a typical day in Normal since the arrival of Phillip Nelson in early 1946. And no one knew that better than an exhausted and desperate Police Chief James McCloud. He stared down into his third cup of coffee, lamenting the fact that he was still waiting for the effects of the first one to arrive. He blinked hard as he set it down and glanced over at an occupied but silent jail cell.

Denver was still sleeping off the results of the previous night's successful disaster.

In many ways (minus the probable concussion) the Chief almost envied him. Face down, dead to the world, free room and board, three squares a day…what more could a guy want? Add a pretty blonde to the list and McCloud might even *volunteer* to trade places.

He laughed inside as he contemplated it. What the heck was he thinking? He already had a pretty blonde. If he could just find a way to get to her. Helen was about 600 miles away as the crow flies, and right at forty years as time flies.

The Chief always joked with the other Jumpers saying "It wasn't the *distance*, it was the *time*." It could have been funny if it weren't such a sad reality. But unfortunately, he hadn't thought much of Helen of late. The frenetic events of the past few weeks had dominated his waking moments, leaving little time to reminisce about his wife or his boys, Trevor and Zach.

Since he had arrived in 1950, he had held an unshakeable confidence that he would find a way to get back home to them. But today his confidence was being eroded by violent waves of doubt. He looked over at his unconscious captive. Even the very idea that Shep was right was both an unbearable yet undeniable conclusion.

For the second time in just over three years he faced horrific choices.

But regardless of where his decisions landed him, he honestly wondered if his humanity would survive the fall.

McCloud shook his head and grabbed a small flask out of the bottom right drawer. He spiked his coffee twice. It may have been way too early to drink, but it was the perfect time to be drunk.

Perhaps as a small mercy, his grim cogitations were interrupted by the arrival of Officer O'Connell with Betty Larson in tow. Billy held the door for her.

The visibly-fatigued newspaper editor glanced over into the cell. "Any update on the mystery man behind jail-bars number one?" she asked.

McCloud shrugged. "What you see is what you get, Betty."

She walked closer to the cell. "Has he come around at all?"

McCloud rose up and set his cup down. "Oh, he's moaned and fussed a few times." He strolled over to the sink area. "You want some coffee? I know we all had a long night." He held up a mostly-empty pot. "It's my special law enforcement blend."

She looked over her shoulder. "Oh, no thanks, Chief. I'm fine, or fine as can be, I guess."

Billy didn't need to be asked twice, and he hurried over and poured himself a steaming cup. "Everything was pretty quiet over at the paper last night," he reported to the Chief. "I rigged the back entry, and Ike Sanders dropped by this morning. Said he felt bad about the front door and he helped me put up a sheet of plywood. It'll hold for now til Hank gets there."

The Chief slapped him on the shoulder. "Couldn't ask for a finer deputy."

Betty looked up. "Oh, yeah, definitely. Thanks again, Billy."

He blushed as he took a hot sip. "No problem, Ms. Larson. I almost felt like I was on a stakeout. My pleasure."

She finished studying Denver. "You, uh, said there would be some paperwork?"

McCloud looked up. "Oh, of course." He pulled out his chair and sat back. "Gimme a sec…yes, right here it is." He slid a page towards her and pointed. "Just fill out this part, and give us a list of what was stolen. Obviously the amount of cash, and then the, uh, other items."

Her eyes darted up at him. "Other items?"

McCloud paused. "Well, uh, remember that big hole in the wall? I assume you want to report at least a safe was stolen. And, uh, then, whatever was inside it."

She searched his eyes for a moment and then glanced down at the form.

Right then something caught Billy's attention and he moved toward the front window.

Betty picked up the sheet. "Can I bring this back, Chief? I still need to do a little inventory."

"Oh, yes, Ma'am, absolutely. You can just get that back to me whenever it's convenient. As long as I have it before John Doe over there stands before Judge Seyer, we're good."

She stashed the form away in her purse. "Thanks, Chief."

McCloud nodded and glanced over at his deputy. "Alright, Billy. What's so interesting?"

The young officer adjusted his hat. "Dark sedan just pulled up. Government plates." He paused. "A couple o' suits are getting out. I'd say Feds if I were a bettin' man."

The Chief tried to conceal his concern as he stood up. Betty raised her eyebrows. "Oh, are these your friends you were telling me about? The ones that you said would know what to do?"

The Chief was blindsided for a few seconds. She elaborated. "You know, about my *items*. Our meeting at the bridge?"

He connected and recovered. "Oh, *those* friends. Gotcha. No, no, not those guys. No, not them."

She appeared deflated. "Oh, okay, well, just let me know."

He was so distracted that he didn't even respond to her. She headed for the door. "I'll see you officers later."

The Chief looked over. "Oh, yeah, Betty. We'll be in touch."

She started to reach for the handle when the door popped open. Betty retreated as two men brushed past, clad in matching suits, matching sunglasses, and matching hats. The second one apologized and held the door open for her. "Ma'am."

She smiled and nodded back as she walked out. The second man forcefully pulled the door shut behind her.

Betty paused for a moment on the sidewalk and glanced over at the like-new government vehicle. Her reporter's instinct wouldn't let her just walk away.

Connect the dots, she thought.

Betty scurried down the empty concrete, going well past their car. She turned, walked out into the street, and then came up to the vehicle on the driver's side. She glanced over at the police station window. Only Billy was visible, and he was obviously looking at the VIP's. She took a deep breath and inched up right beside the driver's side rear window.

The sudden influx of hot tires, hot engine, and warm asphalt caught her senses by surprise. She choked back a quick round of coughing.

These boys must've come straight from the Big City.

Betty peered inside the immaculate car and spotted a briefcase in the backseat with a folder lying next to it on the near side. The folder sported a large stamp across its surface which read: CONFIDENTIAL – FBI. She glanced down. The door was unlocked. Her pulse quickened.

The opportunity was just too irresistible. She scanned the street.

No one.

She gazed through the car windows at the police station once again. Even Billy was nowhere to be seen.

It's now or never, Larson.

Betty paused for a moment.

It's now.

She pried the door open and knelt low, sliding the folder across the seat to herself. She took another breath and then flipped it open with trembling fingers. The top page was filled with typed information. She perused it and spotted a repeated name: *Denver Wayne Collins.*

She set the first sheet aside and her heart almost stopped beating. Underneath was an artist's sketch of the mystery man she had seen passed out in the back of the squad car several hours before.

Why is the FBI after a petty thief?

She concentrated on the sketch, mulling over various scenarios.

Unless Denver Collins is more than just a two-bit burglar.
But how did they already know he was here?

She looked up at the police station.

What is going on, Chief James McCloud? Did you call them in? Why? Is this about my collection? Did you lie to me, Chief?

The rumble of an oncoming car broke her internal investigation and Betty shut the folder in haste, sliding it back precisely where she had found it. She waited for the car to pass, keeping her face hidden, and then shut the car door with care.

Betty scurried away from the encounter with only one answer, but at least a dozen new questions.

"Mornin', gentlemen," the Chief began as the two visitors paused and surveyed the area. In unison, they removed their sunglasses and their eyes were as void of expression as their pale faces. McCloud wondered to himself if maybe they were just both having a bad day, or worse yet, perhaps these were their happy faces. He had met a few Feds in the past—smiles didn't seem to be standard issue.

The taller of the two men, who was carrying a file folder, broke the tension. "Police Chief James McCloud?"

The Chief nodded and stepped forward. "Guilty as charged, gentlemen, that is, unless the charges are serious."

He smiled.

They didn't.

He tried to salvage the introduction. "James McCloud, at your service." He turned. "And this, this is my deputy, Officer O'Connell." They acknowledged him, but only in the academic sense and continued looking around.

The shorter agent broke away and headed down the tiny hallway. He checked the bathroom, and even opened the storage closet. He glanced over at the other agent and signaled. His partner reached into his vest pocket and produced a golden FBI badge. "I'm Agent Simmons." He motioned towards the other, who displayed his credentials as well. "This is Agent Jameison."

The Chief grinned. "Well, Agents Simmons, and, uh, Jameison, what can we do for the Bureau today? Can I interest you gentlemen in some coffee?"

Simmons ignored his offer. "Are we alone, Chief McCloud?"

The Chief looked around and nodded. "Just the four of us, Agent Simmons. Well, I guess *five* if you include our, uh, *sleeping* guest over there."

Agent Jameison walked from the storage closet over to the cell and inspected Denver as he lay there, face down, almost snoring. Jameison looked back at his partner. Simmons cracked opened his folder and produced the artist's sketch and the driver's license photo of Denver Wayne Collins. He handed them to the Chief. "Have you ever seen this man before?"

Billy moved casually beside the Chief and they stared at the two images. Years of poker were finally paying off and McCloud began shaking his head. He glanced up from the sheets and made eye contact with the deputy. "How about you, Billy?"

The young time Jumper looked like he was about to throw up, but played it cool. "I, uh, I don't believe so…no, no, Sir."

McCloud acted like he was concentrating. "Doesn't seem to ring a bell here either, gentlemen." He handed them back, "What's he wanted for, if I may ask?"

Simmons glared down at him. "You *may not*."

Jameison rejoined his partner and Simmons continued. "His name is Denver Wayne Collins. Approximately five feet eleven inches tall. Medium build. Blue eyes. Brown hair. May or may not have a beard, probably not."

The sleeping inmate began a fresh round of groaning and mumbling, and both agents zeroed in on him. The Chief panicked at first but then smiled. "Well, gentlemen, I could put those pictures up at the Post Office, if—"

"Out of the question, Chief McCloud," Simmons snapped. "This investigation is to remain a strictly *internal*, law enforcement affair. No public, no press."

Agent Jameison made his way back over to the occupied jail cell. He studied the unconscious convict and waved over at his partner. Simmons closed the folder and joined him. Jameison whispered something and Simmons nodded.

The Chief noticed that Billy was getting paler by the second. The deputy's eyes displayed a primal fear and the Chief discreetly pointed at the door.

Billy's voice cracked. "Chief, gentlemen, if you will excuse me, I have to see if Betty needs any other assistance at the *Journal*." He grabbed his hat and car keys.

The Chief glanced over at him. "Uh, sure, Billy." He raised his voice. "That is, unless you two gentlemen have any further need of my deputy?"

Simmons spun around. "Wait. Deputy. You said *Journal*. Is that the local newspaper?"

Billy was almost to the door, and was probably seconds from losing his breakfast (and most of his dinner). McCloud covered for him. "Uh, yes, but my deputy has some unfinished business there. They, uh, had a small break-in last night. Nothing major, some vandalism, probably kids' stuff, you know."

Simmons stared at Billy, and the remaining color fled from the young man's panicking face. The FBI agent assented, and O'Connell grinned and exited in a rush.

Denver coughed, and one of his hands moved up and vigorously rubbed his head. McCloud did his level best to distract them. "So, uh, did you guys hear that the Yankees just got Enos Slaughter, you know, the outfielder from Kansas City?"

It was doubtful they even heard him.

"Good ol' Country, he, uh, he was really something back in, what was it?" He rubbed his chin. "The forty-six World Series? Or was it forty-seven?"

There was no response, because the Chief figured that he—just like sports trivia—had ceased to be relevant.

The agents traded glances but then settled sights on Denver. Simmons motioned for the Chief to join them as he pointed through the bars. "What's his story?"

McCloud took the deepest breath of his life.

So, after all these years—has it finally come to this? Heaven help us all. The police chief took a few reluctant steps up behind the federal agents.

He looked down at his gun.

The End of Book One: Paradigm Rift

EPILOGUE:

The late night air was breezy and cool, but for mid-October it could have been downright cold, especially for this rural stretch of upstate New York. The crimson leaves of the sugar maples released their trademarked fragrance with each fresh gust of wind. For the lone female staring out across the moonlit ripples of the Black River, though, the weather was warm—at least warmer than her childhood home.

"Not quite as wide, nor as deep as the great Dnieper," an accented voice called out, interrupting her silent meditation. She turned and acknowledged the older gentleman navigating the rocky slope down towards her.

"No, no, the Dnieper it is not," she said. "But greatness is not merely assessed in terms of scale or strength, comrade."

He removed his gloves, one finger at a time, and hid them away in his gray trench coat. "Your sentiment, Darkstar, is not always shared by those—who make the decisions."

She pivoted back towards the quiet waters. "Even a tiny stream can carve an enormous canyon."

It was his turn to nod. "Yes, indeed. Given enough time. But, as you know," he hesitated, "one does not always have the *luxury* of time."

She tensed up. "Are you expressing concern about my progress, Commander?"

"What can one say about such things?"

"One can speak the truth."

He appeared to be caught off guard by her sharp reply, but grinned while he adjusted his thin-rimmed spectacles. "The truth? The truth is that the Americans have a strong lead in Chicago. Project SATURN is awakening from her slumber." He paused. "Time is no longer a luxury...it is now a *liability*." He stared into the distance, awaiting her response. The silence grew uncomfortable.

"They may have a lead," she finally asserted, "but I have developed a source."

His eyebrows raised. "Ah, yes, the...*mental* patient. The Directorate is not as enthusiastic about your...*source* at the hospital as you have become."

She was stoic. "Results are not merely influenced by *enthusiasm*, Commander."

He shrugged more or less and fished a folded document out of his inner pocket. He held it up just below her offended face.

"New orders?" she asked as she took it with some hesitancy.

"New *help*," he said. "Perhaps."

Intrigued, she faced him and opened the letter.

He glanced over at her. "Our New York office received this request several days ago. It is from a troubled young man in Texas." The commander searched her eyes. "I thought that, perhaps he could be *groomed*."

She spoke without bothering to look up. "It could be fake."

"If it were, I wouldn't be wasting our time this evening. Our research indicates that he has been in the Civilian Air Patrol. But more importantly...he has plans to enlist with the US Marines."

She finished studying the letter and folded it with care. The older gentleman rubbed his hands together, and picked his way back up the hill. She faced the river once more and gazed across it.

"Are you ordering me, or *advising* me, Commander?" she asked point-blank.

He continued making his way up the rocky incline. "I forget that we are in America, Darkstar. In Russia, there is no difference, wouldn't you agree?"

Within seconds he melted away into the gathering fog, and she was a lone figure once more.

She didn't agree with this unwarranted intrusion on her investigation. In fact, she resented it as a humiliating vote of no confidence. Two people may have been optimum for dancing, love play, and fencing, but assassins of the First Chief Directorate's 13th Department had always worked in groups of one.

One.

She knew that she was on the edge of a real breakthrough in Chicago, but now all of that would have to be put on hold as she traveled to Fort Worth to pacify her short-sighted chain of command.

She checked the bottom of the letter one more time. Her eyes traveled down to his signature. It was simple, unassuming, and only two words.

Lee Oswald.

Coming Soon:

TRADECRAFT

Book Two of the Back to Normal Series

For more information, visit:
www.MovingImagesPublications.com

ABOUT THE AUTHOR

As a science fiction movie fan and insatiable reader from his earliest memories in his birth state of California, Randy McWilson draws inspiration from a wide spectrum of interests and influences.

The reverberating echoes of Cold War espionage, explosions in scientific advancement, and strong, complex themes permeate his literary offerings. The historically-inclined reader finds a thrilling tale founded upon the rich fabric of both actual and alleged events.

He occupies his non-writing hours with a diverse range of hobbies: geology, theology, philosophy, history, and art.

McWilson currently lives in Jackson, Missouri, with his wife, Amanda, three children, and several pets.

Made in the USA
Lexington, KY
12 November 2014